Whatever It Takes
Mack Cameron

William Cameron
Post Office Box 321244
Flowood, MS 39232

Visit our Web site at http://www.msbluffs.com

First Edition: January 2020

Cameron, Mack.
        Whatever it Takes / Mack Cameron. – 1st ed.

        ISBN-13: 978-0-9801434-2-3

Dedicated to all of my family and friends,
without whose support I could have not completed this novel.

Chapter One

Tony Gable had made it in Hollywood. Following his participation in the shoot-out on mobster property in Louisiana south of New Orleans, he had ridden his motorcycle over 2000 miles to Los Angeles. He had gradually made friends and eventually had been given parts as an extra in action movies that needed someone with good karate skills. Tony was a black belt and had kept up his expertise by practicing at least two or three times a week at a workout facility in Beverly Hills. He also continued to ride from time to time the same motorcycle he had ridden to Los Angeles from Louisiana. He always enjoyed feeling the breeze on his face and the freedom while roaming California roads on his cycle.

His good looks and being single led to lots of come-ons by Hollywood starlets who also worked at the shooting locations. Tony had all the money he needed due to what had happened in Mississippi with the Devil's Swamp gas field money. He eventually signed on to do the physical combat scenes of an action-packed movie. He became well-known as a result of that and worked his way up to being cast as the lead actor in a series of action movies.

He stayed single for many years though numerous starlets and female admirers constantly made it known to him that they were available. He became known as one of the most handsome single men in Hollywood. He eventually met a much younger, very beautiful, up and coming starlet named Amanda Kincaid on one of his movie sets. They dated for several months and Amanda began to attempt to convince him that she was the one he needed to marry. Finally realizing that his age was beginning to catch up with him, he decided that Amanda was someone he should go ahead and marry. After months of preparation, they got married.

Unfortunately, though, Tony found out after almost a year of marriage that Amanda had to have attention from men in addition to him, and that she was seeking it from the younger men she worked with on movie sets. One of those men, a famous and very handsome young actor, introduced her to experiencing different drugs while they were having sex. She gradually got more and more into drugs, having started with marijuana and then moving on to harder drugs at the urging of her on-the-set boyfriend.

Tony began to notice Amanda not being the same person he thought he had married. She started not coming home until late at night and, even the few times she would get home at a reasonable hour, she could hardly talk. He decided to check things out and, after a few calls to some of his friends who were working on the same project, he found out about her boyfriend and their drug activity. After confirming what he had been told about was happening with the lead actor in her current movie, he showed up at the set and, utilizing his expertise in karate, broke the boyfriend's nose, putting him in the hospital.

Tony immediately took his wife to the Betty Ford Center, where she stayed for two months. Upon her release from the unit, she behaved herself for about a year until her former boyfriend showed up and got her to start doing drugs with him again while they were having sex. This time she was introduced by the boyfriend, on purpose, to a new, much stronger drug which caused her, the first time she used it, to have a heart attack and die.

Though it was not Tony's fault, he felt horrible about not being able to keep Amanda off of drugs and away from what eventually killed her. Even though assured by the doctors that he had done the best that he could have under the circumstances, Tony still felt responsible for her death.

About two and a half weeks after his wife's funeral, as Tony was sitting at his house just thinking about what direction his life was going to go in now, he got an unexpected call.

"Hello?"

"Tony?" a very feminine voice answered.

"Yes?"

"This is Karen Patterson, in Bay St. Louis, Mississippi."

Tony's memory flashed back to the beautiful woman he had met in the mid-1970's while he had been down in Bay St. Louis closing an estate his father had established. When his father's sister, Madeline Benedetti, had passed away, Tony was the only heir and, after arriving from Sicily in New York City where he had spent a short time, he had traveled to the Mississippi Gulf Coast to deal with her estate. Tony had almost lost his life on the coast, and probably would have, if it had not been for Mark Patterson, Karen's husband. He had left that area because of what had happened, but he had always wondered how Karen was. Karen had been dating Mark at that time and Tony found out after he had left town that they had gotten married.

"Karen! How are you?"

"Hi, Tony. I am fine. Thanks for asking."

"How is Mark?"

"That is why I am calling you. You know that Mark and I got married not too long after you left down here. He ran for Hancock County Sheriff and got elected. He has been Sheriff ever since then."

"Yes, I had heard that years ago," Tony answered. That had been one of the reasons Tony had not been back to the coast. While it had been good for him to stay away because of what had happened in Devil's Swamp, he had thought about the possibility of going back a few years earlier, but he had met Amanda and gotten married. With what all that had happened with her and her recent death, he thought Karen's call was good timing. He wondered why she would be calling him after all this time, and what she said next caught him completely by surprise.

"Tony, Mark is very sick. He probably doesn't have long to live. And Tony, he wants to talk with you before he passes away," she said with a shaky voice. "Would you come down here as soon as you can to see him?"

"What is wrong with him, Karen? What happened?" he asked, sincerely concerned about the man who had saved his life so many years ago.

"He has cancer, among other things, and he only has a few more days to live, if that."

Mark had indeed saved Tony's life and, because he was asking to see him, he was indicating that enough time had passed that it was alright for Tony to come back to the area. Tony knew what he had to do. As soon as he could, the next day if at all possible, he had to fly to New Orleans and then drive over to Bay St. Louis, Mississippi to see the man who had saved his life, his friend, Sheriff Mark Patterson.

Chapter Two

Mark Patterson had enjoyed his training in becoming a Green Beret. Those going through the very stringent, but thorough, training sought to be picked for the honor of joining that select military group, which were the best of the best in the U. S. Army. The men were eventually selected, after over 90 per cent of the applicants had dropped out or not been promoted for the next level of training, and were cross-trained in many things, from repair of firearms to familiarity with various languages to political skills of community organization. Members were assigned to take care of medical problems, both with those inside the unit but also with those they were assigned to work.

A Green Beret "A" team consisted of only ten to twelve men, who had a combination of many different skills. Often, in Southeast Asia, they were assigned to areas that were remote and required special personnel. Such was the case for Mark and his team members. They weren't supposed to be where they were but then, at that point in the South Vietnam, Laos and Cambodia areas, a lot of things were going on that were not supposed to be happening.

As he lay on his bed in Bay St. Louis, Mississippi, Mark struggled to find some position to place his ravaged body so that he wouldn't hurt as much as he did. Gradually he had found himself having less and less success finding such a position and had been forced to rely more and more on drugs in an attempt to dull his extreme pain. At some points, it had gotten to where, when the drugs were beginning to wear off, he began to think it would be a blessing for him to die. He found himself now trying to distract his attention from his pain by thoughts about his time in Southeast Asia.

Finally drifting off into a sleep, Mark's thoughts went back to his group's first assignment to that area, which had been as "advisors" to the Montagnard tribesmen in Northern Laos. The Montagnard's were assisting American troops with the interdiction of supplies coming down from North Vietnam through Laos on what was known as the Ho Chi Minh Trail and then into South Vietnam to the communistic rebels fighting against the government. The land had been beautiful; at least that was what he had thought the first time he landed in that area. The mountains rose sharply in elevation with most of the slopes on their sides being at least 35 degrees or more. Many were just sheer cliffs with a gradual rise in elevation on one side, but there was always a dense foliage covering almost every square foot.

On his initial trip to his assignment area, Mark flew out of Danang Air Base in South Vietnam on a plane with one engine, which he would come to find out was the Pilatus, a Swedish plane with special capabilities of which there were only 26 at that time in the whole world. It didn't bother him too much when, at 11:30 p.m. late one evening, he first saw the airplane on the tarmac over in a remote corner of the huge airbase. He became more concerned when the plane took off, in the pitch black of darkness, with him and Gene, one of his team members, on board along with crates of guns and ammunition. Gene was sitting in the right-side co-pilot's seat while Mark sat in a canvas seat behind the pilot. The plane was carrying almost two thousand pounds of military material to the site to which Mark and Gene would also be delivered. As sick as he was now, Mark could still remember being impressed by how absolutely dark it was for almost the entire flight. He later would find out that they had flown very low, at a little over 1000 feet, for most of the way so as to avoid detection.

He also recalled how the pilot of the plane, whose name was Russ he was told, had only greeted him and his partner with the nod of his head. There was no smile, no conversation, no discussion about anything. Mark, in fact, thought he had noticed a little shake side to side of the pilot's head as if to say, "You guys have got to be crazy to be going where you are."

That had bothered him for a while, but actually only a short while, because it wasn't long and they were rolling down the runway and became air born. While he could see a few lights out of the only window near to where he was seated, after a few minutes it was as black as it could be all around them. Continuing to glance out of the window from time to time did not do one bit of good because nothing could be seen in that darkness.

After bumping around in the sky for a little over an hour and a half, the pilot yelled over his shoulder, "Hold on. We're going in."

Mark remembered, so many times, thinking about that first

landing. The plane slowed its speed and Mark looked out and still could see nothing. He had remembered wondering at that time about how in the world that pilot was going to land in that "soup", as they had called it. He had found out a little about his pilot before they had left and felt encouraged. He had been told that the pilot was one of the best in the Marine Corps and that he had flown the F-4 Phantom fighter plane and other planes for quite some time.

Mark had also been told by his team leader that this particular pilot, Russ, had flown escort for a strike up near the border with China when one of the U. S. planes had been shot down. There had been an attempt by Chinese artillery, along the side of a runway on an island nearby, to shell the pilot who had survived the crash landing. Going against orders, when Russ saw that the Chinese planes were coming onto their runway in an attempt to take off, he had flown in on his own, immediately followed by three of his fellow F-4's. They had destroyed the artillery positions and damaged the runway so the planes could not take off. He would have attacked the planes directly but, that being in 1965 in the early years of the war, he had also been specifically told to not engage Chinese fighter planes. A "Jolly Green Giant", as the rescue helicopter was called, had finally arrived after a 45-minute flight from a U. S. aircraft carrier and had made a successful recovery of the pilot.

Having heard that story made Mark feel a little bit better about being flown in the middle of the dark night to join the remainder of his Green Beret team. He felt better, that is, until he was told that this would be the first time for Russ to make this flight. It seemed that most pilots working for the CIA in the region had decided that this flight Mark was on was too dangerous to make on a regular basis, so Russ had been recruited from the Marines.

As Mark looked for any kind of sign that there was a place for them to land, suddenly he saw two red fires, then two more, and two more and two more, as they became visible in the dark. Mark remembered the shock of seeing that because, of all things, those fires appeared to be in a line going almost straight up and down, but each pair only seemed to be separated by about fifteen yards. They must be located, he thought, on the side of one of the mountains! The thought then occurred to him that, regardless of how good of a pilot Russ was, how in the world was he going to land that fully loaded plane in the absolute darkness, except for those glowing fires that had now appeared, going up the side of that mountain? The other thing he remembered was that he had been told that the runway, or at least the area that served as a runway, was only 40 yards long! It was then that he began to have doubt as he seriously began thinking that they just might not make their landing safely.

As the red fires quickly got closer, Mark remembered again feeling that they were going too fast and were going to end up as some sort of an explosion out there in the middle of wherever in the world they were. He could feel Russ fighting to keep the plane on a path that would take it in between the four sets of fires. Mark could not remember ever gripping something as hard as he was holding onto parts of that foreign plane. He later had chuckled to himself when he thought that, if they had crashed and the opposition had gotten to the site of the wreck first, it was going to be quite a while until whoever got there figured out why a Swedish plane, with Sweden being a neutral country, was flying a complete load of arms into a tribal location in the middle of nowhere. The only things that could have possibly been identified, besides the arms, were the fatigues that the three humans were wearing, but if that plane crashed, there would be little left to search through. They weren't wearing any military identification.

Then it happened. The plane made contact with the side of the mountain but was going in an up-hill direction toward where the sky should have been. Mark was amazed that the plane touched down softly like a feather and settled onto the ground. Then, almost immediately, it came to an abrupt stop.

Mark remembered several small figures immediately running up to the plane. The two passengers quickly opened the one side door and jumped out. The cargo door was opened, and the various boxes of arms and ammunition were unloaded as the plane's engine kept running. After the unloading had been completed, the cargo doors were shut, and Russ began to turn the plane around to the left so that it faced in the opposite direction from which its landing approach had been made. Some of the small figures grabbed the wing on the left side and actually held it up so that it didn't scrape the ground while the plane was being turned.

The plane then took off, going down-hill this time. It didn't take twenty yards before the plane was air born. Russ was now on his way back to the Danang Air Base. From landing on the side of that mountain to takeoff, the plane had not been on the ground over three and a half minutes. It wasn't ten seconds and the fire pots were covered up, thereby extinguishing them. By that time, the plane had completely disappeared into the darkness.

Mark abruptly woke up from his sleep and called out for his wife. He needed some more pills, fast. The severity of the pain had awakened him. It was too much to take for long. Just too much.

Karen knew from the tone of his voice that Mark was really

hurting. He was never one to ask for the pain pills, except when he was really in pain, as he now was. She quickly grabbed a glass from the adjacent bathroom and filled it with water. She took it to him, first taking a pill from its container and, while sitting on the edge of his bed, sliding her left arm under his neck and raising his head as she put the pill in his mouth. She then brought the glass of water to his lips for him to take a small sip to help wash the pill down.

After he had swallowed, she eased his head back onto his pillow. Karen looked at him and could tell by the ever so faint smile that came to his face that he was appreciative. She gave him a gentle kiss on his forehead, stood up next to his bed, and looked at her wonderful husband one more time before she left the room. She never knew when such a look at her beloved would be the last one she would give him while he was alive. Tears began to come to her eyes, as they often did these days, and she hurriedly turned and left the room before he might notice them.

Mark's mind eased back into the dream he had been having before the pain had interrupted his sleep. He thoughts carried him back to when his Green Beret team had later been transferred, because it was experienced, to the Mekong Delta in southern South Vietnam while a new, less experienced team took their place in the mountains. He remembered that it was while his team was in the Delta that he had been exposed to Agent Orange poisoning. The tactics used there by his commander, Col. Bill Hackworth, had been highly successful. His utilization of several Green Beret teams and other units in the art of unconventional ambush and hit and run warfare had been so successful that a large bounty had been put out by the Viet Cong on Col. Hackworth. Higher command had wanted to remove him from the area because of that bounty but "Hack", as he was fondly called by his troops, would not leave until he was finally forced to by his commander-in-chief, General William Westmorland.

Unfortunately, as Mark and others knew, the military had begun spraying a defoliate called "Agent Orange" over the jungle to kill the plants in large areas involved in combat. It was during this time that the Army bosses encouraged soldiers to demonstrate to the local tribes living in those areas that the product would not hurt them. To do that, the soldiers were told that the chemical was harmless and to prove it, they had been told to demonstrate, on occasion, that it really was harmless by drinking it in front of the local populace. Instead, it had proved over time to be poisonous. Mark had gradually gotten sick and became one of thousands of veterans forced to deal with the results of their exposure.

When Mark woke up next, he could tell there was somebody standing with Karen next to his bed, but his blurry eyesight kept him from seeing who it was.

"Mark," Karen said in a very soft voice. "Somebody is here to see you. It's Tony."

Mark blinked his eyes several times in an attempt to focus them on the man standing next to Karen. He gradually began to smile as he recognized his friend.

Tony stepped next to the side of the bed and took Mark's right hand in both of his hands as he said, "Hi, partner. It's Tony."

Mark could barely reply, but he did gently squeeze Tony's hands. After holding Mark's hand for a few moments, with a hint of a smile on his face he said, in a voice barely more than a whisper, "Thanks … for comn."

Tony gave a big smile while saying, "You knew I would. I

mean, I wouldn't be standing here now if it wasn't for you. You saved my life."

Tears began rolling down Karen's cheeks. Both of her hands were covering her mouth and part of her face as she began to sob, trying ever so hard to do that as quietly as she could, so Mark would not sense her heart-wrenching pain.

Mark looked at her and, after a moment, said in now barely a whisper, "Hon, let us … talk … alone …. for a …. moment".

Karen could tell by the pleading look Mark had in his eyes that she needed to do what he had asked and that was to leave the room. She reached out and gently touched the clasped hands of the two men and then turned and left the room.

After she had closed the door, Mark looked at Tony and said, "It's good … to see … ya."

Tony gently squeezed Mark's hand and said, "Am glad to be here, partner. Sorry you are having these health problems. Please tell me what I can do to help you."

After a few moments to catch his breath, Mark began.

Have … a …. favor… to ask …. ya."

Tony answered, "Sure, Mark, anything you want. Anything I can do, I will. What is it?"

Mark looked Tony straight in the eye and, after a pause, haltingly uttered his request.

"Am not … goin ta … be here… much … longer," Mark whispered, with much difficulty. Continuing to look straight into Tony's eyes, he then said, "Please … take … care … of … Karen …. and … our daughter Jean … and our … two grand kids. Our first child …. a boy …didn't … make it. Died … not too … long after… being born."

Tony was shocked. As he thought about what he had just heard, but before he could say anything, Mark continued.

"There... are those ... who may... try to ... harm Karen ... Jean ...the grand kids ... cause them ... problems ... after I'm ... gone."

Tony continued to hold Mark's hand and look at his face as Mark took another pause in what he was saying. Then he continued, in a pleading voice, now more firmly gripping Tony's hands.

"Take ... care ... of 'em ... for me."

Tony was totally surprised by the request. The first thing he could think of to say, and he did, was, "Mark, sure. I will do anything, anything for you. But why me? I mean, I will if you want me to, but surely you have some friends or family here that would be a lot better to do that than me."

Mark gently squeezed Tony's hands and said, "Cause ... you ...." He paused as he began to shake. After a moment, he continued, "...are ... the .... only ... person ...." Tears started coming from his eyes. He finally managed to continue, saying, "that ... I .... really ... trust!"

Tony didn't know what to say. He just kept looking at his friend.

After a brief moment, Mark said, "I know ... you cared... for her. Promise ... me. Please ... take care... of her, ... and ... the kids." Then Mark asked, as firmly as he could, "Ok?"

Tony squeezed his friend's hand and said, "Ok. You know I will, Mark. I promise I will. I will do whatever I can."

After thinking about it for a brief second, Tony could not help but ask, "Does she know you are asking me this, to do this?"

After a pause, Mark replied in a barely audible whisper, "No."

Seven and a half hours after that conversation, Sheriff Mark Patterson peacefully passed away in his sleep.

Chapter Three

Tony spent the night in a local motel not too far from Mark and Karen's house. He learned of the passing of the Sheriff the next morning by a call from Karen. He let her know he would stay for the funeral and try to help her in any way he could.

Later that morning, Tony was sitting in the swing on the screened in front porch of Mark and Karen's house, enjoying a leisurely swing when Karen came from inside the house where she had been making funeral plans on the phone. She sat down on the swing next to him. On this day, which was to be his first full day in town, he had earlier met their daughter Jean's oldest child, a six-year-old son fondly called Junior.

He had also met Jean's youngest child, a four-year-old daughter named Emily, whom he had found out was, unfortunately, autistic and not able to communicate much at all. Both kids were now over at Karen's mother's house so Karen could concentrate on making arrangements for the funeral. Jean, who was a drug company representative, had been notified of her father's death and was on her way back from a sales trip to Knoxville, Tennessee. Tony felt that now was a good time to catch up on things, as much as he could, with Karen.

"So, tell me about your grand kids. Junior seems like a good little boy," Tony said as they began to gently swing back and forth while the big fan hanging over the front porch turned slowly.

Karen leaned back and said, "He is a good boy. He's always been a lot like his grandfather. Even at his young age, he is kind, considerate, and thoughtful. Tries every way possible to make things easier for his Mom and for Emily."

"What happened with Emily? Do you know what caused her autism? How did she end up with that?" Tony asked as he intently looked at Karen. He wanted to know the background behind the severe limitations that he had already seen Emily try to deal with.

Karen took a deep breath, looked away for a moment, and after almost breaking into tears, turned to Tony and said, "They don't really know. The doctors can't seem to agree on what caused her to be like she is. We all thought she seemed to be alright for the first two years of her life. She was just a normal child. Then, right after she went and got those vaccinations, those shots that every child is supposed to have at that age, almost immediately she changed."

She looked away and began to shake her head from side to side. After a moment's pause, she looked back at Tony and said, "I think it was those shots".

"The shots?" Tony said as he stared at Karen. "You think the shots that were given to her caused her to be like she is?"

Karen paused for a second as she looked away, then she turned her head to face Tony.

"It had to be the shots. We have gone over everything, looked at where she had been in the days before she changed. We went over everything she had eaten over those days. Almost everything she ate was from what I had bought at the grocery store. She wasn't around that many people we didn't know. She was with very few kids, just kids from parents we knew, and there was no indication of anything wrong."

Karen turned to look at the area in front of her house. She shook her head again as she said, "We have gone over everything, time and time again, and finally I started looking online for information and began running up on things that made me think."

"Things like what", Tony asked, now interested in finding out more about Karen's granddaughter's situation.

Thinking for a moment, she answered, "Well I don't know where to begin. So, I'll just start telling you things that I found out."

After taking another big, deep breath, she then said, "I found out that in the 1980's there was only about one child in every twenty thousand that was autistic. Today, that number is around one in every eighty children. So, something has to have been happening in that time period."

Seeing and appreciating that Tony was closely listening, she continued.

"There have been requirements for kids to have shots going back to the 50's and 60's, except back then there were only like five or six things included in those shots. Today, there are over 45 different things in the vaccinations."

"That many?" Tony said, clearly surprised by the numbers.

"Yes, and the stuff making up those shots is held together by what they call a binding agent or something like that, which is, of all things, mercury!" Karen exclaimed.

"Mercury? That stuff is poisonous, isn't it?" he asked.

Now sitting forward in the swing, Karen answered, "Yes! Well, it certainly can be. Some doctors who have been looking into all of this think a lot of it goes to a child's brain, and other parts of their little bodies, causing all sorts of things to go wrong as they grow. Now, of all things, they are talking about using a new vaccination more concentrated and intense than any that have come before it, even though it has been associated with high rates of adverse reactions in children during clinical trials."

Tony turned away from Karen to look across the front yard area as he thought about what he had just been told. After a moment, he turned and asked an obvious question that came to his mind.

"Why doesn't Junior have it? Didn't he have to take the same shots, or at least the same types of shots, that she took?"

Karen looked at him and said, "That is the same question we have asked for so long. Why doesn't he have it? We can't figure out why. If the shots are the cause of it, then why don't all of the kids have it? Nobody knows. The only thing they have said back to us when we asked the doctors about it is that they think different bodies with different types of cells and chemical makeup handle the chemicals differently when children get the shots."

After a few moments of silence, Karen said, "Now I am going

to mention something I found out on the internet. I don't know if it is true or not but ohhhhhhhh wait until you hear this."

Tony turned more to face her in the swing. He didn't want to miss any of what she was going to say next.

"I read where the five major drug companies, the ones that produce almost all of the shots and put them together and all, knew back in about 2005 that they had a problem. This article said that they felt they had to do something because all of the families of the kids that began to have all of the health problems they had not had before, were wanting to get with some of those big law firms that were filing lawsuits that could possibly result in big financial awards against them, like what was done with the tobacco lawsuits. You know those people ended up getting millions of dollars against those tobacco companies."

"I remember hearing about all of that when it happened," Tony said as he nodded his head affirmatively.

"Well, according to this article I read, those major drug companies had a meeting at some place about an hour outside of Atlanta and made the decision that they had to do something or each one of them was going to be faced with potentially really big court judgments as a result of what was happening to all those kids."

"So, what did they do?" Tony asked, really interested in what Karen might say now.

"The article said they agreed to go to Congress and get the United States Congress to grant them an exemption from being sued! A limited exemption, but even so, an exemption!"

"An exemption? What happened?"

"They got a United States Senator, who happened to be a very well-respected doctor, to put together legislation to get that exemption for them and to get it passed by Congress," she said as she now sat on the edge of the swing.

"He was actually able to get that done?"

"According to the article, that Senator was able to get exemption language quietly put into a major piece of legislation that was passed by both houses of the Congress during the last few hours they were in session. Are you ready for this? It supposedly happened the last day before they adjourned for the Christmas holidays!"

Tony sat there in shock. There was no other way to describe how he reacted to being told that. Karen watched the look on his face as he quickly ran over in his mind what he had just been told.

After pondering it all for a few moments, he asked, "Do you really think those shots are what caused her problem?"

Karen replied, "I think so and a lot of parents like Jean feel the same way. Why would they go get immunity from Congress, in the middle of the night during the Christmas holidays, unless there was something to it. And they did it in such a way that it could not be overturned by a court, one of the parents told us. Also, some of the researchers who have been looking into things concerning the major companies and raised questions, have apparently been threatened. Others have had problems, some even suddenly passing away."

Karen paused for a moment and then continued. "So, there is no way to get any financial help for these kids or their families. The doctor bills and other charges are so expensive that a lot of families are in financial trouble trying to take care of kids like Emily. Jean's sorry husband ran off with his secretary who was supplying him with drugs. His family, even though they are one of the richest families in New Orleans, did everything they could to limit what Jean got in their divorce. She was able to get a little child support and the house they were living in in New Orleans, but the medical expenses are just so high she had to change jobs and now travels a lot. We try to help her as much as we can, but there is only so much we've been able to do on Mark's salary as a Sheriff."

At that point she said, "I have a lot to do. I'm sorry to have unloaded all of that on you, Tony, but now you know a little more about it all."

"I understand," Tony said. "I am so sorry you are having to deal with all of that, along with everything else."

Karen then, ready to change the subject, asked, "What is going on with all of that property out there in Devil's Swamp that you were dealing with when I first met you on your trip down here back when? Is there anything you have to take care of while you're here concerning all of that?"

"No, not really. That was, for the most part, taken care of during that trip. There are a few things I sort of have to keep up with but nothing on a regular basis," Tony said as he leaned back in the swing.

Karen looked at him and said, "Sometimes I have caught myself thinking about all of the goings on out there. There are so many stories that have gone around, and still go around, about what all went on out there and what happened to people who were out there. Of course, Madeline's name comes up probably more than any other. She lived for so long and lived out there in that small house near where that elegant mansion had been."

Tony continued to gently swing and just listen, while looking at the still very pretty Karen.

"I always wondered," Karen continued, "about what happened to that young boy that lived out there with her for a while."

"A young boy?" Tony asked. He had not known about any young boy living out at the bluffs in Devil's Swamp where the mansion had been.

"Yes. I think his name was John," Karen answered. "Madeline was always having people go out there and do work for her. She had to pay them a lot usually because most people who knew anything about her thought she may have had some mental problems. So, a lot of them were sort of worried about going out there to do any kind of work. She did supposedly have an older black man that lived somewhere out in the swamp go by there from time to time and do a little work."

Tony turned his head to look, through the screen covering the front of the porch, at the street in front of the house, wondering about what he had just been told as he continued to listen.

"At one point in time, this nice-looking young kid, I'm pretty sure his name was John, started showing up out there. I believe he was about 14 when he was first noticed as being out there. Some thought he was just part of one of those work crews that used to go out there, but he didn't leave. He stayed out there. People wondered if maybe he was a relative."

That comment caught Tony's attention since that would have meant that the kid may have possibly even been some sort of distant relative of his. He thought all of that had been checked out when he had first come over from Sicily to resolve all the claims against Madeline's estate when she had passed away. Nobody had ever stepped forward during the process of settling that massive estate.

Karen continued, "Boaters and other work crew members

would see him out there, but everybody else would always leave. The only way anybody knew that he was still around was we would see him with Madeline sometimes when she came to town to do some shopping. He would be with her from time to time and apparently lived out there for about three years, until he was about 17 or so."

Turning to face Tony a little more, she said, "I heard it said that after the kid was not seen for a while, that older black man, the one that did some work out there, was asked what had happened to the kid. He supposedly said that the kid had left and gone to live in San Antonio."

Karen shifted her position in the swing and put her right hand on one of the chains holding the swing. She then looked at Tony and asked, "You never heard anything about that young boy being out there? He wasn't going to school, he didn't come to town by himself, and I don't know if he ever had any friends. I know that Madeline was the only person I ever saw him with. And he always, always was wearing a faded, old red shirt and old blue jeans. He never said much, but was very polite, and just seemed, I guess you could say, to be shy. I wondered about him, about why she at least didn't have him in school if no one else was responsible for him."

Tony said, "This is the first time I have ever heard about this. I don't know anything about it, who the kid was or where he went or anything."

"Well, I just wondered if you knew anything and wanted to ask. It was sort of a strange situation. The kid just looked so sad all the time."

Tony then said, "Well, if you ever hear any more about him, please let me know. I would like to know who he is."

27

Tony then turned more towards her and, changing the subject, said, "Tell me one thing. What did Mark think caused Emily to be like she is? Did he think it was the shot?"

Taking a moment before she replied, Karen then said, "He was kind of like everybody else. He thought the shot could have caused it. He also wondered if it might have been caused somehow by Jean taking drugs at some point, but he was convinced she was not taking any illegal drugs. And I think he felt that way because he checked that possibility out every way he could have and didn't find anything. The only other thing that might have had something to do with it, and I just have run up on this recently, is that she began taking anti-depressants while she was pregnant with Emily. That sorry husband of hers was starting to act strange and that began to put a lot of pressure on her. We finally found out that was about the time his secretary had gotten him to start taking some of the same drugs that she was taking, and also smoking marijuana. They ended up getting intimately involved, which I think she had planned all along."

After taking a moment, Karen said, "There was one other thing that Mark thought might have been involved. You know our first child, a little boy, died not too long after he was born. The doctors all said it was from natural causes. Mark thought it might have been because of some of the chemicals he had been exposed to while he was in Vietnam. They sprayed stuff all over everything over there and even had them drink some of those chemicals sometimes to show the Vietnamese that it was all safe. He thought that may have had something to do with our son's death. We had a hard time having a child after going through all of that with our son but finally we had Jean. He never could find anything though that showed that what had happened over there had any connection with our son's death."

Tony thought over what he had just been told as he looked out through the screen over the front yard. The only sound was a slight creaking noise cause by the gentle motion back and forth of the swing.

"How did Jean meet the boy that became her husband," Tony asked?

"She met him at LSU while in college there. They began dating each other about the middle of her second year there," she answered with obvious displeasure in her voice. "I never did ever really like that boy. He just always seemed like a jerk to me, but Jean thought he was so cute. He was fairly nice looking but drank a lot, and always seemed to be a smart aleck because of a lot of the things he said."

She shifted her position on the swing as if to show that talking about her daughter's former husband made her feel uncomfortable. After a moment, she continued.

"They eventually had a very bitter divorce. His parents are in the upper high society of New Orleans. They have long been involved in a very successful shipping business there, going way back to the early 1800's. They are one of a small group of families that is sort of in control there. When they were going through their divorce, that family made things so difficult for Jean and the children. In fact, they somehow had her husband able to end up with custody of their son, even though that sorry excuse of a human being was taking drugs with that new wife of his, as he is doing almost every day now. I worry about that little boy being around all of that, but there is nothing I can do. Jean tries so hard to do everything she can for their daughter, but it is so hard on her financially. I don't know how she handles it, but she tries."

Though starting to sniffle a little, Karen managed to say,

"That little girl of hers is so sweet and tries to do things but has such a hard time, with just about everything. She gets so frustrated just trying to do simple things. She eventually loses patience because everything she tries to do is so hard for her. Sometimes she just loses it and starts throwing things and screaming. She sometimes gets out of control because there is almost nothing she can do easily."

Looking at the porch floor as the swing glided back and forth over it, Karen said as she looked over at Tony, "The one thing the little girl does love, of all things, is sometimes listening to some country and western music." She softly giggled following that comment.

After the quiet passage of a few moments, Karen said, "There is another problem that I have to deal with now in the middle of all of this."

Tony turned his head to look at her as he said, "What problem is that?"

Karen looked back out towards the street and said, "I hate to even mention it. I need to spend my time on getting the funeral planned and all and trying to get it paid for. The funeral home has not been understanding at all about us not having the $18,000 they want paid to them before they help with the arrangements. And on top of that, one of my credit card numbers was stolen and has been used to run up a $14,000 bill on it. I don't know what to do about that. Things are a complete mess. I just don't know if I can handle it all." With that, she started to gently sob, bringing both of her hands up to cover her face and hold back her tears.

Tony reached over and put his left arm around her shoulder to comfort her. He did not want to see the wife of the man who had saved his life crying like she was. It was at this time that he also remembered the day when her husband's mother had told him, under a promise to never disclose what she was going to tell him, that Mark was in fact his half-brother, a fact that Mark did not know, and his mother had not wanted him to know. She had told him that fact only in case there may come a day that he might have to help Mark stay alive, and that exact situation had happened oh so many years before. Tony had pulled Mark out of a car only moments before a bomb Tony was aware of in the car exploded. Tony had done that because he had just found out about their having the same father. The next day, Mark had paid him back by saving Tony's life in a shoot-out at a local mobster's mansion south of New Orleans.

Remembrance of all of that was brought on by Karen's tears. Then he remembered what Mark had asked him to do the last time they had talked, just before Mark had died. He knew what he had to do.

"Karen, Mark asked me in his bedroom that last time I saw him to take care of you and his family."

She sat up and looked at him through tears as she, trying to say her words but stuttering and barely able to say anything.

"He … really… asked you…to do that?"

Tony took both of his hands and put them on each of her upper arms and said, "Yes. And Karen, I'm going to do what I told him I would do. So, get ahold of yourself. Now, go inside and get the numbers off of your credit card and give them to me. I will make contact for you and try to get that straightened out."

She looked back at him and, realizing what he had just said, she really started to cry.

Seeing her reaction, Tony gave her a little of a hug and then said, "Now, Karen. Karen. Listen to me. One more thing."

She caught herself for a moment and, after wiping her tears away one more time, she looked at him to see what was coming next.

Looking straight at her, he said, "You go in there and get the telephone number of who you have been dealing with at the funeral home and bring it to me. I will have a little talk with them also."

She looked at him now almost in shock. She couldn't say anything, and he quickly tried to put her mind at ease.

"Also, Karen. Don't worry about paying for this funeral."

Tony had to catch himself from saying something about his blood relationship with Mark, about how Mark had saved his life, but he knew he couldn't explain it. He had promised Mark's mother all those years ago that he would not ever say anything, and he wasn't going to break that promise.

"Now, go on and get me the numbers off that credit card and the telephone number for the funeral home. And I particularly want the name of that man that you have been dealing with at the funeral home."

After a moment's pause, as she was looking at him with tears coming down from her eyes, she managed to say through her sobs, "Thanks, Tony. Thank you so much." After again wiping her tears away from her face, she leaned over and gave Tony a kiss on his forehead.

After she had gotten up and walked back into the house, Tony pondered what all had just happened. Going over everything for a few moments, he decided that, after the funeral, he just might need to get in touch with his relatives and friends in New York. It would be interesting to hear what they might have to say about what he had just heard. He would go ahead and get his office assistants in California to help him with Karen's credit card problem. But he hadn't seen any of his relatives since his first arrival in the country so many years ago. It would be good to see them again.

* * *

The ceremony for the Sheriff took place at their church and was attended by over five hundred people. It was a proper military funeral for a war hero, complete with an honor guard, flags and the playing of Taps. Tony had wanted to stay in the background, but Karen insisted that he sit with the family at the church and then go with them out to the cemetery.

At the burial plot, he sat in the second row under the canopy for the casket. At the end of a short service, Tony waited his turn and then walked up to the casket of his friend. He looked down at it, touched the casket holding the man who had saved his life, and then briefly bowed his head in prayer.

Upon finishing his prayer, Tony walked away from the casket so other members of the burial party could pay their respects. He walked out from under the canopy and over to a nearby tree. Reaching that location, he turned to glance around the area at those in attendance. As he surveyed the crowd, he noticed a black man looking at him while standing next to a parked car. Looking around the crowd as he waited for the family to talk with attendees, he again looked over at the black man and it was then that something clicked in the back of his mind. The man continued to stare at him, so Tony decided to gradually make his way over to him. The man's eyes followed him as he made the effort to move nearer to him.

When Tony got close enough, the man said, "Welcome back."

Tony was shocked. He looked at the man more intently and

33

it was then that he remembered who he was. This was the man who had broken into Tony's house when he had first gotten to Bay St. Louis. Tony had been there sitting in the dark in his house by himself and had eventually ended up breaking the man's arm. He had ended up taking the intruder to the hospital. Tony had eventually even paid the man's hospital bill but had told him, the last time he had seen him back then during a visit to the hospital, that he should not break into anyone else's house or he, Tony, would be back to see him again. That had happened oh so many years ago.

"Thanks. How are you doing?" Tony answered, now genuinely interested in what the man was going to say next.

Still looking intently at Tony, the man said, "Saw a picture of you in da paper. When I saw dat, I wanted to come sees ya." He then shuffled his feet as he looked for Tony's response.

"Why would you want to see me?" Tony asked as he almost wondered if he should prepare himself for something else to happen. Looking at the man more closely now, he continued, "If you are the guy I think you are, you may not really want to see me."

The black man continued to look only at him and said, "I wanted to tell you, thanks." Looking away for a moment, the man then looked back at him and said, "I wanted to thank you for what you did for me." The man again shuffled his feet a little bit, glanced around at the various people now beginning to leave the funeral area, and continued.

"What ya did changed ma life," the black man said as he put his intense stare back on Tony. "If ya hadn't did what you did, I probably wouldn't be here rit now."

Tony was hard to impress. Hollywood had helped him get

that way. He had seen so much in his life, all the lies, all the misrepresentations that he had witnessed, all of the insincerity, so when he heard what the man said, he could tell it was coming from his heart. He really did not know what to say in return. He could only glance around quickly and even caught himself looking at the ground for a moment as he evaluated what had just been said to him. He then looked back at the black man.

"If something I did may have helped you or provided some guidance to you, I am glad. I really am. What has happened with you since then?" Tony looked deeply into the eyes of the man. The man could tell Tony seemed to be genuinely interested in how he might respond to that question.

The black man glanced around quickly and then said, "What ya did ta me caused me ta change ma life. I started out doing a littl' yard work. It helped keep me out of trouble. With the help of a minista, I got a job as a yard man at tha black Baptist church on da edge of town. I managed ta keep my nose clean, all the time, everywhere, in everythin ah did. Stayed away from all dat bad stuff, da drinkin, da stealin, da hangin out in da wrong places, all da evil thangs out thar. It was hard, but ah did it, and every now and then ah thought about ya, what ya had told me. Afta a while, a few years, ah became custodian of da church. After some time, ah even began to teach a littl' Sunday school."

The man paused for a moment, glanced around at the diminishing crowd, and then looked back at Tony. It was then that he got just the hint of a smile on his face as he said, "Ahm da preacha thar now." With that, he pulled the top of his coat back to show his preacher's collar.

Tony could not help but grin. He stuck his hand out as he said, "That is great! It really is. Congratulations!"

35

The preacher extended his hand and they shook, each now smiling at the other.

The preacher then continued, "Ya don't know how much it means ta me ta be able ta do this. Ta see ya. Ah really didn't know if ahd eva would see ya agin. But most of all, ta shake yor hand and tell ya, thanks."

Tony responded, "It means a lot to me too." He then gave the black preacher a hug. As he pulled back away, he said, "You are going to have to tell me your name, preacher man."

"Martavious Lewis," he answered, with the few remaining teeth he did have now fully showing.

"I am glad it worked out well for you, Martavious. I really am," Tony said looking at him, and then around him to make sure their conversation was still private. Seeing Karen looking at him with a somewhat quizzical look on her face, he could tell it was time for him to move over closer to where she was when she casually tilted her head toward the area where she was standing.

"I have to go now," he said as he stuck his hand out for another handshake. Looking at the preacher, Tony said, "Thanks so much for coming to see me and telling me what you did. That means a lot to me. Take care of yourself and, maybe one day, I'll make it out to one of your services."

Sticking his hand out and joining Tony's hand, the preacher said, "Ah would consider dat an honr. You'd be most welcum any time ya could make it."

Tony stepped away from the black preacher, took one final look at the man, and turned to begin making his way towards Karen. After taking a few steps, he looked back over his shoulder and saw Martavious walking down a long row of cars away from the burial site.

Once in Karen's presence, he was introduced to some of her relatives, usually being identified only as a "good friend" of her deceased husband, though most of the people already knew that Tony was now a famous actor in Hollywood due to his successful movie career. Several people in attendance came up to him to say "hi" and to thank him for being there.

The funeral also gave Tony the opportunity to briefly meet Jean, who was Karen and Mark's only child. He did not know much about her and had only found out that she even existed while he was checking in at the motel in Bay St. Louis.

Chapter Four

Jean had been born to Karen and the politically important Sheriff in June of 1983. Her birth had finally come after the couple had experienced a lot of difficulty as they attempted to have a second child following the death a year earlier of their first child. The first child, which had been a boy, had passed away not too long after his birth. Jean was the only child the couple would be capable of having.

Jean loved her dad so much and was so proud of him but, as she grew up, she had a hard time finding a boy that matched up to her father. In junior high school, she was considered as being very pretty. By the age of fourteen, she was already attracting the attention of males, both boys and men, and the comments of women, both girls her age and older. By the time she got to high school, she was thought of by everyone who saw her as being beautiful. As she got into her junior and senior years of high school, she began to win local beauty contests. Going through high school, she won a total of seven, in addition to her selection at her high school as Homecoming Queen during her senior year. She had a good personality, but it was her figure, 36DD-24-36, that was the subject of most of the discussions about her.

She began dating the captain of her high school's football team, Bobby Jim Franklin, the summer before her senior year. During the fall of her senior year, she had made the decision to celebrate her winning the highly contested position of Homecoming Queen by engaging in sex for the first time with her very popular and handsome boyfriend. They had come so close several times and, that night, she finally gave in to something she had thought about so much and really wanted to experience. Such activity became a regular event on their subsequent dates, usually taking place in Bobby Jim's old, beat up 1964 Ford, while it was parked in a vacant parking lot next to a group of tall trees near the 16th hole of the local golf course.

The couple even once arranged for the young paramour to come in the back door of Jean's family house one afternoon after school when her father was out of town and her mother was not due home from her part time job until 5:30. That was supposed to be her schedule, except she came home after being excused from her work an hour early that day. The young man barely escaped getting caught by Jean's mother by quickly leaving out the back door while partially undressed and racing to his car, which was parked nearby in the alley. Karen came into Jean's back bedroom looking for her daughter, who was trying to quickly get herself dressed.

Immediately noticing a definitive odor in the bedroom and the rumpled-up sheets on the bed, her mother had quickly gone to the back door of the house and scanned the alley. After closing the door and walking back into the bedroom, she looked at the expression on her daughter's face. She immediately knew what had been going on and also what had to be done. She turned around and walked into the kitchen, picked up the phone and called her doctor. When his nurse answered, Karen very firmly asked for an appointment for her and her daughter for the next day. Hearing the firmness in the caller's voice as she made her request, the nurse readily made an appointment for the next morning at 9:30. At that appointment, Karen very tactfully made sure that her daughter was put on birth control pills. She was not going to let Jean's life be potentially altered by an unplanned and unprepared for pregnancy.

Karen had never been comfortable with Bobby Jim being her daughter's boyfriend. She did not think that he was good enough for her daughter and, once experiencing the remnants of what she felt was an exit by him from their house, she became even more insistent that Jean should go to college somewhere other than where Bobby Jim was going to be. Karen made sure and guided college conversations in that direction. Mark did not question the decision for Jean to go to Louisiana State University, or LSU as it is commonly called, once it was determined that she could get enough academic scholarship help so that her parents would not have to pay much money for her to get a college degree. Upon graduation from high school, it was agreed that she would go to LSU.

Bobby Jim got a full scholarship offer to go play football at a small college in south-western Louisiana. Since he had to have a scholarship to go to college and that offer was the only one he received, it was off to that area of the state for him to pursue a college degree. He had to leave not too long after graduation so that he could get an early start at his college due to the early practices of the football team. Because he was worried about making the team and therefore keeping his scholarship, he did not have time to return but once to Mississippi to see Jean. He had already met a cute, friendly cheerleader at his new school, and she made sure that his interest in girls was kept satisfied.

Jean felt disserted. She had heard about Bobby Jim's new cheerleader friend and felt that she just had no choice but to find someone new to date at LSU once school started there. Besides, that summer while Jean was competing in various beauty pageants, some of her competitors had become envious. Jean noticed that envy and made up her mind to do everything she could to promote it. At the summer parties given by the sororities that were rushing her, she made sure that she was as friendly as she could be. She especially made sure she was introduced to boys being rushed by the top fraternities.

Because she was already taking summer courses at LSU, Jean was allowed to compete in various contests. She won three of the contests to bring her total of beauty contest wins to ten, but she came in as runner-up in Lafayette, losing to the daughter of a very wealthy family from New Orleans, Melanie Duchain, which nobody could believe. It wasn't long before she heard a rumor that Melanie had managed during an event to become personally involved with the lead judge of the three-judge panel.

The next pageant Jean had entered was a beauty contest held in New Orleans, one of several held in that area, but also the one that local observers felt was the most important. As part of the activities of the beauty contest, contestants spent time alone with each of the judges during which they were interviewed. The head judge, a prominent businessman from the area, let Jean discretely know during her interview with him that, if she were to meet him at his room on the edge of the downtown area, she could spend additional time convincing him that she would be the appropriate contestant to win the crown. She asked the judge if Melanie was going to get the same opportunity to meet with him, to which he answered that she wouldn't if Jean agreed right then to meet with him. Jean decided, especially since by that time she was not seeing Bobby Jim anymore, that she was not going to let Melanie take the crown in this one too. After spending two hours with the head judge late that evening, she left his room. The next evening, she was named the winner of the beauty contest.

During her freshman year in college, she signed up for classes in General Liberal Arts. She felt she had plenty of time to decide what she might want to major in. She pledged to one of the top two sororities at the school, which made most, but not all, of the members of the sorority she picked happy. Each weekend, she would have multiple different dates with mostly freshman boys but, as the first semester went forward, word about her beautiful face and fabulous body made its way around campus. Using her personality to tease almost every boy she met, she began to have more and more offers of dates with upper classmen mixed in with freshmen. Though some of her dates were interesting, most of them did not meet up with her expectations as their dates progressed. They seemed unpolished, poorly dressed and, in some instances, a few seemed totally ill-mannered.

She finished her first semester with all A's and one B, in English. The second semester, she continued her dating habits, having many dates with those similar to boys she had been out with the first semester.

There was one event that happened during the second semester that was somewhat different. She and a Sophomore sorority sister of hers, Mandy Jo Wilbanks, agreed to let one of the Sophomore boys Mandy Jo knew, Elton, pick them up in his car and take them out for burgers and a few drinks. He was an average looking guy and seemed to be just someone Mandy Jo knew well enough who would sort of look out for them while they were drinking.

The two girls were picked up at their dorm entrances and taken out for a quick meal. Since there were the two girls and Elton, the boy driver, the two girls sat in the back seat. While Jean had taken her first few drinks of beer and liquor with Bobby Jim, she had only gradually begun to drink more regularly with some of her dates in college. They had each already had a few drinks at the bar where they had eaten, and Jean was a little tipsy by the time they subsequently stopped at an out of the way rural bar that sold cheap booze. Elton would not have any problem purchasing additional drinks there for all of them. At some locations, their age might have made such purchase a problem.

While waiting for Elton to come back to their car with their drinks, Mandy Jo leaned over and said, "I am so glad we came out tonight. He is somebody that I think we can count on to keep getting us what we want as long as we want it, and not be a threat to us. Don't you think?"

After thinking a moment, Jean said, "No, I don't think he will bother us. Would not have come if I did. He is enjoying being with two girls at once. He probably has not ever even done that." They both chuckled at that.

Mandy Jo continued, "We are probably the only girls that would go riding around with him. You know how shy he is."

After pausing for a moment, Mandy Jo said, "You know you really do look beautiful tonight."

Jean looked and her and said, "Thanks for saying that. That is really nice."

Mandy Jo said, "I have wondered what it would be like to kiss another girl. Have you ever wondered that?"

Jean looked at her and said, "No, I have never really thought about that."

Mandy Jo said, "Would you like to try it? Before he comes back out?"

Jean looked at her and said, "Ok. Why not?"

Mandy Jo sat forward and then leaned over until their lips met. The kiss was a good solid kiss from which Jean did not quickly pull away from. After a few moments of a complete kiss, Mandy Jo pulled back and Jean said, as soon as she could, "Oh myyyyyyyyy." After smacking her lips a little, Mandy Jo said, "Oh, my goodness."

After a quick pause, Mandy Jo continued, saying, "That was good. Oh my, that was so good."

Jean looked forward and, seeing their driver approaching, said, "Here comes Elton."

After finishing their drinks, their driver took them to their respective dorms, dropping off Jean first. The two girls never really spent any more time together during the rest of their college days. Not too much later, Mandy Jo met and began dating the man who became her husband during her junior year in college.

For most of the remainder of the second semester of her freshman year, Jean basically continued her very active dating. Her beautiful face and her standout figure on her five-foot, six-inch frame was enough of an attraction to anyone who saw her.

When she took the time to properly deal with her shoulder length brunette hair, her overall appearance was even more striking.

As the semester came closer to its end, she was confident from the comments she was receiving that she needed to further refine her criteria for a date, limiting her willingness to spend time with someone based on his looks, his status in his fraternity, and the financial background of his family. She also made it clear to her dates that she was not going to have sex with them just because they had taken her out and spent some money on her. She was looking for someone special that she could spend the rest of her life with and that meant that she did not want the word going around campus and elsewhere that she was easy to get into bed.

Many of her sorority sisters had the idea that if they could have sex with a date that they liked, then their possibilities of getting such a boy to eventually marry them, support them for the rest of their lives and have children with them was much better. Others were looking for someone to fall in love with. Such a search was difficult for many of them for various reasons. It was quite the opposite for Jean. It was not hard for her to have prospects simply because her beauty had become so well-known around campus.

Not too long after the beginning of her sophomore year, Jean met the man, Dalton Johnson, who would become, after college graduation, her husband. She had a class with him and noticed him since he was rather handsome. Many of the girls made it quite obvious that they wanted to go out with the somewhat dashing young man with the good personality. Jean asked several of her sorority sisters about Dalton and she immediately found out that his family was extremely wealthy as a result of their highly successful shipping business at the Port of New Orleans. It was rumored that they were one of the six most wealthy families in New Orleans, which meant that he had gotten into the most well-known fraternity on campus. When the 5-foot 10 inch, one hundred and seventy-pound Dalton walked over to her on Friday of the second week of classes her Sophomore year with a smile on his face and began talking to her, her quick evaluation was that he had possibilities.

Jean and Dalton had begun dating and enjoying each other's company. He liked being the envy of the guys by dating a girl who was widely now known as one of the most beautiful girls on campus, if not the most beautiful. She enjoyed being with this always well-dressed student who had a really good sense of humor. He seemed to take a special delight in making Jean laugh, which he did on a regular basis. After seeing Jean on the football field as one of the Homecoming Court members, he determined it was time to move things further along in their relationship by becoming intimate, which they became one weekend at one of the most elegant hotels in the French Quarter in New Orleans.

From that evening on, any time they got together, usually at his apartment just off campus, they both enjoyed drinking more and more and sex was almost always part of their evening. Eventually, most weekends would be the time of raucous fraternity parties and at some point, during the evening, as much sex as possible. While Jean had a more than healthy appetite for sex, her boyfriend was not as enthusiastic, mainly due to his often times heavy drinking. As a result, Jean was usually left very unsatisfied, sometimes not even enjoying the activity as much as she had with her high school sweetheart.

Their senior year, it was commonly thought that Jean would be Home Coming Queen. At a sold-out football stadium, the winner was instead none other than her competition from earlier years, Melanie Duchain. Nobody could believe it. Everybody was surprised. Weeks later, Jean ran into Melanie at a fraternity party after one of the football games. Having had a few drinks, Jean went ahead and asked her if she had fixed the judges up with girls for that selection. Melanie calmly answered that, no, girls had not been used this time. It had been something different, a male ballet dancer, and that had been only for the head judge! Jean almost slapped her.

Jean and Dalton got married after graduation in an elegant wedding in Jean's church in Bay St. Louis. Though Jean was concerned about Dalton satisfying her sexual needs, he was nice looking, and his family did have a lot of money and status in the New Orleans area, so she decided to go on through with the marriage. Hundreds attended the widely publicized event and afterwards, Jean and Dalton took their honeymoon trip to Hawaii.

Upon their return, using money provided by her husband's family, they bought in both of their names and moved into a well-known, very expensive ante-bellum home in a very exclusive area of St. Charles Street in New Orleans. Dalton went to work in his parents' shipping business. Jean began her efforts to become involved in upper society events and organizations in New Orleans. She soon joined the neighborhood garden club, which had been in existence for many years. She attended the regular meetings of the exclusive group and tried to make friends with as many of its members as possible. However, she always felt like she was the outsider who really was only allowed to attend their meetings because of the family she had married into.

She also began learning how to play tennis by taking lessons at the New Orleans Lawn Tennis Club. She became friends with three other girls about her age that played the game at about the same level as she did. She and her husband became members of the Tennis Club and she soon had regular matches set up with her three friends at least every Saturday morning and sometimes Wednesday afternoon also. She soon began to be competitive with the group of girls with whom she was playing.

After three years of trying, the couple had finally welcomed their first child, a boy that was fondly called Junior. Initially, Dalton and his family seemed very happy about the new arrival. The male heir to their business was established. However, Dalton's two older sisters, Gertrude and Josephine, both very matronly in their looks, were not as excited. In fact, they were not happy about Jean's inclusion in their family at all. The fact that Jean was still very beautiful did not prevent them, every chance they got, from making disparaging comments about Dalton's "hick from Mississippi."

Gradually, Jean began to feel that she was not welcomed in the family, thanks mainly to the attitude of the two sisters. Dalton went from heavy drinking to smoking marijuana almost every weekend and then to including more smoking during the week. Jean thought that if they had another child, maybe Dalton would become more responsible again. She was happy when she found out she was pregnant. Gertrude and Josephine, and eventually Dalton, were not. They made things very unpleasant for Jean and she became so depressed that she went to see her doctor. He prescribed anti-depressants and other medications to try to help her deal with her situation.

When their second child, a daughter they named Emily, was born, she was beautiful and seemed perfectly healthy and normal. It became obvious after her second birthday, within three hours of getting her shots, that something was not quite right. It was shortly after Emily got those shots that Jean and Dalton found out they were the parents of an autistic child. Jean was devastated. Dalton went back to his office to take more drugs, which he was now doing regularly, unknown to Jean, with his pretty blonde office assistant.

Within two years, Dalton filed for divorce. He and his family filed for custody of Junior, agreeing to let Jean have custody of the autistic daughter. Neither Dalton nor his family wanted to have anything to do with the daughter. Their feelings crushed Jean, making her really despondent and depressed, especially so because Dalton and his family's efforts left her financially under pressure due to the high medical expenses. Jean was having to spend so much time and effort to take care of Emily, but Dalton and his family could care less about the poor child. They were proud of the little boy, who they had helped Dalton get custody of, but wanted to leave Jean with very little financial support because she was the mother of a child they would just as soon not have anything to do with. They knew that the child was very limited and was talked about despairingly among the upper level of families they associated with in New Orleans. Also, the two sisters felt that their portions of the massive family estate, that they might eventually be entitled to, could possibly be significantly adversely affected by the "hick from Mississippi" and the medical requirements of Emily.

Because of their political connections, the female judge assigned to the case, who initially seemed to favor Jean and care for Emily, shifted her preference to Dalton when funds for support of the mother and her child became the topic of discussion. It soon became apparent that the judge must have been friends with or influenced by the other side. Her decisions and comments concerning funds for Jean and support for Emily became more and more directed towards limiting what the family should make available for the two.

The family even went so far as to find a young dock worker, Sammy Jeffery, who testified at one of the preliminary hearings that he and Jean were very involved sexually, which statement was false. The two sisters, Gertrude and Josephine, had discretely arranged through the shipping company to make sure the dock worker would receive, after his testimony had been provided, a "bonus" of $28,000 that was to be paid over a four month period, supposedly for his extra hard work for the company on the waterfront. The two sisters had always been jealous of Jean's good looks and wonderful personality and had continuously worked to cause problems while the couple had dated and even more so after the marriage ceremony had taken place. With the actual worth of the family being well over one hundred and fifty million dollars due to the family's highly successful shipping business with China, the concerns of the two sisters, especially those of Gertrude, were more due to envy than any real need for financial support. Instead, Gertrude in particular liked causing her younger brother's wife any problems she could and was constantly making disparaging comments concerning Jean to members of the elite garden club of which they were both members and to members of the exclusive church to which the family had long belonged.

Jean had remained loyal and true to her husband, though she had been on edge and not satisfied sexually for quite some time. She had been approached numerous times during their marriage about becoming involved with various men who were attracted by her beauty, but she had continuously rejected such offers. Jean was horrified by the young dock worker's claim during his testimony of sexual involvement with her. Yet, Gertrude

51

made sure to include all sorts of various rumors about Jean and Sammy in discussions with her friends.

When one of Jean's former sorority sisters let her know about Dalton's involvement with his blonde office assistant and agreed to testify about that relationship, Jean finally was able to get the judge to allocate half of any money that would be received from the sale of the house to Jean, but only upon a completed sale of the house since title was in both Dalton and Jean's name. The judge agreed to provide Jean with a monthly payment from Dalton of a limited amount of money. However, the funds allocated were much less than funds she normally should have been provided and not enough for the support of Jean while also paying for her daughter's extensive medical needs. That situation meant that Jean was going to have to go to work, which was really what her ex and his family wanted. It also meant that the two sisters were going to have significantly more money made available to them from the estate than normally would have been the case. Jean began attending nursing school and worked hard enough to finish her education requirements as soon as she could.

Through her tennis contacts, she was then able to get employment at one of the local hospitals. Being as smart as she was, she became proficient with her nursing duties and, at the first opportunity, was able to convince the hospital administrators to let her attend classes at a local college so that she could work toward a better paying job as a surgical nurse. The judge agreed to have Dalton provide some limited additional funds for her education efforts but refused to provide more than a minor increase in money for the child's care. However, Jean was ordered by the judge to immediately terminate her membership in and usage of the New Orleans Lawn Tennis Club facilities. The judge told her that she could, instead, start using the public tennis courts at the City Park of New Orleans. The girls she was playing with did not agree with the way she was treated by being excluded from the Lawn Tennis Club courts and agreed to move their somewhat regular doubles matches to the City Park tennis courts.

Jean's mother tried to help her by taking care of her autistic child as much as she could. Special care for autistic children in New Orleans was also utilized as much as could be afforded. The elegant house on St. Charles was put on the market for sale, but no one had looked at it so far. Jean began to believe that Dalton and his family were putting the word out that whoever looked at the house was going to have a hard time dealing with them. She felt they wanted to cause her as much of a problem as they could as she tried to get that house sold.

Because of how expensive the care for Emily now was, and going to be even more so in future years, Jean decided to try to become a drug salesperson. She was told that, if she was able to become a successful agent for a drug company, she could make a lot more money than she would working in surgery in a hospital.

After several discreet inquiries at the hospital, she found out that most of the drug companies were looking for attractive, smart young women who could market their products in that very competitive industry. Soon she was able to identify the regional representative for one of the top nationally known drug manufacturers. Once she had the chance to talk with him, he was more than happy to include her in the next class of potential female sales reps who would be involved in a three-day class at a large, modern hotel in downtown Houston. Her performance in that class would enable the drug company representatives and instructors to determine if she would be successful as a drug salesperson for them.

After convincing the representative to give her a chance to participate in the classes, she was selected for inclusion with seven other very nice looking, smart young women with great figures who had indicated they had the drive the company was looking for to succeed. The company was ranked fourth nationally and was hoping that a more aggressive sales group could be developed out of upcoming classes. Success would lead to an increase in sales and a higher ranking financially for the company. Stockholders would of course be pleased with any increases in sales numbers but, equally, would not be happy with no increase or, especially, any decrease.

As the classes began at their hotel in Houston, Jean was quick to realize that she was in a class with a group of very intelligent women. While four of the seven females seemed to be very smart and quick to understand the various technical makeup and terms of the company's products, Jean had to work very hard to keep up with the descriptions and discussions of performance of the company's products. She became much more serious about making her effort to learn in the classes when one of the instructors mentioned that a successful sales representative in any of the positions for which they were being considered could make anywhere from $150,000 up to $325,000 a year!

Jean was shocked. She had heard that these types of sales reps made good money. That was why she had pursued becoming one of them. But she had no idea it could be that much. If she could get anywhere in that range, she would be so much more able to take care of herself and look after her daughter and see to it that Emily got proper care and attention.

What she did not have to be concerned about as much was how her looks and appearance compared with her competition. While two of the women had been involved previously in beauty contests at their various high schools and while in college, Jean felt only one of them could really compete with her in total overall looks and figure.

During the late morning session, the subject matter of how the female reps should dress for their meetings with their clients and potential prospects came up. The rather nice-looking female instructor began by saying that, if selected to represent the company, they should always look the best they possibly could. Business suits were appropriate dress attire along with silk or satin or other matching blouses. Their skirts should be formally tight but also definitely not too long. Hearing this made Jean wonder exactly what the instructor meant. The instructor quickly tried to clear things up by saying specifically that the skirt should never be longer than mid-thigh in length. Heels should always be worn but never be higher than four inches.

Specific attention was paid to the discussion of hair style. Several examples were shown as to what might be an appropriate hair design when meeting with an already existing client, but there was a definite change in the style shown for meeting with a potentially new client.

At the end of the presentation, pictures were shown of how the total look should be considered for both categories of clients. Jean thought the suggestions fit right in with what she already might wear for high society parties and gatherings in the New Orleans area and was not particularly surprised by what was shown. Some of the other girls were and immediately questioned how they were supposed to pay for such first-class clothing. It was then that they were informed that the company would provide them with a certain amount for a clothing budget, the level of which would be discussed more in detail after the selections were made.

At the end of the second day, Vern Whitley, the lead instructor, told the group that on the third and final day of classes, each prospective employee would be questioned and basically interviewed by him on a one to one basis. The group was informed that the interviews were intended to be conducted in the relaxed atmosphere of the instructor's personal Cadillac as he took each one of them on a trip around the downtown area. Jean was immediately concerned, having experienced what she had previously in her life with the judge at the beauty pageant. She worried about the upcoming "interview" all that evening.

The next morning, after who she thought was her main competition had gone first on her ride with the instructor, Jean was notified that it was her turn to go. The first girl had been gone for about forty-five minutes. Jean met the car and its driver at the front door to their hotel. She felt less concerned about Vern when she saw him now dressed in a very expensive suit and wearing a tie. She also knew that the remaining women all were waiting for their time to meet solo with him.

After the doorman for the hotel opened the door for Jean to get into the front seat of the car, the door was shut, and Vern pulled away from the hotel and onto the street. As he blended the car into the traffic, he began their conversation by saying that he hoped to hire four from the class and wanted each girl to have the opportunity to ask him questions about various aspects of the positions for which he was hiring. After going over some of the requirements for the successful performance of the job, he mentioned that he was very happy with Jean's progress in the class over the past two days, as he had been with some of the others in the class.

After other comments about Jean's performance in the class, all of which were generally complimentary, he asked her if she had any questions that she might not have felt comfortable asking him in front of the others. He said that his experience in the past had often showed that prospects had sometimes wanted to ask certain questions but usually felt that they should not. This opportunity was being provided to each one of them individually so that they might ask those questions, if any, that may be on their minds. Vern said that the questions the prospects might have that they were really concerned about would give those doing the evaluations, including him, a better idea as to whether a candidate was willing and able to handle the job.

Turning yet another corner in the light traffic, Vern said, "For example, what are you going to do to make a difficult sale? There are going to come times when our competition is going to have done a good job of getting an office manager or doctor or representative of some type to not want to do business with us because of a connection of some sort with someone else. How would you deal with that?"

Jean thought for a quick moment about one of the main points of a particular presentation that had taken place late in the evening of the prior day. The idea of persistence had been presented, but persistence that was not offensive to the person to whom the presentation was being made. An in-depth discussion had taken place and the instructor had emphasized when it was important to be persistent, while at the same time not being offensive.

The instructor had eventually set forth in the class that what they wore to their presentations was always vitally important to their potential success. They were to always dress with class and act with class, but they should not forget that while each one of them was a very beautiful person, both outside and inside, they should never forget that most of the people they would be dealing with were men who had been successful in getting their positions by being smart, observant, and aggressive. The instructor had closed by saying that, "It will never hurt you to be a classy, intelligent sales lady who also happens to be, at the minimum, subtly sexy. That is the least you can do while making all of that money that you can earn in your sales position."

At that point, along with all of the information that had been provided to them about the company's excellent products, the instructor had provided subtle guidance as to how to sit, how to walk, how to talk, and, yes, how to pose and tease. What had been mentioned was almost like what Jean would have thought would be included in a course on how to begin a stripping routine in a strip bar in New Orleans. That presentation had surprised her and was now, at this point in the conversation, what she brought up.

"I know how to get someone's attention, Vern. I mean, I won several beauty contests and was able to win most of the ones I competed in. I've never had any problem getting someone's attention," she said as she looked over at him for his reaction, as he was driving, to what she had just said.

Vern smiled and said, "I bet you have been able to do just that, Jean. But there is one thing I want to ask you because at some point in time, you may have to deal with it if you are selected to join us."

Jean looked at him, wondering what Vern was getting ready to bring up.

Pulling the car over into a vacant parking lot, Vern came to a stop, put the car in park and, with the motor and the air conditioner still running, turned to face her. He then slowly said, while looking directly into her eyes, "Jean, there may come a time when you have to make a decision just how far you are willing to go to complete a sale."

After pausing for a moment, he continued, saying, "There may come a time that you have to do whatever you are comfortable doing to close a sale. But there also may come a time when you may have to make a decision to go beyond what you are comfortable doing and do whatever you have to do, to close the deal and make a sale."

Jean immediately felt she knew exactly what he meant by what he had just said, or at least she thought she did, but she did not want to let him know she knew that for sure. She didn't know what to say next.

After a pause of a moment, with the engine still running, the car still in park, Vern took a breath and said, "At that moment, you have to realize that there are those who want the same job you would have and who are willing to do whatever it takes to be successful at that job." After pausing for a moment, he next slowly said, "If you won't do what it takes to be successful, at that job, to get the job done, then we will just have to get somebody else who will because, Jean, there are those out there who will do what they have to do to make these sales."

Jean immediately responded, "Are you saying I may have to use sex to make a deal?"

Vern replied, "No, I am not saying you have to go to bed with someone to get a deal closed. I am not saying you have to do that. I am saying that you, you Jean, may have to make that decision yourself in order to conclude a deal. You are the person that will have to make that decision. But Jean, if you don't make those sales, if the sales you are working on are not successfully concluded, we will have to get somebody else into that position who will be willing to do whatever it may take to make those sales."

After a moment of silence, Vern then took his eyes off of Jean and straightened up in the driver's seat. He put the car in drive and pulled back out onto the street. As they drove on a route that would take them back to the hotel, Vern changed the subject of their conversation and talked, in a more everyday tone, about how all of them would be getting ready to leave now and go back to their homes. The company would make its decision within the next few days and would let each one know what that decision would be as soon as possible.

After a few moments, Jean spoke up, saying, "Mr. Whitley, I need this job. I really do. I have a child with special needs who I have to support. I know I can do this job. I know I can be successful doing this job. I promise I will not let you down if you will just give me the chance."

Jean was so desperate she was almost about to cry. She stopped talking so her voice would settle down and hopefully she would stop shaking. After a moment's pause, she continued, saying, "I promise you I will make you proud of me. Just please give me the chance to do it."

She looked over at him as he turned his head to look at her. What she saw was his evaluation look. He had given that look to so many people. He could evaluate a person, especially a woman who was a prospect for a job in the sales of his company's products. He had to make the decision as to which job applicants would be the most likely to get the job done. His bosses had made it clear to him that they wanted their company to move up in sales and now was the time that they wanted it to happen.

A week later, Jean got a call from Vern. He told her he was going to take a chance on her and give her the opportunity to be successful. At the end of the conversation, he said, "Jean, don't let me down."

She quickly responded, "I won't. I promise I won't."

He didn't think she would. His review of her records and his evaluation of her led him to believe that she was not only very smart, but that she also had a lot of common sense. He felt that her beauty had probably led people to underestimate her intelligence. That's why he decided to take a chance on her. She might actually do quite well, depending on how far she was willing to go to be successful.

Within two weeks, she started making the rounds of those areas assigned to her. Her territory would be in parts of east Tennessee, the western half of North Carolina, parts of South Carolina, and part of northern Georgia. As she became familiar with her new contacts and with those she would have to get to continue letting her company service their needs, she felt that she could handle the demands of her position without too much trouble. She could feel several of the men looking at her like other men had done in her life, admiring her still beautiful face but especially checking out her still fabulous breasts and, as she was sometimes told, her almost perfectly shaped hips. She made sure that she wore matching skirts and blouses along with business jackets and heels. She also had remembered the suggestion in her original class about how the length of her skirt should never be longer than mid-thigh. She was most concerned about her long brunette hair, which she usually wore up in some type of sophisticated bun arrangement.

Only two of the men she made presentations to were somewhat obvious about checking her out, but of course she acted as if she was totally unaware of their looks. She did have to pose more for one particular buyer at a rather large hospital in east Tennessee and did have to make a repeat trip to visit with him in order to close the deal. She made sure her white blouse underneath her jacket was rather sheer and that, when she unbuttoned and removed it prior to her presentation, her lace trimmed bra was somewhat visible underneath.

A deal was eventually reached. She felt good about it once their agreement was concluded. At one point later as she went over in her mind what had happened, these men that she was dealing with as buyers for the businesses they represented reminded her of some of the boys she had dated in college. None of them, just like those boys had been back then, could keep up with her. She was feeling, as she had back then, like she was so far ahead of these poor males she was dealing with. They just simply could not keep up with her.

A few months after she had begun her job as a sales rep for the drug company, her job was putting an enormous amount of pressure on her, along with requiring her to do an extreme amount of travel. Though she had been successful with some of the smaller accounts that she was responsible for, two of the larger accounts had proved to be hard to deal with. She had finally managed to bring that east Tennessee account on board and that had helped her total income somewhat. But the manager of the largest of the accounts, a man who represented six very large hospitals in North Carolina, had not even agreed to meet with her yet. They were under an existing contract with a competitor, but that contract would soon be expiring. She had been told to get back in touch with them in about a month and that they may want to have a presentation made by her to their decision maker at that time.

While she had managed from her efforts to bring her income up close to $90,000, she needed to get more than that in order to take care of her daughter's increasing medical bills. She planned to pursue the North Carolina group as soon as possible and to try to develop more contacts for her products in the other state areas assigned to her. She felt sure the reason that her predecessor had been dismissed was because she had not been able to increase the market size in her area. She could see where it might be difficult to expand the area that was being taken care of.

She could also see from the contacts she had already made how difficult it was going to be to do better than her predecessor. Some days, the attitude of the men she was having to deal with was so arrogant, and in some cases outright offensive, that she could not believe they did not know how difficult they were being. She often felt like the one thing they seemed to think they were due was total effort on her part to play up to them. It got to where she began to feel like she had to do more and more to make and increase her sales and her quota. She was beginning to get fed up with the total arrogance of several of the men she was having to deal with.

Because of all the pressure she had been under, but also because she had been somewhat successful so far, she felt she needed a break. It was at this time that she received a call from one of her college sorority sisters who asked her to be a bride's maid in her upcoming wedding. Thinking that she would get that break and probably see at the wedding many of her sorority friends that she had not seen since college, she decided to go and try to enjoy being in the event.

Upon arriving in Dallas, Jean checked into the downtown hotel where most of the out-of-town attendees and participants had been provided with rooms. During check-in, the sorority sister she had shared a kiss with, Mandy Jo Wilbanks, also arrived to check in. She was there to also be a bride's maid. They agreed to get adjoining rooms next to one another on the tenth floor. Along with others staying at the hotel who were also in the wedding or attending it, they were able to catch rides provided by the bride-groom's family to the church for the wedding rehearsal on Friday night and for the actual wedding event early Saturday evening. Jean and Mandy Jo agreed to do some shopping together in downtown Dallas late Saturday morning.

Early Saturday afternoon, they sat by the swimming pool sunbathing before they went to their rooms to get ready for the wedding ceremony. During this relaxation time, the two girls were able to bring each other up to date on what all had happened to each of them since their college days some fifteen years earlier. Jean shared her experiences while she was married, and Mandy Jo provided information on her childless and loveless marriage, which had only lasted four years. Mandy Jo was now a sociology instructor at one of the local colleges in New Orleans, having gotten her undergraduate degree at LSU before getting married and then going to Texas to get her master's degree after she had gotten divorced. She was now working on her Doctorate while she was teaching to put herself through school.

After a lovely wedding ceremony Saturday evening, a very large and lively wedding reception and dance was held in the main ballroom at their hotel. During the progression of the reception, the vibrant music led to dancing that never slowed down.

Numerous men were continuously offering to dance with the still beautiful and sexy Jean while the very nice-looking Mandy Jo also had her share of dancing opportunities. Between dances, they both had several drinks that they enjoyed during the early part of the evening. Finally excusing themselves to visit the lady's room, Mandy Jo was able to guide the, at that point, very tipsy Jean upstairs to her room. It was there that Mandy Jo was able to do what she had thought about from time to time for so many years, and that was taking Jean further into what had started with a kiss in that car during college.

At about 2:30 in the morning, Mandy Jo left Jean and went back to her adjacent room. During all the time they had spent together, she had made sure that Jean had to do nothing but lay back and enjoy all of the almost constant attention shown her by Mandy Jo. While at first Jean had been a little resistant, she too had wondered about the other activities that might have followed that original kiss. She was also very frustrated sexually due to her long-time horrible relationship with her ex-husband, a fact that Mandy Jo had picked up on from their conversations during the day.

Mandy Jo had been continually watching Jean all day long, listening closely to what she had said as the day went along, and wondering if it might be possible to hook up with Jean later in the evening. She made sure that Jean had been drinking as much as she could handle and, once Mandy Jo had the opportunity, she made sure that Jean was enjoying the attention being shown to her.

What Jean did not know was that Mandy Jo had spent a lot of time since her divorce becoming very experienced in the art of lesbian sex. She had been with twenty-six different women and was now very experienced with, and thoroughly enjoyed, introducing straight women, which is what she thought Jean was, to the various excitements of lesbian sex. By the time Mandy Jo left Jean's room, Mandy Jo felt she had figured out the best combination of ways to keep Jean's attention and continually take her over the edge. During all of the experience, Jean was never made by Mandy Jo to do anything except lay back and enjoy. By the time Mandy Jo left the room after a couple of hours, Jean was very exhausted, and more than satisfied. She also felt like a sleeping giant had been awakened inside of her.

As Jean was packing her luggage the next morning for her return trip, she realized something. The white thong that she had been wearing the evening before was nowhere to be found. After going to the airport to catch her flight to New Orleans, she checked in and then sat down at the end of a row to wait for being called for boarding. After a few minutes, she could wait no longer. She called Mandy Jo, who answered her cell.

"Hi there," Mandy Jo answered. "How are you doing?"

"Hi," Jean said. "Wonderful. Really wonderful."

"Am glad to hear that. Are you on your way back?'

"Yes. Are you?"

"I just arrived back. I'm now driving from the airport in New Orleans to my house," Mandy Jo said.

After a brief pause in the conversation, Jean said, "There is something I have to ask you."

"What is that?" Mandy Jo was really interested to hear what Jean was going to say next.

"Did you happen to take something of mine when you left my room?"

Very coyly, Mandy Jo answered, "Now just what would that have been?"

"I think you know what I am talking about," Jean coyly answered, "and I would like to have them back."

"Mmmmm. Let's see. Give me a little hint."

"You know exactly what I am talking about," Jean said softly.

"What do you think I have, honey?" Mandy Jo had decided long before the call that, if she did get a call, she was going to make good use of it.

"I was missing this morning a personal item and I thought you just might know where they are," Jean said.

Mandy Jo giggled and answered, "I was wondering how long it would take you to realize they were gone. And I just love having them."

"Well, I would like to have them back. They do belong to me, you know," Jean teased.

"Oh, I know. That's why I wanted them. They belong to a beauty queen that I have gotten to know much better," she said.

"Well, I was a beauty queen once upon a time and I am now missing the white thong that I wore to this wedding I just went to and I thought you just might know where it might be."

After giggling again for a moment, Mandy Jo said, "Ok, I think as a matter of fact I may actually have something I happened to pick up in your room last night and they may just belong to you. But for you to get them back, honey, you are going to have to earn them."

There was a pause on the phone for a moment and then Jean said, "Promise?"

"Ohhhhhhhhhh myyyyyy goodness," Mandy Jo said. "Ohhhhhhhh myyyyy! Yes, honey. I promise. You are going to have to spend more time with me. The question is when! How about today? You want to meet me after you get off of your plane today?"

"I can't do it today. I have to go home and quickly pack for a trip for my job. I will be gone for a several days but will be back in about a week or so. How about I call you when I know I am coming home and maybe we can get together then," Jean said with some anticipation sounding in her voice.

"Ok. Great!' Mandy Jo answered with some excitement in her voice. "Try to give me a day or so notice so I can make sure to try to get free so I can meet with you. And I will try to take good care of that sexy little thong of yours in the meantime. I want to make sure I have it available for you to earn back."

After she hung up from finishing the conversation, Mandy Jo began thinking about what all she might be able to come up with to get Jean more interested in lesbian sexual acts. She had done such planning many times before and was looking forward to plotting and planning the taking of the former homecoming queen more deeply into the world Mandy Jo had just introduced her to.

This next time, Mandy Jo wanted to try to make sure that Jean was taken much further into her new world, so much so that she would have a more difficult time not being totally consumed by her new levels of excitement. She smiled to herself as she thought about how responsive Jean had been for what Mandy Jo was relatively sure was Jean's first complete lesbian experience. She wanted to get Jean converted into being a full time lesbian and their next meeting would be the perfect opportunity to take her further into it all so that could happen. Maybe this would be a good time to get her comfortable with possibly being with more than just one other woman at the same time.

Out of the three girls who had participated with Mandy Jo in successful seductions for the past three months, Ronnie was probably the best one to work with. Together she and Ronnie had been with six other women who had initially been targeted when those women had walked into the Green Tomato bar, which was not too far from the airport in New Orleans. Though not well-known outside of New Orleans, that bar was locally known as a hangout for women looking to explore "other" sexual experiences.

Very few knew that the four of them, Mandy Jo, Ronnie, Susan and Katie, had seduced a total of nineteen straight women over the past two and a half years. They had eventually passed those conquests on to more permanent lesbian partners and relationships. Except for three, each one had been taken from their initial contacts into additional experiences by the woman who had introduced that particular girl to the scene and were eventually passed on to other more experienced women.

Mandy Jo planned to do the same thing with Jean, but only after she had taken Jean into further experiences with her and most probably with Ronnie. Ronnie was the somewhat masculine but very nice looking, short haired, thirty-eight-year-old weightlifter, who worked as a bartender at the Green Tomato. She was physically very strong, working out at least three times a week and was an experienced lesbian. She also happened to live about two blocks from Mandy Jo, who rented a small house three blocks off St. Charles Avenue out past Tulane University. Ronnie living so close to Mary Jo had proven on several occasions to be very advantageous for their seduction adventures.

Thinking about various possibilities, Mandy Jo felt that, if she could introduce Jean into a scene with her and Ronnie, maybe it wouldn't be too long, and she could also introduce Jean into a scene with her and the young, very pretty 21-year-old former student of hers, Lindy. Hopefully soon, it might even also be possible to have her be with the two very masculine, somewhat heavy, but very experienced, lesbian women from Lafayette, who both had special sexual talents. After Mandy Jo got Jean deeper into things, she could then spend more time on Lindy, whom she had recently found out was putting herself through college as a stripper.

But first she needed to get Jean more comfortable with the lesbian side of things when she got back from her trip. Yes, Jean could earn her thong back, but Mary Jo was going to try to make sure Jean got more sexual experience at the same time. She wanted to eventually make sure that she got Jean into the picture game.

* * *

After packing in New Orleans for her first business trip following the wedding, Jean quickly traveled over to Bay St. Louis to see her daughter before leaving that evening. Tony managed to spend some time with Jean that afternoon on the front porch swing of the house where she had grown up. He had arrived at the house and, as he was walking up to the front door, he heard the screaming of a young child. He guessed the child was Emily as he was able to overhear Karen and Jean trying to comfort the young child in the front bedroom. Emily was having none of the comforting and was continuing to scream literally at the top of her lungs. Jean began crying, so distraught by her daughter's actions.

When Tony walked to the doorway of the bedroom, Karen asked him to take Jean and go out on the front porch while she continued to try to calm the young child down. Tony encouraged Jean to sit with him in the swing and handed her a handkerchief he was carrying to dry her tears. She sat on the swing and tried ever so hard to quieten her own sobbing. Karen's efforts finally began to have some effect on Emily in the bedroom as Tony put his arm around Jean and tried to comfort her.

After a few moments, Jean said, between sobs, "I'm …. so … sorry."

Tony replied, "Don't you worry." After a few more sobs by her, he continued, "We will be here for you. Just know that." As Jean began to calm herself somewhat, he continued, "You know your mom will be there for you and will always try to help you." Giving her a pat on her shoulder, he continued, "And I will help in any possible way I can. I promised your dad that I would do everything I could for your mom and you and your children, and I will."

After a moment, he continued, "I thought the world of your dad. He was such a fine person and was a true friend to me. So please know that you have people around you who care about you. And your little ones."

She leaned back a little and gave a quick glance toward Tony as she gave a little nod of her head. After a moment, she said in a low voice, "My little girl didn't ask for this, to be like this, and she is going to be like this for her whole life." Jean started slowly moving her head side to side in a negative motion and said, "The doctors tell me she is going to always be like this. Always." And she started to sniffle again as she said, "And there is nothing, nothing at all, that I can do about it. Nothing. Except love her and hug her. If she will even let me do that."

Tony just sat there and listened, figuring that was the best thing he could do at the moment. Jean slowly continued, "They say she might … at some point … might … get a little better… but …." After taking a moment to stare off in front of her, she then hesitantly said, "But they … they told me … not to … not to count on it, and that … that she will never be normal." She then started sobbing softly again, while dabbing at the tears coming from her eyes.

After a few moments, she sat up and said, "Thanks for what you just said. That means a lot." After pausing for a moment, she said, "I need to go see how she's doing. Mom is so good trying to help me and all. I feel so badly about my whole situation, but I feel so much worse about poor Emily. Then she stood up, and said, "Thanks for listening." Bent over and looking down, she opened the screen door and walked back into the house.

The next day, Tony went back over to Karen's house to see if there was anything he might be able to do to help Karen and her daughter and grand-daughter. He was only able to watch as Karen and Jean tried to get a reaction of any sort from the child. Sadly, Emily was almost totally non-responsive, completely opposite from the way she had been the day before, which caused Karen to cry deeply in his arms.

Tony decided to go ahead and take care of the two items he had told Karen that he would. The funeral home he dealt with directly and was able to convince them that the cost of the funeral should be reduced because of the Sheriff having been an outstanding veteran. After he mentioned that he was sure they would want the community to know they honored veterans and would not take advantage of their families at such a time of grief, the funeral homeowner agreed to lower the cost by $4,000.

The credit card fraud was more complicated. Since he was already halfway across the country, he decided to go on up to New York and see his relatives. He had not been there since he had first come over to the United States in the 1970's to deal with the complicated estate situation left by his Aunt, Madeline. He had kept up with the family and knew that they were now in legitimate businesses in the world of jewelry. They had previously been the subject of federal investigations and had gotten out of the crime business at just the right time. Federal agents had come into the New York area and dealt serious blows to two of the larger crime families in the area.

Once he was able to get a contact number, he placed a call to his cousins and asked if he could come up to the area for a visit. His call was very favorably received. They were glad to hear from him and told him that they would be looking forward to his visit. They were very happy that he wanted to come see them.

There was one more thing Tony thought about that he knew he was going to have to deal with. Realizing that he would probably be spending a lot of time on the Mississippi Gulf Coast until things settled down somewhat with the situation there, he contacted his office in LA and had them make arrangements to ship his motorcycle down to New Orleans. Once it got there, he would pick it up and ride it over to Bay St. Louis. He had asked Karen if it was alright that he kept it in the garage next to her house. She knew how much it meant to him to have it there on the coast, having ridden it with him when he had lived there before, so she readily agreed for him to keep it there in her garage.

74

Chapter Five

The leaders of the top five drug companies made it a point to meet every quarter of the fiscal year at some place convenient and interesting for the group. The meeting this quarter was being held at a huge hotel in the Charlotte, North Carolina area. The presidents of three of the companies were in attendance as they usually attended the meetings, as did the Chairman of the Board of one company and the Executive Vice President of the remaining company.

The purpose of the meetings was to discuss their efforts to make sure profits stayed up, even though some of them knew that there might be problems with their products. They all were in agreement that the profits should be kept as high as possible, regardless of any adverse results that might take place on the public from taking their products.

The unofficial chairman of the group was understood to be the president of the company with the highest gross income. That individual was not in question since the gross income of President Martin Zucoff's Tuckerman Corporation had been in the $48 billion range for the past twelve months.

Though President "Buzzy" Chatwood's Garwald Company was not too far behind in second place at around $42 billion, his company was more the subject of a lot of conversation because of its manufacture of several pills, one in particular, that had attracted attention as possibly being the cause of autism in children. "Buzzy" was continually defending his company's product by claiming that no proof had ever been clearly shown indicating that their product was the direct cause of autism in children. In fact, numerous studies, extensively financed by Garwald and other industry units, continuously failed to find any connection.

The third-place company, Shetland Rohrback, was usually represented by its hard charging Executive Vice President, Stanley Rohrback, the son of one of the company's founders. SR, as it was usually referred to by its competitors, maintained its gross income at around $37 billion but also had a high profile constantly pushed by Rohrback as he tried to show his father and the industry that he was really the smartest company head in the group. He was often urged by the group to not make too many public statements or do things publicly that would draw attention to the industry.

The fourth-place company, Fenton and Oswalt, usually was represented by their President, Martin Powell. The company often remained in that position with about $32 billion in gross income but had a much lower exposure to the youth market.

The fifth-place company was always Ballard, Tinkersly and

Lowell, represented by their Chairman of the Board, Bruce Rushton. With their annual gross being at around $28 billion, though such figure would be very attractive in many industries, it was considered as a weakling when compared with the other companies.

"All right, fellows. Let's get this meeting started and see where we are. Brandy will give us our update," Zucoff said.

The professionally dressed Brandy Chaplin, who had been giving the update presentations for over three years now, began and gave a rather thorough, though time limited, presentation. Only a few questions were asked since the attendees had seen the information before the meeting due to a rather complete circulation of documents containing available information prior to the meeting.

Near the end of the meeting, after Brandy had left the room, Zucoff asked the question that he had recently begun to ask at the end of each meeting.

"Is there any news that the rest of us need to know about from "Buzzy" concerning potential litigation regarding the legislation?"

"Buzzy" immediately responded, "No. Everything is quiet, as it has been now for some time. We anticipate it will stay that way."

Rhorback immediately followed, saying, "Things are the quietest they have been for some time." Looking around the room, he then said, "I would like to invite each of you to join me at a party in Miami at the convention coming up down there. There usually are some interesting things to see and do at this particular convention."

With laughter and smiles around the room, the meeting soon broke up.

* * *

The drug companies had decided back some time ago that they needed people they could count on and who were loyal to them but, at the same time, were somewhat separated from them. They wanted individuals who would make progress on investigations, doing what might be necessary to find out things, get leads and bring matters to a conclusion that others, such as law enforcement, might not be able to conclude. As they had ever so discretely let the people that had initially been interviewed know, they were large companies involved with huge bank accounts and they did not want anybody, anywhere, at any time, thinking they could do things that the companies would not deal with somehow, in some way.

That particularly held true for anybody who thought they could take advantage of any of the companies. When a preliminary investigation indicated that one person might need further attention, they would sometimes decide to get their lead private investigator, Robert Stone, involved in dealing with the individual. In this situation, the person needing further attention was an accounting employee, Linda Robertson. Linda was a pleasant looking, middle-aged, divorced mother of two who was employed in the accounting department of one of the major drug companies. That company had found out that Linda had been embezzling money from them each month for almost two years for a total of over $90,000.

Robert's office was located on the edge of the downtown area of Louisville, Kentucky. Working with him were two computer experts who were able to do extensive research on the internet and, when needed, in person. Robert used the computer expertise of his two associates to get access, with their help, to the drug company accounting records. Without the passage of too much time, they were able to figure out how Linda was taking the money and when. He had then contacted her by phone.

"Linda Robertson?"

"Yes?"

"This is Robert Stone. I am an investigator for the Morgan-Wilson Company and need to arrange a time to get with you. Are you available, say Thursday of this week, to meet with me after you get off of work?"

Linda had heard about Stone and was shocked that she had been called by him. The fact that she had been called was not good.

"Can you tell me what this is about? I mean, I don't know you and have no idea why we should be meeting somewhere after I get off of work."

"Let's cut out the crap here, Linda. You know exactly why I want to talk with you and I highly suggest that you meet with me Thursday, at say 6 after you get off from work, or I can go straight to the guys in the uniforms. Is that what you want me to do, Linda? Just go ahead and talk to them? I am trying to talk with you first."

Linda knew exactly what he was talking about. Quickly thinking about it, she said, "Ok. You said this Thursday, at 6?"

"Yes," he answered. "Meet me at the Mountain Inn on the north side of town. There is a bar there right next to the restaurant. I'll be the guy wearing black blazer and grey slacks."

"Okay."

"And Linda, so that I will recognize you, wear something red and sexy. You really need to wear something very sexy."

"Well I don't know. I mean, I don't even know you," she says with a tone of hesitation.

"Linda, you better wear something that will convince me to not send you off on an extended trip to a place for people who have done what you have. Do you catch my drift here, Linda? It would really be to your benefit to wear something really revealing for this meeting. You know, something low cut, tight and short. You know what I mean."

"Well, I guess I can try to find something red, if that's what you want."

"Yes, that is what I want, so do it. I will see you there at 6. And don't be late."

"What if I can't ...", she tried to say, but he had already hung up.

Three nights later, at a little before 6 pm Linda walked into the lobby of the Mountain Inn wearing red. Seeing the entrance to the bar, which was to the right of the lobby, she walked over to that area. She had spent a lot of time trying to do something with her medium length, blonde hair and had ended up just having to be satisfied with doing the best she could with it. She had other things to think about, such as feeling so obvious about being too over-weight to be wearing what she had on: the red, low cut, one-piece dress with a short, full skirt.

She knew that she was literally bulging out of the dress, which she had often worn at other times a few years back when she had been trimmer and on the social circuit with her then husband, with whom she had had two kids and from whom she was now divorced. She had not been out much in the past couple of years because she had purposely tried to keep a low profile for certain reasons. Now it seemed that this person, this caller, seemed to know a few things about what she had been doing. She had to find out what he knew and that was why she was there.

Looking around the room, which had probably fifteen people in it, she noticed a rather rugged looking man, just over 6 feet tall, stand up and motion her over to his table. Since he was wearing a black blazer, and no other man in there was, she walked over to him with the hint of a smile on her face and asked, "Are you Mr. Stone?"

"Yes, I am. Please call me Robert. And you must be Linda," he answered as he ran his eyes down over her cleavage and then to her hips.

"Yes," she answered, feeling very conscious now about literally bulging out of her dress, especially in the area of her waist.

Looking back up at her face now, Robert motioned her to a chair at his table as he sat back down in his seat.

Up walked a waitress, who said, "What may I get for you two?"

Looking at Linda, Robert said, "What would the lady like?"

"Vodka on the rocks," Linda said.

"And bring me a Vodka tonic."

After the waitress left, Robert said, "I am glad you came to meet me. I didn't want to make this hard on you, which I could have done, but it definitely is in your best interest to have come here and have this conversation with me."

Linda noticed that his eyes again glanced at her cleavage before he continued.

"I am an investigator for major drug corporations and have

been for some time. They asked me to look into a few things that seem to be happening at one of the companies. While checking into it all, I found that over the past almost two years, an amount of over $92,000 has come up missing."

Linda was shocked! From what he had told her over the phone, she definitely was afraid he knew something. Now, she was finding out he seemed to be aware of it all! She just looked at him, not knowing what to say, and didn't want to say anything until she knew more.

"I am sorry to hear that you have found that out, but what does that have to do with me?" she asked with as calm a voice as she could muster.

The waitress came up and put their two drinks on their table and quickly left to attend to other patrons.

Robert held his drink up and said, "Cheers", after which both took a sip from their drinks.

He then leaned toward her and said, "Look. I am not going to waste my time with this. You know why I contacted you. It is because I have all the evidence I need to send you away for embezzlement and theft for about ten years, at the least."

Linda was shocked. Robert knew she was shocked because a look of absolute horror came over her face when he had completed saying what he just did. This was not the first time he had seen a woman working for one of the companies react like that. He had caught six other women over the past three years as an investigator for the companies doing the same things that Linda had done. He had found that the best way, to save time for everyone, was to get right to the core of the problem and let them know he knew about them and what they had done. He had to admit that Linda had gotten away with her efforts longer than most of the others had but the result was the same. He had figured it out and now, just like the others, she had a decision to make. He was going to deal with her just like he had the other six.

Linda took a big sip from her drink, and then said, "You are mistaken. You don't know what you are talking about."

Robert quickly responded, "Oh yes I do, and you know it. The big question is, what are we going to do about it?"

After taking a sip from his drink, he continued, "There are two options." He leaned over closer to her and said, "I can turn you in and you will spend at least ten years in prison." He then paused to gage what the effect was on Linda of his last sentence. Seeing she was almost trembling, he said, "Do you want me to do that?" He paused again, and then said, "Answer me! Is that what you want me to do?" Linda still did not answer. After a moment, he continued.

"I guess that means you want to know what the other option is for you."

He took another slow sip from his glass and then said, "The other option is you can go with me to my room, right now. I have a room down the hallway here and you can go there with me right now." Robert paused to watch her reaction, which was to stare at him and see if he was serious.

After a few moments of silence, Robert said, "Well? What is your choice?"

"Look, I haven't done anything …."

Interrupting her, he said, "I am running out of patience here, Linda. I can't believe I am even giving you an opportunity to deal with this."

Seeing that Robert did seem to be getting upset, Linda said, "Ok. Ok. If I do go with you to your room, what happens next?"

For the first time, he seemed to be making progress. He had to laugh to himself because it was at this same time, with four of the prior six he had dealt with like this, that those others had come around to his way of thinking. The other two had agreed to his offer much sooner, one of them, the oldest, had done so within just a few minutes. This one, he had found out during his investigation, was in her early forties but had worked for the company for only just over two years.

Sitting back in his chair and, while again staring at her cleavage, he said, "You will make yourself available to me whenever I am in this area." After changing his glare to now look at her face, he said, "I am not in this area but maybe two or three times a year, but I would expect you to be available for me when I am here."

Looking first at him, and then away at the bar and then around the room, "I don't knowwwwww," she said as she brought her eyes back to him.

Robert answered as he raised his hand to signal for the waitress, "Look, this offer is not going to be available to you much longer. I am going to get up after I pay this bill and I am going to my room."

The waitress came over as he took a couple of bills out of his wallet and gave them to her. After the waitress left, Robert looked back at her and said, "If you go with me, I know what your answer is. And that would be that you don't want to go to jail. You get to go on leading your life as it now is. The company does not know what I have found yet and I will take care of that." Then leaning across the table, he said in a low, firm voice, "But if you don't come with me, I know what I will do, and you do too."

He leaned back in his chair looking at her. Then he slowly stood up and took a step around the chair he had been sitting in as he slid that chair back to the table.

Linda was distraught. She felt she had no choice. She had never thought she would get caught. She thought she had hidden everything so well. To some extent, it had even given her a good feeling to successfully do what she had been doing. She worked hard, well, some of the time. The company should have given her a raise anyway. So, she had done what she did, and had intended to keep on doing it. But now, this had happened. He wasn't that bad looking, she reasoned, and she did not want to go to jail, that was for sure. She had her two kids to worry about, her reputation to think about, and what would her friends think if they found out.

Robert took a step towards leaving the table and glanced back at her one last time. Linda made the decision. She would go with him. She would do this to at least give her more time to figure out how deal with the situation. She needed more time to at least talk with him, get to know him better. Who knows, maybe she could even get him to fall in love with her. She was good in bed, or at least that is what her former boyfriends and her ex-husband had told her.

So, she stood up and grabbed her bag, as she watched Robert turn and slowly begin walking toward the entrance to the bar. She followed him out of the bar, purposefully not looking side to side to see who, if anybody, was watching her as they left. They walked down the hallway and Robert stopped in front of the fifth room on the left, room 124. He used a room key to open the door, letting her go in first, then watching her from behind as she walked into the room. After shutting the door, Robert said,

"You need to see to it that you do everything possible to make me happy. Do you understand?"

Linda got that message and for a little over the next two hours, she did everything he wanted her to do to make him happy.

When Linda announced she was getting up to go to the bathroom, Robert knew the time had come. After she had closed the restroom door, Robert reached over, got his cell phone and dialed a number. Once it was answered, he said, "Time to rock and roll," and disconnected from the call. He then got up and began to put his clothes on.

He had his pants and shirt on when Linda opened the door to the bathroom and walked out. She was only wearing a short, white bathrobe tied at the waist, which had been folded up in the bathroom.

"You're dressed. Where are you going?" she asked with surprise in her voice.

"It's time to leave," he said as he pulled on his coat.

Then, as he grabbed the doorknob of the door to the room, he said, "And it's time for you to leave also." He opened the door and there stood two uniformed policemen. The biggest one walked through the door holding out a pair of handcuffs in his right hand.

Linda was shocked and began to stutter, finally uttering "What are you doing?" as she looked at the two policemen and then back at Robert. One of the policemen grabbed her left wrist and snapped a metal handcuff on it.

As her other wrist was next being pulled behind her and the other cuff attached to it, the officer said, "Ma'am, you are under arrest for embezzlement and for theft of funds from your company. You have the right to remain silent. You have the right to an attorney and if you cannot afford one, one will be provided for you."

Linda screamed out, now glaring at Robert, "You said you wouldn't do anything if I went with you!" She began twisting and turning in an effort to try to get to him, even trying to kick him until being pulled back by the officer, which caused her robe to fall off of her left shoulder, exposing her breast.

Now being firmly held by the officer, Robert walked over to her, smiled and said, "I lied. You were so bad in bed, I couldn't imagine coming back to town and being with you again."

"You bastard!" Then she spat at him. After dodging her spittle, he reached over and pulled the other side of her robe down off of her other shoulder so that both of her breasts were now exposed.

"Let her put her heels on so her feet don't get hurt," one officer said as he grabbed her shoes and gave them to the second officer. That officer bent over and put them on her feet as Robert gathered her clothes, rolled them up and put them in a plastic bag now being held by the first officer.

"Thanks, officers," Robert said to them as he nodded his head to first one of them and then the other one.

"Any time," the first officer answered. "Thanks for letting us know about her."

"That's the hotel's robe she has on. Tell the front desk that I'll reimburse them for that robe when I check out. Just get her on out of here," Robert said as he shifted his eyes from one officer to the other.

"Will do," the first officer said as he made a half-hearted effort to pull both sides of her robe up so that her shoulders and breasts were at least somewhat covered.

She was then escorted out of the room and, with an officer on each side, walked down the hallway, bending her head down trying to hide her face as much as possible. At the front desk in the empty lobby, one of the officers stopped her and again pulled both sides of her robe up to make sure her breasts were covered. Then they walked her on out to their waiting police car. Linda would not be allowed to put her clothes on until after she had been placed in the back seat of the police car.

Robert watched from the hallway as the two escorting officers had walked Linda down to the hotel lobby. He knew he was going to forget to make that reimbursement payment for the robe at the front desk. Somebody else was going to have to worry about that. That was too unimportant for him to spend time fooling with.

He was at the stage of his career that he only worried about important things. This had all gone just like most of the others had. The only difference was that some of the other women had lasted a year or more before he had turned them in. Now it was time to find the next one. He was looking forward to it. He hoped the next one was better looking and lasted longer before he turned her in.

Chapter Six

After arranging with his office for his motorcycle to be shipped by air freight from LA to New Orleans, Tony had Karen take him over to the freight area at the New Orleans City Airport to pick it up after it had arrived. Once Tony was dropped off at the proper location and got the motorcycle unpacked, Karen went to do some shopping while he mounted up and rode his cycle over to Bay St. Louis. It was such a good feeling to be riding on his mechanical beast and feeling the wonderful fresh air in his face as he rode it over to the Mississippi gulf coast.

A few days later, Tony called LA and told his secretary that he would be going to New York City to see some friends. He said that he would be back in touch once he knew how long he was going to be there and where he might be going next. Before he left Bay St. Louis to go to New Orleans and catch a plane to New York, Tony took some time around dusk to ride his motorcycle around the little town of Bay St. Louis to see how much it had been changed by the massive Hurricane Katrina since he had been there. He had been told that Katrina had devastated most of the Bay St. Louis area. He found out that what he had been told was correct, that the downtown area was almost completely blown away, except for the massive County Court House which had originally been built in the early 1920's.

While riding around, he decided that he would try to find the church he had visited in downtown Bay St. Louis the night before the shootout that had taken place so many years ago over in Louisiana. He was eventually able to locate the general area and, as he rode around the corner of where he thought it might be, there it was. The church, and a few nearby buildings he remembered, had not been destroyed by the hurricane at their site several blocks from the waterfront.

Tony pulled his cycle into a parking space across the street from the church, turned his motor off and sat there to take a long look at the building. With it being dark, but still early evening, the church had an allure that almost beckoned him to come closer. He noticed that, as it had looked so many years ago, there seemed to be a hint of light coming from inside the building. He decided to try and see if anyone might be inside.

After kicking the parking stand down in place, he got off and walked across the street. He could not take his eyes from the quaint, white, wooden structure. The bell tower above the entrance to the building had impressed him the first time he had seen it and it did so again. As he climbed up the five stairs to get to the entrance, he guessed that the door would probably be locked. To his surprise, the door opened and inside there was one faint light near the altar that was providing limited lighting.

Closing the door behind him, he walked down the center aisle and stopped at the second row to the left from the front, the same row where he had sat so many years before. He slid in and took a seat, immediately running his eyes around the sanctuary and the choir area to the front of him. He sat there, thinking about so many things but mainly about how he had talked back then with a figure that was seated on the opposite side from him a few rows back. He had not heard the man come in, much less be seated where he was, but he was there. He remembered that so clearly, because he had talked with him. It may have only been briefly, but he had talked with him. He had never forgotten that moment. The more he thought about it now, the more he wished the man would show back up again. The longer he sat there, the more he realized that such encounter was very unlikely to ever happen again.

Finally, after saying a prayer for his friend, Mark, Tony decided it was time to leave and get back to Karen's house. As he made his way up the aisle, he stopped at about the location of the row where the visitor had sat so many years ago. He was just able to look at the area and decided to again say a prayer of thanks. He had always felt that the experience he had witnessed in the church that night years ago was in large part responsible for his safety the next day and his eventually being able to come out alive from the shootout that had taken place.

Turning around, he took one more look at the altar area and then bowed his head as he quietly said a brief prayer of thanks. Upon completing his prayer, he turned around and made his way to the front door. Opening the somewhat massive door, he paused to take another last look at the area where his visitor had been seated before. Again, not seeing anyone, he turned and walked through the doorway, easing the door shut behind him. He was disappointed that he had not somehow been able to see that individual again but knew that, regardless, it was time to move on.

Chapter Seven

Jean's initial contacts as a representative of one of the larger drug companies had led to her finding out just how to approach contacts to make sales. She had picked up right where her predecessor had left off as she had been removed from her position. The sales agent was nice looking and was well spoken but over time was only able to increase her sales at a very limited pace. While the predecessor had been somewhat successful, she had not been able to move the sales level above a specified threshold that her supervisors had wanted. That had led to the hiring of Jean.

When Jean took over the accounts of that area, she was told that there needed to be an increase in the overall accounts for the area and that it needed to happen rather fast. The supervisor for the reps working in that area, who had run out of patience with the former sales reps, made clear to Jean that something had to change rather quickly because the former agent was getting outworked by her competition. Her main competition in the area was a girl who had graduated from a well-known college in the Washington, D. C. area with honors and always made sure she was dressed in very expensive clothes. Her presentations were made in such a manner that the people representing hospitals, clinics, and other medical facilities were usually impressed. The only problem was that she usually made sure the people that she was making the presentations to knew how smart and how successful she had been in college, and was now in her business, and just how much more she knew than they did. While men and women were appreciative of her knowledge of her products, they were unimpressed by her rather bland appearance and self-serving arrogance.

Jean made sure she studied her market area thoroughly before she had gotten out on the front lines. She also spent a lot of time working with her computer skills, making sure she improved and continually was getting better with those skills. Being as intelligent as she was, she was able to explore internet avenues of research and exploration so that she was continually being exposed to more and better computer skills and resources. She did extensive research not only on the entities she was dealing with but even more so on the people in key positions with those companies. She made sure she was continually expanding her widespread knowledge and expertise in medical areas, but she also made sure that she was specifically ending up from time to time seeking and exploring additional medical and administrative information. Some of her research involved not necessarily the care of a patient as much as the effects of and the end results of some of the drugs that she had been provided with information about. Gradually, she became more and more proficient with her use of the computer.

Jean also made sure she was dressed to impress when she went to make presentations of her products. Though she was now thirty-six, she had maintained her outstanding figure through her tennis and occasional exercise classes. No wrinkles had yet made their appearance on her face or around her neck area. Her legs and arms remained fashionably firm. Then there was always her 36DD assets that she made sure were prominently and tastefully displayed. She also continually followed the advice of her instructor who had said to wear skirts that were appropriately short, pleasantly tight, and accentuated the flair of her hips and rear. When she was dressed in a way that she knew would tastefully display her figure, she felt that she still was really in a league of her own.

The Highlands Medical Group, commonly known as the Group, consisted of six very prominent hospitals and numerous associated clinics. Their headquarters in Charlotte, North Carolina, was the center of their operations and was continuing to grow at a surprising speed due to the aging of the baby boom generation. The Group had major facilities in North Carolina and Tennessee and was looking to expand into Virginia and South Carolina.

The man responsible for product purchasing for the Highlands Medical Group, Tyler Washington, was well-known not only in North Carolina but also in many east central states. Washington had been born and raised in eastern North Carolina and had been a well-known black high school football player. He had grown to be 6 feet 2 inches in height and weighed around 185 in high school and up to 220 pounds his last year in college. He had played defensive back on a highly successful two-time state championship high school football team. Upon graduation, he had numerous scholarships offered from prominent universities and eventually decided on attending a well-known North Carolina university that was part of a major conference. While having been a nice-looking young boy in high school, by the time he graduated from college he was a very handsome young man. He had even posed for some of the athletic advertisements for his university. He had started steadily dating one of the school's cheerleaders his junior year in college.

He majored in Business Management during his college years though he wanted to play professional football if possible. He kept his grades up and made every effort to do as well as he could academically. His father and mother never married and had split up during his junior year in high school, leaving his mother to raise him and his younger brother, Leon.

Because of Tyler's athletic abilities, his mother was able to get a good job as a receptionist at the athletic department, first in high school while Tyler was receiving All-State honors and next in college where Tyler received all conference awards his junior and senior years. He was selected as a second team All-American his senior year. During the second semester of his junior year, his cheerleader girlfriend got pregnant. A baby boy was born, and the couple began living together with his mother.

He was drafted by a nearby professional football team and received a nice bonus. It was about this time in his life that he would occasionally have dates with white girls. They were usually girls available who followed the team and hung out at bars that team players were known to visit. Unfortunately, his playing days only lasted two years because he suffered a career ending injury to his right knee during a game at the end of his second year of play.

At the conclusion of his playing days, he looked for a job where he could use his college degree. With the help of some of the college alumni from his school, he was able to get a position in a new medical corporation started by some of those alumni. They were very happy to have Tyler come to work with them since he was so well-known due to his athletic accomplishments.

Tyler worked for the company, which became known as the Highlands Medical Group and was promoted over the next fourteen years until he became Vice President in charge of product purchasing for the corporation. He had now held that position for six years and was known for his calm demeanor and athletic frame. He made sure he worked out at least three days a week and took part in numerous touch football camps throughout the south.

When Jean began her research on him, she found him to be quite handsome for a forty-four-year-old black man. She read about his having been selected as a second team All-American football player. She found out that his son had grown up to be a successful athlete also and was now in college playing football in a nearby state. She also heard that Tyler was not married and was not now living with anyone, as far as she could find out.

Jean began to have several discussions with her supervisor about getting Tyler's account for their company. She knew that the large corporation he worked for was under contract for at least another two months to the same company that his corporation had been under contract with for the past two years. She tried to make arrangements to meet with Tyler but was unsuccessful. The reason given by Tyler's associates was that they were already under contract and there was no need for any sort of meeting. Jean did not give up and kept trying, telling Tyler's associates that, since it was her understanding that the existing contract they had would soon be coming up for renewal, it would be a good time for them to have discussions with her company.

For weeks, there was no progress made in setting up a meeting. Her bosses were running out of patience. Only because she did manage to have some small increase in her production in other parts of her area did her supervisors have any patience with her. They finally did tell her though that she had to have some significant additional increase in production, or they would have to seriously consider finding someone to take her place.

Two days after being told that, she got a call from Tyler himself. He suggested she come make a presentation the following Thursday at 10 am at his office in downtown Charlotte. She was ecstatic. Now at least she had her chance, but she had to get the business from Tyler's group. She had to. If she were not able to get it, she would probably be removed and someone else put in her slot. She could not lose her job. She needed to keep her job so she could help pay for her daughter's medical bills, which were continually increasing. She was beginning to get more income from her position, but it was not what she needed to make her supervisors happy or enough to fully take care of the demands of her daughter's bills. It had only been a minimal increase so far.

On Thursday, she was present at Tyler's office on the 6th floor of the office building where he had said that they should meet. After being made to wait for almost forty-five minutes, she was taken into a conference room where she met three of his assistants. After they introduced themselves, they all sat down to wait for his appearance.

After about five minutes of small talk, in walked the former All- American athlete. The first thing that impressed Jean was how handsome Tyler was. The next thing that she noticed was how polite and well-mannered he seemed to be. It wasn't long into the meeting before she noticed how well-spoken he was. Two and a half hours later, her presentation along with an extensive question and answer session was completed. After all the other attendees had left the conference room, she invited Tyler to dinner that evening at a restaurant at the nearby hotel where she was staying. He accepted her invitation to dinner but said that they should instead go to an excellent restaurant with a beautiful view of the city, which happened to be on the top floor of the well-known hotel where he was staying.

That evening, she made sure she had her hair down and wore a tight blouse and short mini skirt with matching heels, which outfit, she thought, was very appealing. She made sure that she did her best to look as good as she possibly could.

He was very handsome in his nice, expensive light grey suit and was, she discovered, so easy to talk with. During a very cordial dinner during which they discussed her company's efforts to get the business of the Group, the big corporation he had long worked for and represented, she constantly made sure that he had the best views of her always smiling face along with her tight blouse which emphasized her ample assets. She also made sure she crossed her legs in a way where he had good views of her legs and of her constantly graceful attempts to keep her short skirt from riding up too high.

At about ten-thirty, Tyler made the comment that it was time for him to be getting to his room. It was at that point, as they were waiting for Jean's credit card to be returned, that there was a hesitation in the conversation. It was the question she then asked that she had thought about having to ask if he did not invite her to his room. He waited for her to say whatever she was going to say because he had made it clear that she was going to have to be the one to say anything about what direction the night was going to take at that point. He had long before decided with other women that he was not going to put himself in a position to be accused of any type of unwanted behavior.

She took her returned credit card and put it away as he closely watched her deal with her purse. She then looked up at him as he looked at her face. He had said nothing about his family, only once referring to his son whom, he had said, was on a football scholarship. He had said nothing about being married and, indeed, her research had indicated that he was not married. She wondered if he had checked out her status before they had met. What she had finally decided she had to ask next, if he had not said anything, she did.

"Will you come with me for a drink?"

He looked at her, hesitating for a moment, and then slowly said, "I am going to make a drink for myself in my room."

She looked steady at him and said, barely without a quiver in her voice, "May I join you for a drink?"

He kept his look on her and said, "Are you are sure that is what you want to do? We don't have a deal yet."

She looked back at this very handsome, very refined black man, with everything going through her mind that she had already thought about if their being together had gotten to this point. She realized that, if she was going to be with him, it would have to be on her initiative. He had not initiated an offer and it did not appear that he was going to. She was sure he probably had many opportunities with other women just like her. Not only was he so model good looking and in great physical shape, he worked in the key position that involved potentially a huge amount of money for her company, if she was able to conclude a contract with them.

She also knew that she had gone this far, and that she had considered his being a black man so many times, but that she just had to have this contract. She just had to, in order to keep her job, in order to take care of her precious daughter, and in order to keep, to some extent, her lifestyle. She also caught herself thinking about the possibility that being intimate with him might not be so bad. He was extremely nice. He was so drop dead handsome. He was so well-dressed. He was so well-mannered. And she kept coming back to the bottom line. She absolutely had to have his company's business. She had to have it. After all, she had gone to that beauty contest judge's room way back when she felt she just had to win that contest after losing a prior key contest in the finals.

Yes, this was so different because so much money was involved and, yes, he was so black. But she now had an autistic child, whose care was expensive. It was costing her a lot of money, thanks to her no-good husband and his family. She had never thought she would go to bed with a black man, but for her it now was so important. Besides, he hadn't even indicated he would be receptive to that because he certainly had not given her any indication that he had an interest in her. She certainly hoped he did have. This was at least his first opening. She had to pursue it. She just had to have it.

"Yes, I am," she finally said, almost with a little nervous tremble in her voice. Then she added, "Maybe I can convince you that you should make a decision in our favor."

He looked at her and then, after a moment, slowly stood up.

She followed the handsome football star as he walked to the elevator doors in the hallway outside of the restaurant, with not a word being said. Thank goodness, for her she thought, there was no one on the elevator as it took them to his floor.

She followed him down the hallway to the door of his room. He used his card, opened the door and stepped back to allow her to enter first. She walked in, again thinking about what she was doing, but quickly noticing the elegance of the room. It was a huge, first-class suite with a living room, a bar area, and a large bedroom with an adjacent bathroom and shower.

After walking in, he made her a drink, telling him when he had asked that she wanted a bourbon and tonic. While making it for her, he made one for himself. After he walked over and gave it to her, they each took a sip while looking at one another. One thing led to another and it wasn't too long that, after brushing her right breast against his upper left arm as she now stood closely next to him, he took her into his arms, and she kissed her first black man. It ended up being a long, deep French kiss. After that kiss, she put her drink on the bar counter and left the bar area to go to the bathroom. He took a seat on one of the bar stools in front of the TV set and turned on a replay of a ballgame from the immediate past weekend. He began to slowly sip his drink.

After less than five minutes, when Jean walked out, she had nothing on but a large towel, which was wrapped around her above her breasts and tied just below her right armpit. The towel was big enough to just barely cover her from her breasts to her upper thighs. She walked over to him and was handed her drink when she got close to him. After taking another sip of her drink, she felt she had to do it again, so she edged closer to him. She then kissed her first black man a second time and a long, deep French kiss it ended up being also. He then took her hand and led her into the bedroom.

After he had stripped off his biker shorts, he slipped the towel off her and eased her onto the bed. After more prolonged kissing, he gently made ready to enter her. Noticing that her eyes were closed, he said, "Open your eyes. I want you to remember what this looks like."

She opened her eyes and looked down. It was exactly at that point that she began to watch herself have sex with a black man for the first time in her life. He had wanted her to see it, knowing it was probably her first time with a black man, and he had wanted her to remember it, for the rest of her life. During the next two hours, the sex only stopped for a trip to the rest room or to change positions.

Towards the end of the third hour, she began to hope it would not stop. The sleeping sexual giant in her that Mary Jo had awakened had now been re-awakened. She could not believe she was feeling that way. She also realized that Tyler was making sure that she had sex with him every way possible. She could tell that this man really knew what he was doing as he guided their intimacy. After now three and a half hours, he took her over the edge again.

After a rest period, she finally was able to get up and get dressed. Before she left, Tyler told her that her company would get a six-month trial contract to see if things would work properly between her company and his. He also told her that he expected to see her up there in Charlotte at least once a month during the six-month "trial" period. She left his room at about two-thirty in the morning, without anyone seeing her depart. It was a good thing nobody saw her because she had a hard time walking to her room.

As she made her way down the hallway, she knew she had done what she had to do. On top of it all, she could not believe it had all felt so good, and how much she had enjoyed it.

She now felt, though, similar to how she had felt after she had met with the beauty contest judge back when. The reason she had been in the room, just like then, had been accomplished. But she was glad she had anticipated, when she had started the job, that something like this might happen and had gotten back on the pill.

When she finally eased her way back into her room, she was so mixed up that she could not go to sleep. It had been so naughty to do what she had done. In one month's time, a total of four weeks, she had been with another woman and now she had been with a black man! The more she thought about both of those experiences, the more she could not get either one of them out of her mind. The more the former beauty queen realized that she had enjoyed each one of them, the more she thought about both them. She had not wanted either one of them to stop. Thinking more about them, she realized she wanted them both to happen again. But she also thought about how bad she had been to have done either one of them, much less both of them. She began to wonder if there was something that might be wrong with her. She concluded she had done what she had to do.

Her daughter's condition had caused Jean to be in the situation she was now in. It was her sorry ex-husbands fault, she felt, that he had made her feel so badly that she had to start taking something just to make her feel better. Even more so, it was that sorry drug company's fault that the condition of her poor daughter was due to at least one of their products she had started taking while pregnant with her daughter. The more she researched on her computer information about products that the drug companies had produced and results that had happened to those taking their products, results that the hugely successful profit-making companies knew all about, the madder she got at what they had continued to do. She was convinced that her daughter's condition was a direct result of their continued production of bad drugs. They had no idea of knowing how hard it was on her daughter and others like her, and on those children's parents like Jean, because of their products. Somehow, they need to experience what those affected by the drugs were going through.

Chapter Eight

Tony had called his cousins in NYC and told them that he would come up in the next three days, if that was alright with them. He was told that was fine and for him to just call them to let them know his arrival time once he had gotten his flight reservation from New Orleans finalized. Tony had been able to set his travel arrangements so that he could arrive at their compound on Long Island the following Thursday at around 2:30. He notified them of the time he anticipated being there and was told they were looking forward to seeing their famous Hollywood cousin.

On Thursday after he settled in for the long flight to New York, he began to think about some of the various stories his father, Nick, had told him while they both sat on the bench on the hill overlooking the straits between Sicily and Italy. He remembered being told once about a trip his dad had taken from the gulf coast area of Mississippi to Hot Springs, Arkansas in late 1926. He had gone there to meet with Al Capone, the well-known gangster who was the head of massive, highly successful, illegal booze shipment operations in numerous locations that included activities in Mississippi. His dad had gone by train from New Orleans to Hot Springs and had ridden in a cab down from the train station over to the exclusive, first class hotel, the Arlington Hotel, where Capone and his men stayed during their trips there. Capone usually reserved the whole fourth floor there for himself and his men.

After paying the cab driver, Nick had taken his bag and walked up the stairs at the front of the hotel and into the lobby. Walking over to the front desk, he placed his suitcase on the floor as he said to the desk clerk, "I'm Nick Gable and I'm here to check in."

The desk clerk smiled and said, "Welcome to the Arlington Hotel, Mr. Gable. We've been expecting you."

The clerk immediately slid a registration sheet to Nick as he said, "You already have a room assigned to you and can go on up to your room, if you would like."

"That would be fine," Nick responded.

The desk clerk said, "Bellman!" Nick saw a nearby bellman step forward to take his bag, as he also took the offered key from the desk clerk.

"Please follow me, sir. You are on the fourth floor," the bellman said as he began walking toward the location of the row of elevators over to the side of the lobby away from the desk. After arriving at the elevators and beginning to wait, Nick looked around the lobby and recognized four men sitting there not too far away that he knew were Capone men. He slightly nodded his head towards them as he looked in their direction.

They each did likewise and quickly continued their surveillance in all directions of the lobby area.

Nick was surprised at how big the crowd was in the lobby. He was also surprised at how packed the elevator was once he and the bellman had gotten aboard. The bellman discretely indicated to the elevator operator the floor they wanted to go to by raising four fingers.

Arriving at the fourth floor, they stepped off when the elevator operator opened the door and held it open for them. Nick quickly noticed one thing. He and the bellman were the only ones getting off that elevator at the fourth floor.

Nick saw that there was a man sitting in a chair next to the wall at each end of the row of elevators. Upon seeing him, one of the men immediately began to stand up and speak.

"Nicky! How are ya?" asked a big guy as he began moving toward Nick, now with a smile on his face.

Walking over to the man, Nick answered, "Hello, Ricky. How are you?" The two men gave each other a hug as the other man sitting in a chair also stood up and said, "Where have you been? We've been asking and asking about you, but nobody knew anything. You been alright?" He gave Nick a handshake as all three of them were smiling.

"Hi, Arnie. Good to see you guys," Nick said. "Oh, I'm good. Been doing a few things the Boss wanted me to check out and here I am," Nick said as he twirled his hat in his hands. "You two are looking like you haven't missed any meals or anything," Nick said as he motioned his hand towards them.

The two men chuckled, each saying almost at the same time, "No, no, not too many."

"What's been going on with you guys?" Nick asked.

Ricky answered, "A few new things happening. You probably heard about that assassination attempt on the Boss back in '22. Now, a couple more attempts have happened. So, he decided to go ahead and get himself an armored car. Got one that looks like a Chicago Police car."

"Good! That should help out," Nick said.

"Yeah. It has, but we still have to be on the lookout," Ricky answered. "You just never know these days."

Ricky then leaned closer to Nick and said, "Al told us that you would be up here. He wanted to talk with you as soon as you got here."

"Okay. Let me drop my bag off at my room and I'll be right back." Looking at the waiting bellman, he then moved in his direction, saying, "Good to see you boys. I'll be back in just a second."

"I'll tell the Boss that you're here," Ricky said.

"Okay. I'll be right back."

After walking past three doors, the bellman opened the door to the next room and, handing the key to Nick after its use, carried Nick's suitcase into the room. Nick gave the bellman a couple of bills and the young man departed as he expressed his thanks. Nick put his suitcase on a nearby chair and took a quick look around the room. He then went out into the hallway, shutting the door to his room behind him.

When he got down to where the two men were, Ricky said, as he motioned towards the second door on the right, "He's waiting for you there in his room. Just knock on the door to let him know you're here."

Nick nodded, walked over to the door and knocked. He used

the same knock he had used that first night a few months earlier at the Pine Hills Hotel in Hancock County, Mississippi.

"Come on in," said a thick voice from the other side of the door. Nick opened it and walked into the room as Ricky closed the door behind him.

"Nicky, Nicky, Nicky," said a standing Capone as he stuck his hand out for a handshake.

"Hello, Mr. Capone," said Nick as he stepped over and grasped Capone's offered hand. Nick noticed the two men in the room standing back a little bit behind Capone.

"Good to see you, my boy. You remember Kenny and Charles," Capone said as he turned to glance in their direction.

"Yes, sir," he said as he nodded to them. He remembered them both from their war with the Purple Gang in Detroit. "Good to see you, boys." They both nodded their heads towards him.

"You want anything to drink?" Capone asked.

"No, Boss. Thanks, but I'll wait 'til later."

"Okay. Boys, let us have some time here by ourselves."

Each of the men immediately took their cue and proceeded to leave the room, with the last one saying on his way out, "Good to see you, Nick."

"Good to see you too, Kenny."

"Well, did you have a good trip up here?" Capone asked after the door was shut behind the two men and he began to move through the entering room area into an adjacent room with three large glass windows. Capone motioned Nick to a sitting chair near the couch that he then seated himself on.

"It was a good trip. The trains were really nice, and fast," Nick said as he sat in the chair. "It was mostly a very smooth ride."

"Good. Good. So, tell me how it's going down there. How are things in the quiet little area of Hancock County, Mississippi?" Capone asked as he now intently stared at Nick.

"Things are going very well. As you know, we have all of the land we need under control. We finally got the cooperation of all of the lumber shippers that we wanted. My office in Bay St. Louis is set up and serving its purpose."

"Has anybody asked you any questions about what you are doing down there? What kind of business you are going to be in?"

"No, not really. The only questions I have gotten mostly deal with somebody wanting to sell me some property they have, or their family has, out in that swamp."

"How are you dealing with that?" Capone asked, still with his focus entirely on what Nick had to say.

"I tell them, like we talked about in Chicago before I went down there, that I made a lot of money in the stock market and I came down here because I want peace and quiet. I don't want any neighbors close-by."

"How are you coming with getting ready for the shipments of the booze?"

"The two bunk houses and two barns are already built on the back side of the highest of the three bluffs. Those were built first. There are five horses out there now and they are in the barn that is the most visible. That provides some coverage for the other barn, which is mainly for storage. We're working on a small guest cottage that overlooks the bayou and is not too far from where the front of the main house and the pool will be. The worker's quarters in the bunk houses in the back are not too far from the main house. That way we can get them quickly to the docks should any guests come up unexpectedly from the water area."

Capone looked at Nick and smiled, saying, "That's good thinking, Nick. That really is. I knew I picked the right guy to go down there and set that up."

"Thanks, Boss. I appreciate that."

"No. I mean that, Nicky. After what happened in Chicago, I was a little worried about you, but I went ahead and trusted you with that project."

Leaning forward towards where Nick was sitting, Capone then said, "Nick, I've got these things setting up all over the country. What you are getting started down there is the key to that whole southern area. It's important to me that it gets done and done the right way. Understand?" he asked looking straight into Nick's eyes.

"Yes sir, Boss. I do, and it's being done that way," Nick answered, looking right back into Capone's eyes.

"Good!" Capone said and then eased to lean back on the couch.

Taking a moment to look at Nick, Capone then said, "One of the things now being set up is in a place called Trinidad, Colorado. It is nestled up next to the Front Range mountains out there about twelve miles north of the Colorado-New Mexico border. Right now, we are slowly beginning to put a big tunnel under the main street to help us with our shipping. Other tunnels under streets there will eventually be connected to the main street tunnel. That little town will end up being a key shipping point for that whole area out west there."

Seeing he had Nick's full attention, Capone continued. "You

know how serious our so-called 'war' with the Purple Gang in Detroit has been. Well, I have been trying to work that out with the bunch of Jews that run that group. Getting your sister's double-crossing husband taken care of has certainly seemed to limit what they know about our operations. I am glad you took care of that. But I just get the feeling that we are not at any point of winning that so-called "war" thing in Detroit, at least not right now. Both sides are killing each other's guys almost weekly. We get some of theirs. They get some of ours." Capone shifted his head slowly side to side as he mentioned his point.

He then looked directly at Nick and said, "You need to keep our site there in Mississippi well-protected. I don't think the Purple Gang would try to get any of their people down to the gulf coast to try to hurt us, but you never know. They may try to get somebody from down there to do something instead of doing it themselves. But I really wouldn't put anything past those guys from the north side of Chicago."

Nick nodded his head in the affirmative and said, "We'll stay as alert as we can, but we are going to need a few more guys as soon as you can send them. We are getting close to having our shipment numbers increasing on a regular basis."

Capone answered, "Okay. You are getting to the point where you're gonna need some more men. I will see to that and will let you know who I'll be sending down there and when, so we can get'em hooked up with you."

"Thanks, Mr. Capone. It will be good to have whoever you can send. I would rather have that side of things covered than to need them and not have them."

Directing his look next towards the view in the middle window, Capone said, "Now, your sister, Madeline, is in Sicily?"

"Yes, sir. I let her go over there to do some shopping for that main house that we're building. It was good for her to get away at this time."

"You know, Nicky, you are going to have to keep a close eye on her."

"Yes, sir. I know."

"As I have said before, get her involved in some things. Maybe she can do some things socially in the Bay St. Louis area. You never know what she might find out. Maybe also over in New Orleans. If she could get involved in some things over there, you never know what she might be able to find out or who she might get to know over there."

"Yes, sir. That's true. There is a lot of association between the two areas. A lot of the upper class, high society families have places in the little town of Bay St. Louis that they go to in the summertime to get away from the heat and mosquitoes in New Orleans."

Capone thought for a moment and then asked, "How is that big house in Devil's Swamp, the mansion, coming along?"

"It is almost finished. When it is, I was thinking about having a big party out there, if for no other reason than to let everybody see it now, before we get heavy into having the shipments out there. That mansion will be good cover for what all we'll have going on out there. That way, once they see it, they may not be as interested in what may go on out there as much."

"That's a good idea. Do that. Invite everybody. Let them see it. How close did you say is the nearest road?"

Nick chuckled and answered, "About fifteen miles."

Capone chuckled at that answer, and said, "Well, that was what we wanted when we planned that thing, right?"

Nick nodded his head in agreement as he smiled.

"You just have to make damn sure those big barges work down in that swamp," he added.

"We will," Nick answered. "We're going to use them to take all those party goers out there for our big party."

"What are you going to say when they ask you why you have such big barges out there?"

"I am going to tell them that we have to have a way to get those horses out there and back. We're going to put a race track in behind the big house and have races out there during our parties."

"Nicky, that is great thinking! Just great! You are doing a great job, Nicky. You really are."

"Thanks, Boss."

After a moment's pause, Capone said as he began to stand up, "I want you to come meet me tonight at that restaurant down the street, 'The Wolf's Den'. It's just a few doors down on the right. Be there about 9."

Nick got up and walked over to the window to look down the street. It was a good view of the center of town with lots of people walking down its sidewalks.

"I'll be there," Nick said.

Capone turned to look at him and said, "I have someone I want you to meet there tonight. Be there about 9"

"Ok. I'll see you there then."

Capone turned and began walking towards the hallway door to the room.

"You've done a great job, Nicky. You really have. Now, let's get those shipments started as soon as you can."

With that, Nick returned to his room. After notifying the front desk to wake him at 8, he took first a shower and then a much-needed nap.

At 9 that evening, he walked into the first class, crowded "Wolf's Den" and looked for one Al Capone. He quickly found him at a table towards the back of the room but not far from the bandstand. Capone motioned him toward the table, where there were two other men and three empty chairs. Capone was sitting on a bench with a man sitting next to him that Nick had seen a picture of once before.

Motioning for Nick to sit next to him on the bench, Capone said, "Nick, you remember my good friend here, don't you? This is Lucky."

Nick remembered "Lucky". That was Lucky Luciano, the chief mob boss of all of New York. He was one of Capone's long-time friends.

Not seeing a hand offered by Lucky, Nick nodded his head to the man as he was sliding onto the bench next to Capone.

A bar maid in a very skimpy outfit appeared and asked, "May I get you something?"

Nick said, "Vodka tonic mixed."

She smiled and said, "One of my favorites. I'll have it right out for you."

As she turned and began to walk away, up walked three large

men. Nick recognized the man in front right away and could not believe it. Capone greeted the group.

"Glad you could make it. Have a seat. Gentlemen, you all know Lucky. This is Nick. Nick, this is Babe Ruth and two of his teammates."

Nick almost fainted as he was shaking the hand of probably one of the most famous athletes of all time. He still could not speak as he shook the hands of Ruth's two Yankee teammates.

As the additions sat down in their chairs, Capone said, "They are down here on a pre-season tour. We have tickets if you want to go watch them play a game here tomorrow afternoon against a local team."

Tony came to his senses, initially taking a few moments to gather his thoughts. Then he thought back to what his Dad had told him. Watching the New York Yankees and Babe Ruth had been one of the best experiences of his life.

* * *

Upon arrival after sleeping for most of the remaining portion of the flight to the LaGuardia Airport in New York, Tony took a cab ride of about forty minutes out on Long Island to meet with his relatives at their walled family compound, which he noticed consisted of five buildings behind the one large, wrought iron gate entrance to their twenty-three-acre estate.

Arriving at about 2:15 p.m., Tony pushed the intercom and announced himself, asking to be let in. He was immediately welcomed by a voice he recognized as Paul's and told to have his driver pull his cab up to the main house, which Paul mentioned was the largest of the buildings in the compound. Tony directed the cab driver to pull up before the obviously largest building, which the driver did. After paying for the cab, Tony immediately got out and was met with smiles, hugs, kisses and handshakes by five men and three women, who had all been told to expect him by the now acknowledged leader of that family, Paul Vacallo.

Tony and Paul had known each other since Tony's original trip through the area to deal with the estate down in Mississippi back in the 1970's. Though the grandfather of the group, who had served as the godfather of the five New York mob families at that time, was now deceased, the succession of family members being the head of that unit had been through such tough times that things had changed. Now Paul was greeting him as the head member of that family group, but not as the head of all five mob families in the New York area.

After being guided into the main house, Tony was shown a bedroom where he could leave his luggage and adjacent bathroom in which to freshen up. He was told they would look forward to talking with him around the massive table in the large dining room adjacent to the kitchen. The three women, each one a wife of one of the brothers, all enjoyed meeting such a famous Hollywood star as did some of the men.

After dropping off his luggage, he was guided to the large dining room table where he took a seat. He then began an enjoyable session talking about what all had happened to him since some of them had last seen him just before his initial trip to Mississippi years before. Some of them remembered when he had first come to the United States after his aunt, Madeline, had passed away and left a huge estate down near Bay St. Louis, Mississippi back in the 1970's.

After an hour or so of catching up with one another and asking about so many relatives, Tony began asking about them. He found out that several mostly successful FBI investigations had convinced this family that they should put their money into legally safe businesses, one of them being the jewelry business. It seemed that each one of them was good at the jewelry business, but of the five brothers Paul was the best. He seemed to have a way of always getting the maximum income for their business in most situations.

Paul's brothers, Basil, Conrad, Gordon and Lazard, or "Laz" as he was called, all seemed to get along well with one another. The one thing about the whole situation was that all of them, male and female, seemed to be genuinely proud of Tony and so glad to see him. This was one of the few times ever in his life that he felt proud of himself and what he had been able to accomplish with his movie career.

As the discussion went on, there was a casual mention made that Conrad was a recently retired technical specialist with the Central Intelligence Agency, or CIA as it was universally known, who had been with the Agency for over 35 years. Hearing that, Tony immediately became all ears, listening to every little piece of information he could hear about Conrad and wanting to find out more. While not knowing much about the CIA, Tony did know that they were responsible for international intelligence activities for the United States, performing their work all over the world. Even he had heard that, while Great Britain's MI 5 and Russia's KGB intelligence networks were good, it was generally agreed that the CIA was by far the best.

When Paul said, "Conrad knows everything about how to find out information, which he used to do for the Agency. He became such a special person that extreme precautions were taken to protect his identity and his location. We have lived with that concerning him for numerous years around here. I think I speak for everybody when I say we are proud of him and of everything he has been able to do for our country during his career." All of his brothers, and the three wives, favorably responded to that statement, some even with applause.

Tony immediately commented, "I may want to talk with you about a few things." With that he let out a slight chuckle. "You may be able to help guide me with something I have just run up on, if you would."

Conrad gave a glint of a smile and said, "Well, I don't mind hearing what you might need a little guidance with. Just remember though that I signed a secrecy document which does cover a lot of things, but not everything."

With that comment, several of the brothers laughed and began humming different tunes of famous movies dealing with spies and investigations, all immediately laughing after a few notes. Tony laughed along with them and began thinking that any discussion he might have with Conrad was going to be really interesting.

"We've seen some of your action movies," Paul said. "Do you still keep up with your black belt requirements?"

"Yes, I do. I work out about three or four times a week for at least an hour or hour and a half or so. How about any of you?" Tony asked out of genuine interest.

Paul smiled and answered, "As a matter of fact, you inspired us." After looking arond the room he coutinued.

"All of us went to that same school you did in southern France and originally learned that self-defense art while we were there, just like you did. When we got settled in over here, each one of us decided that we had spent so much time learning that stuff and getting our black belts that it would be a shame to just give it all up. So, each one of us still has our black belt in karate and we still practice it as much as we can, sometimes wearing the full body, solid black outfits each of us earned getting those black belts. Conrad has probably not stayed as active with it as much as the rest of us, but he has been busy a lot of the time with other things. The number of workouts each week depends on what each one of us might have going on, but we all stay active with it. You just never know when you might need to be able to use it." With that comment, most members of the group laughed and all smiled.

Basil then said, "I also practice my expertise with diamonds."

Tony laughed as did some of the others. Several quickly commented about how Basil's interest in jewelry had been so valuable to them during their efforts to get established in that business.

After a few more comments, Paul said, "Conrad, why don't you take our relative friend out to your hangout and show him around. The ladies and the guys have a few things that they need to take care of. We can all get together right here for dinner tonight, at around 7, if that is alright with you, Tony. That would give you a chance to spend a little time with Conrad and get whatever answers that you can. I am sure he will give you some guidance, if possible."

"That sounds good to me, if it is alright with you," Tony said as he looked around the room.

At that point, Paul got up, immediately followed by everyone else, including Tony. Conrad motioned for Tony to follow him, which Tony immediately did after again giving his relatives and the three wives more hugs and handshakes. After Tony had completed his round, Conrad guided him out a back door of the house.

As they walked towards one of the two large barns located on the back side of the compound, Tony said, "I really appreciate your willingness to see if you can give me some guidance with a couple of things."

"What does it deal with?" Conrad asked as they walked.

"A good friend of mine down in southwest Mississippi was the Sheriff in Hancock County. That county is right next to the Louisiana state line and about an hour or so from New Orleans. He helped me so much when I first went down there to deal with that estate my aunt had left. The truth of the matter is that he actually saved my life at a particular point during all of that."

Conrad took a sideways glance at Tony and said, "Oh, my. Now that is serious."

Tony looked back at him and said, "I see you have an appreciation for what I just mentioned."

Conrad slightly nodded his head affirmatively and said, "A person who puts it on the line for somebody else, especially to that extent, is really a very special person. Most people, during their lives, do not have that experience take place. Those that do almost always never forget it."

As they neared one of the large barn-looking building, Tony said, "He has now passed away. He got agent orange disease and died a horrible death. I was able to see him just before he died and am so glad I was able to do that. He had his wife call me and ask me to come see him before he passed away. I went down there immediately and was able to see him. He was in really bad shape but, just before he died, he asked me to try to take care of his wife and family. They had only one child, a very beautiful daughter, who had two children by her now ex-husband. I think he was worried about something concerning them."

Now arriving at a door leading into the building, Conrad

flipped up a small cover over a keyboard on the side of the door and pushed in a few numbers. He then reached down to slide the metal latch on the door to the side so the door could be opened.

Looking back at Tony, he said, "Let's talk about it more inside."

Conrad opened the door and entered the building, pushing a button on the wall next to the door, causing a few lights to come on inside. He then waited inside for Tony to enter so he could close the door behind them. Tony walked in, rapidly shifting his eyes around the interior as they got adjusted to the dim lighting.

Conrad then said, "What you are about to see, cuz, you are sworn to secrecy and promise to never tell a soul about."

Tony could tell by the way he was now staring at him that Conrad was as serious as he could be.

"Sure."

Then Conrad pushed another button and the entire wall off to the left began to slide by motorized sled off to the rear of the building. Behind that wall, there were numerous tv screens. Tony quickly counted a total of fourteen. Conrad pushed a button on a now apparent panel and one of the screens jumped to life. He then put a finger to his mouth, indicating Tony should not speak, and motioned Tony to follow him over to what looked like a smaller building located inside over to the right side of the larger, open area.

Conrad brought out a special small card and ran it by a blank black square on the side of the wall next to what looked to be a door. Another panel appeared next to the door and a soft beep sound went off. Conrad reached down and opened the door to the small building. The two of them then walked into a windowless room as Conrad pushed a button that caused a single light in the top of the small room to come on. Conrad then quickly closed the door behind them.

Tony didn't know what to think. Here they were in this very small room which had no windows at all and only a small table and two chairs in it. The walls, including the back side of the door, and the ceiling appeared to be made of some type of gray padded cork or foam, which were in small eight-inch square sections. Each individual section had the appearance of having a six-inch reversed cone protruding from it. Tony could only guess that the shape and the material absorbed all of the sounds generated inside the room so no one outside of that special room could hear any discussions that took place inside.

When Tony looked at Conrad, he was motioned by him to sit down in one of the chairs. As Tony sat down, Conrad joined him by sitting in the remaining chair. Tony didn't know what to expect next.

"You know I worked for the CIA for a number of years. I was on the front lines at first and actually spent quite some time there. They sent me all over the place, doing a lot of things that had to be done, and in a lot of places that are, shall we say, difficult to get things done in. I managed to stay alive, though a few times it was in serious doubt. That is why I appreciate what you had to say outside about your friend. I would not be here today if it had not been for a friend that I had who had started working for the Agency at about the same time I did. Over time we were able to get some things done that others had had serious problems with. After a while, I ended up in one situation where I was not going to come out of it alive and only because of his personal effort am I sitting here today."

Looking over toward the one screen that was now on, Conrad said, "My friend did not make it out of one he was put in later on.

A man supposedly working for us was playing both sides of the street and ended up compromising my friend."

Moving his eyes back to Tony, he continued, "My friend was caught, tortured for almost a full week and died. As you can tell, I still remember him and what he did for me and when something like what you said is mentioned, well, it just brings it all back to my mind."

Tony shook his head and said, "I am so sorry. I really am."

After a quiet moment, Conrad said, "I am too. He saved my life. I am just sorry that I could not do the same for him."

After another quiet moment, Conrad continued, "Eventually I was promoted and ended up spending a lot of time on things in Afghanistan and Iraq. When I ended up being made the head of one of those high-level technical units, I was so busy that they just decided to build me one of these secure rooms here instead of having me travelling going between Washington and New York all the time."

Tony said, "I was wondering about this."

Conrad said, "You should. I would be wondering about you if you weren't. This is a secure room. There are very few of them around. Technology has gotten so good that we were having to be very careful. This room is built from material and in a form that will not allow outsiders to listen in on what is said in here. That had to be the case with what I was doing because the other side has gotten good at listening in on things, tracking people and individual cell phones, and intercepting calls and messages."

Tony thought for a moment and then said, "So you were having a sort of constant battle going on with folks who were trying to find out what you and your people were doing and saying and where everybody was."

126

Conrad leaned back in his chair and answered, "Yes, constantly. They got to where they were using things commonly known in the everyday world as Stingrays. Those things work by tricking mobile devices into locking onto them instead of legitimate cell towers. That enables them to reveal the exact location of a particular cellphone, which in some instances as you might guess, may not necessarily be good for our side. The newer ones can eavesdrop on calls by forcing phones to step down to older, unencrypted wireless technology. Some even try to put malware in certain places. Things have gotten so advanced that some of them are the size of a briefcase. Others are even the size of a small cellphone."

Casually leaning back in his chair, Conrad said, "So what's on your mind today?"

Hearing that said, Tony knew it was time to get to why he was even bringing this up.

"Something about why my friend, who passed away, called me to his bedside has been bothering me ever since. It wasn't like he would worry about every little thing. He was as calm and cool as he could be. I mean, he had basically been a hero in Vietnam. He was a highly successful, and well-liked, Sheriff. Yet, he contacted me, of all people, to have me go there and to ask me to watch out for his family. For him to do that, he had to have had some idea something was not right, so much so to the extent that he was worried about his family. Is it possible for you to maybe take a look at their phone lines or the people they have been in contact with to see if there is something they need to be worried about? Can you even do something like that and, if you can do it, could you maybe monitor the situation and see if there is something potentially dangerous going on?"

Conrad looked at him, thought for a moment, and then said,

"It is of course possible to monitor individuals and groups and their conversations and meetings. The abilities of someone or some agency wanting to monitor individuals and groups, their conversations and meetings are numerous and varied for someone or an entity that really wants to find out something. Any determined person can get into anything. Every phone call made in the United States goes to Washington, D. C. every 24 hours and has for over 35 years. Our capabilities included things such as reading radio waves, reversing cameras to watch places and people, using television set receptors to convert to cameras by remote direction, having a targeted tv set appear to be off when it is actually on. Our programs had the capability to actually turn the microphones in tv's into listening devices. Things like that. At any point, we were able to read communications sent by computers all over the world. And we could listen to anybody, anywhere, at any time."

Tony said, "We have had a few discussions down there about what role, if any, the major drug companies may be playing in the autistic child area of medicine. His daughter had a normal son for her first child, but her second child is very much autistic. It is such a sad situation. My friend's wife and daughter both think something is not right about there being so many autistic kids now when back in the 1980's there were not nearly as many. They both are adamant that it is the fault of the drug companies. If you would, take a look at that situation as it relates to some of the more successful companies and see what you can find out. For example, see if you can find out if they are knowingly responsible somehow for the excessive rise in autism. It has been so heart wrenching to watch my friend's wife deal with her autistic grandchild."

Conrad looked at him and saw how troubled Tony appeared to

be about what he was discussing with him. He looked at him and said, "I'll take a look at a few things and see what I can find out."

Shifting in his chair, Conrad then asked, "Was there anything else you wanted to discuss?"

Tony said, "As a matter of fact, there is. That is the most important thing, but there is one other thing. His wife, the Sheriff's wife, has a credit card that somebody spent a bunch of money on without permission. It was somewhere around $18,000. Now that might not be much money for some people but for them, especially with all of the medical expenses and burial expenses they have had to take care of, it is a lot of money. I have the credit card number, name and address here on this sheet of paper." He then leaned forward and gave Conrad the sheet.

"Is there something you could do about helping me with that? I would love to find out who did that to them, if possible," Tony said as he leaned back in the chair.

Conrad looked at the information and said, "I can tell you right now I can probably help you with this."

"Oh, great! When should I check back with you about this? In a week or two?" Tony asked.

"No, it won't take that long. That is something I think I will be able to help you with in about thirty or forty minutes." Tony almost fell out of his chair.

Before dinner that evening, Conrad gave him the names of the two individuals involved in taking the money from the credit card account. The additional piece of information Conrad was able to give him was what Tony really appreciated. Conrad was able to give him their address in Los Angeles.

Tony left the next morning to fly to LA.

It was a quiet night in Bay St. Louis. Karen was by herself at her house which made her very lonely. She could not help but think about her deceased husband, the Sheriff. He had been a fine man and a good husband. Her daughter, Jean, was beginning to seem to make a good living with her business dealing with the sale of various drugs at several different locations in North Carolina, northern Georgia, western South Carolina and eastern Tennessee. The bad part of her job seemed to be that she had to travel so much, almost always a long distance away from her home in New Orleans and from her kids. Jean's son, Junior, was living with his father, Jean's former husband who had remarried and lived in New Orleans. Jean's autistic daughter, Emily, had lived mostly with Karen and the Sheriff, Mark, in Bay St. Louis so they could watch out for her and take as good a care of her as possible. That took a lot of effort, and money, but the child seemed to have her own inner sweetness, which at times made such care easier. However, most of the care effort fell on Karen, even more so with the passing of the Sheriff.

On this night, Emily was not at the house, which was quite unusual. Normally she was there, and Karen would have a difficult time getting her to go to bed, especially since her Grandpa, as she had called the Sheriff, was no longer there to also comfort her and make her feel safe. She just seemed to now be afraid of going off to sleep each night. Fortunately, another couple in their church had an autistic girl about the same age as Emily and the two of them were going to spend this Saturday night with one another. At least this way, Karen would have a chance to gather her thoughts and try to do some planning about what she should do next with her transition into life by herself. She found herself laying in her bed, unable to go to sleep and constantly tossing and turning as she thought about various problems she was having to deal with, now by herself.

Casey and Elrod were two black men who had become friends in jail. They were both a little older than 19 and had previously been sent to jail in Texas for theft. They had both received only minor sentences and had recently been released from jail in Houston. They decided that it was time for them to leave Texas and go to Georgia. They had been told by one of their jail mates that, if they could make it to Georgia, he would give them the name of a friend of his that could help them become one of his group that stole things, such as copper, that could be sold for nice amounts of money.

The funds the two had with them as they left Texas did not allow them to pay for some sort of ticket past New Orleans so they could make their way to Atlanta. So, they did what they had to do to get on their way past New Orleans to Georgia. They stole a car. It wasn't much of a car, but it was available, in that the doors were not locked, and it was located on a side street in downtown New Orleans. Casey was able to get the car started and they drove it to a nearby small shopping center, where they went into a quick stop. They bought some hamburgers, which they were able to pay for, and took some soft drinks, which they did not pay for.

Arriving in the nearby city of Slidell, they did the same thing again. They stopped at a quick stop and took a few more things that they didn't pay for, such as socks, shorts, a few shirts and some chewing tobacco, just before they slipped out of the busy quick stop. They also broke into one of the nearby parked cars and found a gun, which they immediately took. Slipping into their car, they took off towards the Mississippi gulf coast. Along the way they agreed that, once they crossed into Mississippi, they needed to find some residential areas that had a few houses they could break into in order to find things they might sell once they got to Georgia. Elrod had been very familiar with selling stolen copper wiring before he had been caught in Texas and convinced Casey that copper theft would probably lead them to get a quick income from their former fellow inmate's friend in Georgia.

Elrod told Casey that, if he would just find a neighborhood on the edge of one of the rural Mississippi towns they were beginning to come up on, Elrod would show him how to get into some of the houses that might look deserted, since it was late summer and so hot that some of the people on the coast may be traveling. Then they could take what they wanted. Nobody would ever catch them. After all, they had stolen the car in New Orleans and other things, including the gun, in Slidell and nobody had even looked twice at them. They agreed with one another that they were smart enough to avoid any place that might be a problem. Besides, they had that gun now, if they did run into a problem.

Sure enough, as the two approached the small town of Bay St. Louis, Mississippi, they pulled off the Interstate highway and soon spotted a house on a deserted road that looked like no one was around. It was around 1:15 in the morning and no moon was out. No lights were on and no cars were in the carport. They stopped and, after knocking on the front door and there being no response, they broke the door lock. With Elrod leading the way and carrying the gun, they got inside what ended up being a furnished but vacant house. Once inside, they were able to scout around and were eventually able to load up their car with sacks of jewelry, clocks, and even what appeared to be three new batteries from the garage. They were on a role.

It was about 1:40 in the morning when they left and eased on over to an adjacent street. They noticed that the small houses on that street also looked deserted. Almost all of the houses were on one side of the street and the streetlights were not working. The area around these few houses was even darker, being a little further away from the Interstate and there still being no moon out to provide any sort of light.

Seeing in that block a screened in front porch on the second house on the right, Elrod decided they should try that one. There was an older car in the open garage but, if they were to slip in, they would probably be able to get the jump on whoever might be in there. They agreed that, if they got lucky and there was a woman in the house alone, if she was attractive enough, they might spend some time enjoying themselves sexually with her before moving on. It had been quite some time since either one of them had been with a woman since they had both been in jail for over a couple of years. They agreed to what all they might do with a woman if one was indeed in the house.

Quietly opening the front screen door, they eased onto the wooden floor of the front porch and moved up against the wall next to the front door. Trying the door knob, they were pleasantly surprised to find the door unlocked! They were in luck.

Elrod opened the door with his left hand, holding the gun up in his right hand at the same time. After they both eased inside and shut the front door, they quickly noticed that there was no light in the front room at all. It was pitch black dark. They didn't want to turn on any light that might let someone know that they were inside this very quiet house. Elrod knew that they needed to find out first if anyone was inside the bedroom off to their right and, if someone was, exactly who was it. Once that was decided, they would know what to do next. They both softly moved towards what had to be the front bedroom doorway. It was as Elrod pushed the door open to the almost completely dark bedroom that it happened.

"EEEEEEEEEEEEEEEEEEEEEEEEEEEEEEEEEEEEE"!

Out from behind the door came the loudest scream either one of them had ever heard. As the scream was being yelled out, two gunshots were fired in quick succession, also from behind the door!

"BAMMM!" "BAMMM!"

With the surprise to the two men of the high-pitched screeching scream, each gunshot sounded like a cannon going off.

Elrod dropped his gun as he turned and tried to run over Casey, tripping on him as he tried to get out of the house. Casey fumbled over Elrod's upper body as he turned and tried to beat Elrod out of the same door. Within a split second, both were running out of the house and jumping into their stolen car.

Inside the house, Karen moved out of the bedroom and went to the now wide-open front door, her gun that she had been practicing shooting with for over 20 years still in her right hand. Holding her gun up ready to fire again, she got to the front porch just in time to see the car the two intruders had jumped into begin to speed off down the street. She fired another shot, this time into the air.

"BAMMM!"

As they were increasing their speed down the street, front porch lights came on at five of the eight houses in that block. Running out onto the front porch of the last house was a man in his undershorts and a tee shirt, carrying a shotgun. As the speeding car continued to pick up speed as it got in front of his house, he quickly raised his shotgun and fired.

"WHAMMMM!"

The glass window in the back door of the car shattered as the car almost instantly disappeared into the dark night.

A few minutes later, the two intruders were stopped by the Mississippi Highway Patrol on Interstate 10 just a few miles to the west of the exit for the nearby town of Pass Christian. They were doing one hundred ten miles an hour when the highway patrolman first saw them.

Back in Bay St. Louis, Karen reloaded her .38 revolver and locked her front door. She then went and sat on the bed in her bedroom. Almost everybody in the neighborhood knew one another and Karen had not felt the need to lock her doors, especially with the Sheriff living there with her. With his passing, that would have to change now.

After a few moments, she looked up at the two holes in the ceiling caused by her first two gunshots. She didn't know how she was going to explain those holes. If her husband, the Sheriff, had still been alive, he would have wondered why she didn't shoot at least one of the intruders. She also knew what he would have done when he heard that she had screamed at them just before she fired the two shots. He would have laughed. He had heard her sing so many times in their church and had once told her he had wondered when that beautiful voice of hers, as strong and as shrill as it could sometimes be, was going to cause some piece of the glass in their church to break.

Chapter Nine

On his flight from New York to Los Angeles, Tony caught himself again thinking about stories his father had told him during the later years of his father's life. As he settled into his seat for the long cross-country flight, his thoughts went back, as they had so many times, to sitting next to his dad, Nick, on the bench on the hillside overlooking the straits between Sicily and the boot of Italy. His Dad hadn't told too many tales of his experiences in the United States, but he would occasionally tell him a story about something that had happened in Mississippi.

This time he began to recall a story his dad had told him about one of the times, around 1928, that his dad and his men had been unloading booze at one of the landing docks that was located in the bayou. His dad had always mentioned how, at certain times of the day during certain times of the year, the bayou could be very beautiful. Various shades of the color gold reflected off the reeds of the swamp land along with various other colors provided by different angles of the sun's light that at times was very massive and at other times was almost non-existent.

His dad had told him that, on the particular day of this story, he and five other men, two of whom were black, were unloading two of the large barges that were utilized to take the booze and other products shipped in from Cuba from the docks located at the ante-bellum mansion to the bayou dock up the waterway. There, the product was unloaded and put on wagons and cars and trucks for shipment to New Orleans and other parts of Louisiana and to other parts of the Mississippi gulf coast as well as to Texas. Eventually, shipments were also made to east Mississippi, Alabama, west Florida and even parts of Tennessee and Georgia.

The barges were of special design so that horses, wagons and other things could be shipped to the docks at the bluffs location of the massive mansion. A racetrack was located behind the house and large parties were held from time to time around the pool located in front of the mansion over-looking the bayou. Such activities provided cover for the real operations out at the bluffs, which was taking care of multiple shipments of booze from Cuba. Horse races would also usually take place during the course of the day's party activities out at the bluffs and could be watched from the back porch of the mansion.

As the sun was setting on the bayou, a fog would often begin to settle in over the docks and the upper bayou. The haze made it hard to see too far around the site, but that was alright with those working there. It wasn't as hot that time of the day and, though there were never any people normally out in that part of the swamp, the shipment activities were hidden even more so.

Nick told Tony that, about halfway through the unloading

of the numerous bottles, kegs and other items from the barges onto the wagons, cars and trucks from the barges, he noticed the reflection of light in some of the area furthest away on the opposite side of the bayou. He motioned for his loading workers to be quiet as he tried to listen more closely. He noticed that the sound coming from the bayou was getting louder and the light was getting brighter. Whatever it was, was working its way closer.

He motioned for his two men at each of the farthest ends of the barges to place their submachine guns closer to them and lay them down on the two ends of the barges. He then motioned for a third worker to take his submachine gun and position himself in the middle, where the two barges were meeting at the dock.

Though they were out in the middle of a normally deserted swamp, they had practiced this positioning before because of the prior attack that had been undertaken at the mansion dock by some of their competitors who had come all the way down from Chicago. Their landing site had been attacked by men with submachine guns and they had only survived because some of their friends with the swamp people had come to help them. Nick had not wanted that to happen again, so he had made sure to tell the men who worked out there what positions they might take, if attacked. He had made sure that enough fire power was in the right places there to protect their unloading and loading operations.

As the lighting on the opposite side of the thirty-yard-wide bayou got brighter, images began to be visible. It gradually became apparent that horses were lining up along the bank. On top of those horses were figures in white outfits wearing what appeared to be white hoods. Each figure was carrying a rifle and four of the riders were also carrying flaming, fire burning torches on wooden poles. After the riders were all lined up adjacent to one another, all ten of them remained almost motionless. Nobody was saying anything, and the horses were also completely still.

After waiting there for a moment, Nick stepped forward into the small area that was open between the two barges.

"Anything we can help you boys with?" he yelled out to the lineup.

There was total silence for a moment. Then a rider in the center of the lineup moved his horse forward a step. He then yelled out across the bayou.

"We are looking for a negro name Leroy."

Nick looked up and down the lineup of his men, who were now evenly spread the length of the two barges.

"We only have two working with us and their names are Roshad and Eddie Joe," Nick said as two of his men at each end slowly pulled out their submachine guns. "They've been with me a long time. Why are you looking for this Leroy guy?"

After a moment's pause, the lead rider yelled back, "Raped a white woman, next county north of here. They said he came this way."

After a moment of stillness, the hooded voice yelled out, "What you boys doing here?"

Nick hesitated a moment, looked up and down the line as he slowly pulled the third submachine gun out, and then said, "We're shipping some booze out to Louisiana and Texas." After a moment's pause, he then said, "You want some of it for you and your boys?"

The lead man took a moment, then reached up and pulled his

white pointed hood off of his head and yelled out, "Now, that would be kinda nice of ya."

Nick yelled back, "Well then, come on across and we'll let you have some. You can ride across right up there," Nick said as he pointed about thirty yards upriver. "May help make your ride back a little easier."

At that moment, a yell went up from the group as they all began to reach for their hoods and pull them up and off of their heads. They then all followed their leader as he moved upstream to cross the bayou.

Nick yelled to his men, "Give them each a bottle as they come by, boys." Motioning to the two men holding the submachine guns, he quietly said, "Keep those handy."

The lineup came down to the barges with the head man taking the first bottle, letting out a loud yell as he grabbed it. Holding his bottle up, he then yelled out, "Thanks, boys. It's been a long ride coming down here."

Nick waved back at him and the man and his group rode out the same way they had ridden in. When all of them were back on the opposite side, the leader yelled out, "Let's give'em an old rebel yell, boys!"

At that point the entire group gave out a very loud, continuous yell as they then rode off into the area of the swamp from which they had come.

Tony tried to imagine how that all might have looked as his mind began to come back to the present time period on his plane trip to Los Angeles.

* * *

The heads of the five major drug companies had one of their

quarterly meetings. Due to recent questions that had been raised about their liability for some of their products, they decided to have a news conference where they would issue a statement on behalf of all of the companies dealing with liability for the kids that were suffering from autism and other related medical problems.

Some of the companies were not happy that they were being included with other companies who were actually making the products that were alleged to be causing the problems. An intense discussion took place during which some companies, not deeply involved in producing products that were being alleged to cause the significant increase in autism, were wanting to distance themselves from those who were more deeply involved in the huge production being undertaken of questionable products. One of the companies in particular was not happy with the situation as it was now standing and made the group aware of that. Such positioning caused a harsh response.

"So, you think you are now going to split off from the rest of us and try to let people focus on the fact you don't make as much money as we do from our products? Are you just trying to set yourselves up so you can have a different image from us on all of this concerning this issue?" asked the president of the company leading in the production of the products in question.

"It is not a question of who is making the most money. It is a question of who is doing the most damage to the public, particularly to the kids of the public," was the response.

"Naw it isn't. It all comes down to you're not making as much money as we are, and you want to see us not make as much so we come down to your income level."

"Lou, it comes down to the fact, recently reported which resulted in all these questions, that now one in about every 80 children has autism instead of one in every twenty thousand, which is what it was twenty years ago."

"Yea Ernie, and we led the effort to get all of us, you included, to have what amounts to a legal exemption from any kind of significant liability due to the legislation we got passed by Congress, led by the guy we got to do it. And that exemption covers you, so what the hell are you worried about?"

One of the other attendees joined in, saying, "Yea Ernie. What are you worried about? You are covered. Lou got that taken care of."

"Yea, Ernie. You got your big bonus last year due to our effort. And we have got to stand together. You know that. If you break off, it will cause all of us problems. Bad problems. You have to stick with us. So, let's let our good looking, professional PR girl go out there and just simply say that what is happening is not our problem. She can say that we are funding studies on what all is coming up, which we are. But we are doing what we can to check everything out. And then she can close out the press conference with the statement that we will call another press conference when we find out from our research if anything we're doing is in any way related to the problem."

Ernie looked around the table and saw that three of the four others were in agreement with what Lou has just said.

Lou then added, "Besides, you know that there is a lot of money to be made in treating this autism thing. You know that. All those kids are going to need various treatments that we all have been researching. Your company, Ernie, is going to make a lot of money dealing with this, just like we are. So, sit back and enjoy the profits from that too, Ernie."

Ernie looked around the table and saw that the rest of the

attendees seemed to be agreeing with Lou and his company's position. He then leaned forward and slowly again looked around the table.

"When I hear our group taking this position, I think about the Ford Pinto. You all know how that was treated. They knew they had a problem with that car. They knew there were going to be accidents that caused deaths and injuries and loss of property because of the problems with that car. And you know what happened. They decided, on purpose, after studying the potential costs of fixing the problem, that it would cost less just to deal with the results of the accidents. You all know how they suffered as a result of taking that course of action. How they eventually had to change and do what they should have done in the first place. Yes, it cost them a lot of money, but they did the right thing after having some bad losses, and they took care of it like they should have in the first place. I just don't want us to have the same bad PR as a result of what we are doing here. I am also not comfortable with us being the possible cause of so much damage to innocent people, almost all of whom are, or in the future will be, kids."

Lou quickly answered, "Ernie, they didn't have somebody like me who got them what amounts basically to immunity from damage lawsuits. The way it is set up, there may be very, very limited payments that may have to be made, but for the most part, we don't have to even worry about that. And that is because of me! Do you hear me? It is because of me! Because I went to the United State Congress and got my doctor friend, the senator, to basically get us all what amounts to immunity. They can't get us like they may have been able to if I, that's me you understand, had not gotten him to get that legislation passed providing coverage for us. Do you understand the difference between us and the fucking Ford Pinto? Do you? You do not, repeat not, have the exposure that the Pinto had, and that is because of me! So, go enjoy your bonus! And I will go ahead and say, 'You're welcome'."

After that, the meeting soon thereafter broke up. Not too long after the meeting, a very short news conference was held during which the position discussed by the group at the meeting was set forth. The public was assured that further research was being done to make sure that, as was now believed, the products produced by the companies simply were not the cause of the huge increase in autism in the country.

* * *

Tony just happened to be watching the evening news on TV when a report on the news conference concerning a meeting of some of the largest drug companies was made. He paid more attention to what was being said when it became apparent that the report was partially about the huge increase in recent years in the number of autistic children. In the 1980's there had been one autistic child out of about every twenty thousand, the reporter said. Now there is one autistic child out of about every eighty.

After listening to the report, Tony sat there and thought about Jean's daughter. He also thought about all of the parents of autistic children. He wondered why something had not been done more quickly to make sure that problem was made to be less of one. The more he thought about it, the more he felt that there were probably two answers to his question. The first answer he felt was what usually was in play when something that big came up: money. If it wasn't money, it was usually because of the second reason: bad judgment. He quickly made his decision as to what he thought the answer was: both of them, money and bad judgment.

* * *

Jean had called to let Mary Jo know she was flying back in and would be arriving at the New Orleans airport at about 4:30.

"Come meet me at the Green Tomato after you get your car. You know where it is, don't you?" Mary Jo asked.

"Not really," Jean had said. But she knew that she had to do something when she got back. The only thing she was able to keep thinking about was what had just happened. She had to have something to divert her thoughts, as soon as possible, because it seemed that all she could think about was what had just happened. She felt so bad about it. After all, it was a black man, of all peple. Yes, a very handsome, muscular, big black man but still, a black man! And she had sex with him, not just once, but several times that night. More than she ever thought she would have or could have. After all, she had never thought she would have ever had sex with a black man. Any black man!

But she did, and the confusing thing about it was by the end of their session, she almost didn't want to leave. It had been so good, but he was black! She had been raised in a southern home. Her parents had always treated blacks nicely, at the very minimum. But he was black! She needed a drink. Maybe several drinks would help make her forget what in the absolute world she had just done! Having thought about it all so much since It had happened, she still could not believe she had done it. She had not slept at all. She needed a drink. Now! So, she blurted out, "How do I get there from the airport once I get back?"

"Take that main four lane road from the airport and go towards town. When you see the Cavalier Motel on the left side

146

of the street, pull into the parking lot behind the motel. The Green Tomato is the bar sort of behind the motel desk. You can walk through the door at the back of the building and a little walkway will take you to the lobby. The entrance is on the back side of the lobby."

"Are you there now?" Jean asked.

"Yes, and I will be looking for you when you come in."

"Are you going to be there for sure? I really need you to be there."

"I am here already. Come on in. You will see me the minute you walk in. I'll be at the second table inside the doorway to the room or I will be at the bar."

Jean said, "Ok. I am leaving the airport parking lot right now. Will see you in a little bit. Bye." With that, she hung up.

Mary Jo immediately turned to the two girls, Susan and Katie, sitting at the table with a big grin on her face. She then said, very excitedly, "She's coming now! She'll be here in about thirty minutes."

Susan said, "Who?"

Mary Jo looked at first one, and then the other, of her two table mates, quickly thinking about the many times the three of them had competed to hook up with lesbian seduction prospects that had walked into that bar. The bar was known throughout the area as one of the prime lesbian meeting places for those looking to explore possible mutual interests.

"My new target, so you two leave her alone," she answered. "This one belongs to me, okay?"

Both girls nodded their heads, with Susan saying, "This must be serious."

Mary Jo said, "It is. You'll see. She is something special. Absolutely beautiful. Have known her since college. So, this one belongs to me."

She got up and walked to the bar. When she got there, a nice looking, five foot nine, short haired blonde with a very firm figure walked over to greet her. The blonde bartender, Veronica, usually called "Ronnie", was known to work out with weights at a nearby gym at least four times each week.

"Hi there. What's up? Need anything?" she asked.

Mary Jo looked at her and said, "A girl I knew in college is going to come walking in here in a little bit. I am going to bring her up here, away from those two. She is absolutely beautiful. May want your very discreet help with her."

"Sounds interesting. Any experience?"

"Only one that I know of. If possible, I'd like to take her further into things. There was no resistance the first time. She needs further encouragement, some guidance. I will let you know with our usual signal if she needs some help with her drink."

"I always like that kind. They never know what happened to them as we bring them further into our little world," Ronnie said with a big smile coming on her face.

"If we can make it happen, you are going to love this one. She's a former beauty queen and is still just gorgeous," Mary Jo said, now also with a big smile on her face.

"Mmmmmm, sounds really interesting," she answered with an even bigger smile on her face. "Can't wait to meet her".

After standing at the bar for about twenty minutes, Mary Jo looked up as the door to the bar was opened and in walked Jean. Looking at the bar area and seeing Mary Jo, Jean walked straight towards her. Mary Jo immediately began thinking about how she was going to hopefully get that very stylish blouse and tight mid-thigh skirt off her, should she get so lucky. As she watched Jean work her way up to the bar, she immediately thought that if she did get lucky with Jean later, she may even let her keep her high heels on during the fun. She always enjoyed doing that these days with her conquests, especially with the new ones. It seemed to sometimes let them feel like they weren't going to get into anything further.

As she watched Jean walk towards the bar, Mary Jo heard the voice behind the bar softly say, under her breath, "Oh my. This is going to be fun."

"Hi there, honey," Mary Jo greeted her with a big smile and then gave her a big hug.

"Have a seat here. What can I get for you? This is on me," she said as she motioned for Jean to come closer.

"This is Veronica, known to us as 'Ronnie'. Tell her what you would like to have," Mary Jo said as she moved so she was standing next to the bar.

Jean slid onto a bar stool as she hung her bag on the right arm rest.

"Hi. Vodka tonic with a twist," she said to Ronnie as she settled in.

"I have to decide what I would like to have. Are you going to be able to stay for a while, I hope? I mean, you are not going to drive to Mississippi tonight, are you? I hope you are staying in New Orleans and not going to try to drive all that way."

"No. I am going to be staying at my place here tonight, dropping off some things, picking up some things, before going over tomorrow to see my child."

Mary Jo side, "Good. We can spend some time talking here then."

With that, she looked at Jean and said, "My usual Jack and coke." As she said that, she looked right at Ronnie and lightly tapped her left fore finger on the bar one time, a signal that specifically meant one thing to Ronnie, who nodded her head and then turned to make their drinks. She made the drinks as she shielded their views of the glasses in which the drinks were being prepared. As she fixed Jean's drink, she very quickly took a small shot glass and sprinkled a little white powder from that glass into Jean's drink in a move she had done numerous times before.

Mary Jo began their conversation by asking about the trip Jean had just taken and if her business efforts were being successful. As Mary Jo was talking, Jean began steadily drinking from her glass and proceeded to down the entire drink.

Placing the glass down on the bar, she looked over at Mary Jo and said, "I need another one."

Mary Jo motioned to Ronnie for another one which she immediately began preparing. "Put it on my tab." She also put her palm face down on the bar, which was her signal to Ronnie to not put any powder into this drink. Mary Jo felt that there had been enough put into the first drink that it would serve its purpose.

Looking back at Jean, she asked, "Are you ok?"

Jean answered, "Yes. It was just a really hard trip."

She then reached for the second drink that Ronnie had now prepared for her. Putting it to her lips, she took a hefty, full swig of it. There was no holding back by Jean. After what she had experienced on this trip, doing something she would never have ever expected to do, she needed to do some drinking. At least she had Mary Jo there with her, but Jean needed something to ease her feelings. How in the world had she ever let herself get into the situation she had just experienced in Charlotte? Being with a black man. The more she had thought about it on the flight to New Orleans, the more she needed a drink. She had to somehow get that out of her mind.

Mary Jo could sense that something was really bothering Jean. Little did Jean know that soon she was not going to be able to walk, much less drive. Jean drank the remainder of the second drink and eased that glass to the surface of the bar.

She then motioned for Ronnie to bring her another one. Ronnie looked at Mary Jo, who placed her hand palm down on the bar while saying, "Bring her another one." Then, looking at Jean, she said, "Honey, you need to drink this one a little slower, okay? Enjoy it. Take your time. You know she makes a good drink."

Jean answered, "She does. I just really need something right now. There is so much going on."

Mary Jo noticed the beginning already of a little slur in her speech. Looking at her, she thought to herself that Jean had no idea what all more may be going on in her life very shortly.

Ronnie brought the third drink over and Jean fumbled a little as she reached for the glass after it was set down in front of her. Jean took it and, now with her hand not moving so smoothly, guided the third glass to her lips. After taking a couple of sips, she haltingly guided the glass back to the bar surface.

Mary Jo then asked her, "Have you heard anything about our favorite Spanish teacher from college? What was her name?"

At that point, when Jean tried to answer, her words would not come out clearly, partially because she could not remember the instructor's name but also because now the powder was starting to have its affect. That was also when Jean first started to tilt a little on her bar stool and Mary Jo quickly leaned over to grab her, so she didn't fall off. She also extended her right arm so that her hand was behind Jean. She made sure Susan, one of the girls at her table, saw her and motioned to her with her hand as if she was turning a key to a door. That was a signal that the group had used many times before in their seduction efforts. The signal meant for one of the girls to go to the front desk and get their special room just down at the end of the hallway from the bar and the front desk. Susan saw the signal, quickly nodded her head affirmatively, got up and left to go to the front desk.

"Hold on there, girl. Are you ok?" Mary Jo asked.

Jean looked at her, now with somewhat glazed eyes and a smile on her face, and mumbled, "Yes, I'm ok." Then she tilted over a little more and Mary Jo again grabbed her. This time, she stood next to Jean to make sure she did not fall over or off of the bar stool. She had seen that happen before and did not want this beautiful woman to end up laying on the floor. It would be so hard to get her back up. That had not been an easy thing to get done once it happened with others. It was better to help her from where she was now.

Looking now at the entrance to the bar, Mary Jo was glad to see Susan come through the door with a room key somewhat hidden discreetly in her right hand. As she reached Mary Jo, she stood close to her so she could discretely pass the key into her hand.

Susan smiled and said softly, "You owe me."

Mary Jo answered, "No. This will get you even with me finally."

Susan smiled and answered, in a whisper, "Maybe you'll let me have a little time with this one in the future."

"Now that might be possible. We'll see what happens. Just not tonight."

Susan continued with her smile and, after glancing at Jean, she said, "I'll look forward to it." She then turned and walked away.

Mary Jo turned to Jean and said, "Honey, we need to get you to a room. We don't want you falling over and hurting yourself, maybe even ending up in a hospital or something. Come on and go with me. There is a place close-by where you can lay down."

Looking at Ronnie, she said, "Come help me with her."

Ronnie then looked over her shoulder at her boss, an older masculine woman, and said, "I'm taking an early break."

Her boss looked at Ronnie, who nodded her head towards Jean. She quickly looked at Jean and then back at Ronnie and said, "Ok, but I'm jealous."

Ronnie turned around so that she was facing her boss, grinned and softly said, "I'll let you know how it goes." She then walked around the end of the bar and took a few steps over to assist Mary Jo with helping Jean off of the stool.

With Ronnie on her left side and Mary Jo on her right, Jean was helped as she staggered from the bar area and down the end of the hallway to Room 123, a room they had used several times before in situations like this. Once inside the room, Mary Jo said, "We're going to take your business suit off of you, so it won't get wrinkled."

Jean was barely able to stand as Mary Jo unbuttoned her jacket and the two women eased it off of her. Next Mary Jo unbuttoned her blouse while Ronnie unzipped and eased off her skirt. She was then led over to the bed and slowly leaned back until she was laying down. They then each laid on opposite sides of her.

Jean was in her twilight zone, caused somewhat by the white powder mixed in with her drink, but also by the experienced touching and caressing of the two women lying next to her. One thing for sure was that, though her recent experience with a black man was still on her mind, it wasn't for long because of the things the two girls were now doing to her. Mary Jo and Ronnie both began to utilize and practice their experience and expertise in taking another woman higher and higher sexually.

After a few minutes, Mary Jo eased herself up from the bed, grabbed her cell phone and quickly took several pictures of Ronnie having her way with Jean. Jean saw the pictures being taken and feebly made an attempt to object to what was happening by trying to move around a little. But she was too dazed and being too deeply affected by the powder. The touching and caressing were also just feeling too good.

Mary Jo left her phone on top of the chest of drawers and quickly took off her tennis shoes, her leather vest, tee shirt and shorts. She laid back down on the bed next to Jean. Ronnie then got up and quickly took off her running shoes, her tee shirt, and then her shorts. She grabbed the camera from where she knew it would be and took several more pictures of Jean with her face clearly showing, now on the bed with Mary Jo. Ronnie then rejoined the two girls on the bed.

Eventually one thing led to another and Jean's previously sleeping sexual giant was awakened again, and it felt so good. Ronnie took her up to the edge, kept her there for a little while and then took her over. She then passed her over to Mary Jo, who again soon got the same response.

Their past experiences had taught them to gradually explore the effects of their efforts and find out which areas of a target's body were the most sensitive and what type of touch and manipulation was most effective on that particular girl. Mary Jo already had some idea about Jean based on the Houston trip. Ronnie found, guided by Mary Jo, that certain things had to be done in a certain way and with a certain touch in order to be the most effective. Soon, little Miss Beauty Queen was beginning to be taken places she hadn't been taken in a while, if ever. It was eventually just up to them as to when they wanted to get Jean to completely lose control of herself. It began to seem, as time went on, that Jean could not get enough of what they were doing.

During one of the times when Ronnie was again taking Jean close to losing her self-control, Mary Jo got up off the bed and used her camera phone again. It was during this point that Ronnie made sure that Jean's face was again showing along with her now completely nude body. Finally able to more clearly realize that pictures were actually being taken by Mary Jo, Jean tried to turn her head so her face wouldn't show, but her effort was again too weak and too late. Ronnie made sure Jean's beautiful face remained showing as Mary Jo quickly took more pictures.

Such an effort by the two girls was something they had done many times before and had really gotten good at, especially with Jean only now finally starting to come out from under the effect of the white powder that Mary Jo had put in her drink. Everything felt so good to Jean that, even as she became more aware that there were two, not just one, women having sex with her, she did not want anything to stop.

She had just left something she had not wanted to do but, in order to survive, she had been put in a situation of basically being forced to do it. Besides, she was beginning to enjoy so much what was happening now to forget about what had happened then, or at least not think about it for a while. She still could not believe she had done it, but she felt it was part of what she had been forced to do due to her sorry ex-husband. She also continued to rationalize that she had been forced to do it because of the physical and mental condition of her daughter, which she felt had been caused by those big pharma companies. The extremely high expense of her care and treatment, and the bad financial condition Jean was now in, were results of it all.

It was not her fault. It was due to one of those sorry manufacturing companies making a product that they knew was harmful and had caused her and her daughter so much heartache and agony. That manufacturing company was literally wrecking so many families and their lives. She wondered how the head of that company would feel if they daily, personally faced the same problems and limitations that her daughter faced. How could they continue to make those pills knowing that there was something about their product that caused so much suffering and disappointment? Why didn't they do something about a product they made that they knew caused problems? Why didn't they? Then her sweet daughter would not have to be going through what she was experiencing and would experience all of her life, and neither would Jean and her family. Nor would thousands of other families. But now they were also having questions about the mandatory vaccination shots that every child was having to take when they got to be two years old.

It was at about that time that Ronnie, who was so good at what she was doing, began doing more things that completely took Jean's mind back off all of that, and also away from her recent first sexual experience with a black man. There was one thing about this girl named Ronnie. She surely knew exactly where and how to touch another woman. Jean immediately thought that it was probably because of many hours of practice, practice, practice. That sleeping giant inside of Jean that had been dormant for so long was definitely being brought back to life now. Oh, was it ever!

A couple of hours later, Ronnie had to leave to go to her second job at a bar downtown on the edge of the French quarter. By the time she did leave, a now totally exhausted Jean fell almost immediately into a very nice sleep.

Mary Jo waited for a few minutes and then eased herself from the bed. She quietly got dressed and, with Jean's panties and her phone with the pictures safely placed in her bag, she left the building. She was very pleased with how the evening had gone, which had been very similar to many other times she and some of the others in her little group had done the same type of thing with other girls they had picked up. Mary Jo was going to make sure the pictures that had been taken were put in her safe storage area in the back room of her closet at her house, so that they would be there along with the pictures of the twenty-six other conquests she had taken since becoming a hunter. Her little group of four girls loved to seduce straight women, have several lesbian experiences with them, then trade the girls around among their group and their friends to find out which arrangements might become more permanent pairings.

Mary Jo was now ready to move Jean on to the next stage of her experience with other women. She wanted to quickly get Jean into that next scene, which she planned to have take place soon at her house. Yes, Mary Jo wanted it to happen sooner than later, since it seemed that Jean had thoroughly enjoyed what she had been taken into. Once some of the other girls in her little circle had experienced being with Jean, a decision would have to be made as to which one would take up a more permanent relationship with her. Initially it might seem the best one for her would be Ronnie, but Ronnie also liked to hunt. She didn't necessarily want to settle down, but maybe being with a former beauty queen would be good enough for her to consider it.

In the meantime, it was on to her next conquest for Mary Jo. At this time, that seemed to be pointing toward the nice looking, twenty-one-year-old student named Lindy, who had just passed a course Mary Jo was teaching at a local college. Mary Jo was making steady progress towards eventually getting her Doctorate Degree in Sociology and Lindy had been one of her really good students in the semester that had just recently ended. Lindy had come up to see Mary Jo many times after class was over and made it obvious, after all of the other students had left the classroom area, that she wanted to spend more time with Mary Jo, privately.

Mary Jo had barely managed to resist the situation, but only did so until Lindy had completed her class. Lindy had come up to see her after getting her grade for the semester at the end of her last class meeting. Mary Jo immediately invited her to come over to her house that very night. Lindy eagerly accepted her offer and, just a few days earlier, they had explored one another for several hours. During their time together, she found out more about Lindy helping put herself through college by stripping late at night during alternate semesters in a bar just off the edge of the French Quarter. The fact that she was a new encounter, attractive and fresh, and so much younger than Mary Jo's other recent conquests, such as Jean, made her a girl that Mary Jo was looking forward to spending more time with. In the meantime, Mary Jo intended to take the former beauty queen further into certain experiences Mary Jo was thinking about and planning that she doubted Jean had ever even thought of.

Chapter Ten

Tony had arrived back in LA with the thought in mind to deal with his deceased friend's wife's problem immediately. She had enough sadness to deal with and didn't need any other problems like the theft of money through a credit card account. The loss of $18,000 may not sound like so much to some people but, for her around the same time as the death of the Sheriff, such amount of money was significant. Karen needed it back and while Tony could have easily written a check for that amount and never missed it, he thought it might be good to bring a little justice to the criminals involved in the theft. Once he found out his New York cousin, Conrad, was able to locate and accurately identify those responsible for the theft, he almost suddenly felt the urge to bring about an immediate rectification of the wrongdoing.

After studying the information packet that Conrad had provided to him, which even included pictures of the two, he decided that it was time for the two perpetrators of the crime, Walley and Walton, to meet a friend of one of their victims. From the looks of the two, he wasn't as worried as he could have been. They both appeared to be arrogant computer nerds who needed some adjustment to their thinking. Their pictures both showed what he thought were funny looking, glass wearing computer specialists who had gotten so good at computers that they became capable of breaking into other people's and company's files. While they had made good grades in school, they had apparently decided that no one appreciated how smart they were technically with their computers.

The two experts became so dis-satisfied with the lack of respect they received that they decided they would start hacking into financial records after Walley's mother was evicted from her house by a bank. They became very proficient at getting credit card information over the internet and started using other people's cards to first buy things and then to withdraw money from accounts in banks or from credit card account numbers. They were totally amazed at how easy it was and that nobody was really checking out things and really putting forth an effort looking for who had been doing what they were into. They gradually began to amass a large amount of money and were totally surprised at how easy it was and how much smarter they were than the people who were supposedly trying to catch them.

What the two had not counted on was that the man who was probably for over twenty years the CIA''s top computer expert, as Conrad was generally recognized by those in the know as being, just happened to have a few of their facts show up thanks to a request by that man's cousin, Tony. After having years of experience utilizing computers and information networks to find and follow anti-American foreigners from all over the world, especially in Iraq, Afghanistan and Syria, it had been basically no problem to find two skinny, glasses wearing, nerdy looking computer geeks. In fact, Tony was impressed and felt that he had to bring the matter to a quick resolution because there may be other things that he would have to pay attention to in the near future.

After scouting out the apartment complex in which the two boys had hidden their operation, Tony went to a nearby sports store and bought himself a baseball bat, cowboy boots and some thick gloves. Waiting until mid-morning, he then contacted one of his long-time friends with the LA Police Department and told him to expect a call from him in about three hours, that he might need his help with a matter in his jurisdiction. He then put on his boots and gloves while in his car parked in a lot near the apartment complex. He then grabbed the bat and worked his way towards the building number that Conrad had provided for the two boys in the complex. He was glad to see that the place was rather deserted with very few people coming or going in the area.

Arriving at the building number, Tony went to the second-floor balcony entrance to the room number provided by Conrad for the two boys and knocked on the door with his glove covered fist. With there being no immediate answer, he knocked again, this time louder. This second time, the front door slowly opened, and a tall skinny boy peered from the other side. The moment there was enough room to see light inside the room, Tony shoved the door open, which caused the greeter to stumble back from the entrance.

"Hey, what are you do …," the figure began to yell out as he pulled his right fist back as if to next swing it at Tony.

It was then that Tony quickly stepped inside and shut the door, locking it from inside. The figure, which Tony could tell was Walton, paused for a moment while looking right at Tony.

"Hey, you're Tony Gable, the actor!"

At that same moment, Tony put his bat in hitting position on his right upper arm and said, "Yeppers, that's right." He then swung his bat against Walton's left upper arm, hearing a loud crack as the bat hit the target and drove him back across the small living room as he grabbed his arm. He fell to the floor as he yelled out a screech.

Now on the floor, holding his left upper arm with his right hand and looking up at the man who had just hit him with that bat, he managed to say, "Ohhhhhhhhh ! Why' ... dddddddd ... youuuuu ... dooooo thattttt?"

"Because you were going to try to hit me, asshole," Tony answered. Walking over to stand next to him, holding the baseball bat in his right hand, he said, "I had to use a hickory cane about like this years ago back down south, when I first got over here. Seems the ole boy wanted to rob me. Broke his arm too."

Walley was in deep pain, which was accompanied by loud moans as he writhed on the floor, trying to find a position he could put himself in that would not hurt as much as the position he was now in, whichever position that might be.

Standing over him as he now grasped the bat with both hands, Tony said, "I am going to ask you one time, and you had better answer me quickly or I'm gonna break some other bone in your body with this bat. Now look at me and pay attention."

Tony leaned forward, got right in his face and said, "I know every computer expert, like you and your buddy, keep a large part of the money you've stolen in cash. So, here is my question.

164

Where is the money that you have stolen that is here in your apartment? And I want you to tell me right now."

The boy continued to moan until Tony said, "I am going to ask you one more time, dipshit. Where have you stashed the money you and your buddy have been stealing?"

Still no answer as Walley now looked up at the man holding the bat standing over him.

The boy, now lying on his back on the floor, was holding his left arm where he had been struck by the baseball bat. His eyes got wider after he heard the question.

After waiting for a moment, Tony said, "If I have to ask you again, I am going to hit your sorry ass, again, with this bat. You are beginning to piss me off." He took a few steps over to the figure lying on the floor in front of him and said, "I don't like thieves, especially when they lie to me." He then pulled the bat over his right shoulder and brought it down on the mid-upper thigh of the boy's left leg. The cracking sound of the bone breaking could be heard, even over his scream after the impact.

Sitting down in a chair, he watched the boy twist in pain on the floor. After a few moments, he said to the boy, "Ok. Let's try this one more time. I am going to ask you the question again and if you give me what I think is a truthful answer, everything will be lovely. But if you lie to me again, I am gonna break some other bones in your body. Now then, where do you keep your money?"

"In the ... closet in ... the next room," he stuttered and then looked up at Tony. In between moans, Walley motioned his head, and the foot-long hair on that head, towards what appeared to be the entrance to a bedroom.

Tony got up and took a few steps in the direction of the

bedroom, while checking down a small hallway that appeared to lead to another bedroom. Going into the first bedroom and then opening the door to what appeared to be a closet, Tony was amazed to see numerous large stacks and adjacent piles of cash leaning against its back wall. These stupid nerds had so much cash they had not spent the time to take care of storing it all or getting it deposited. There was cash money everywhere.

He pulled the knapsack off of his back and went over to the closet. Seeing stacks of cash lying against the wall in the back of the closet, Tony bent over and took those portions of the cash that were already wrapped in paper in what he quickly was able to determine were one thousand-dollar stacks of twenty-dollar bills. He quickly put about twenty thousand dollars into his bag and zipped it up. As he pulled it onto his back, he looked over and could not even tell from all of the money still all over the place in that closet that the money he took was even missing. When he walked back into the living room area, he saw that Walley was trying to get up, but had not made much progress due to his two injuries.

Tony heard the sound of the front doorknob being turned and looked at it. Someone was getting ready to come in. The door was pushed open and in walked a thin, hippy looking young man with extremely long hair. As he shut the door behind him, he looked up to see Tony walking back into the room. He looked over to see Walley on the floor against the far wall.

Tony knew from his black belt classes that he had to quickly evaluate his potential opponent in order to determine what might need to happen next. He immediately noticed that this young man was probably a little taller than his friend now on the floor but was also slump shouldered and appeared weak. He didn't look like he had lifted anything heavier than a computer bag in the past year, much less recently.

"Hi, Walton," Tony said as he took a step towards what looked exactly like Tony would call a computer nerd.

Walton just stood there watching him as Tony took a few steps towards him. He saw the bat hanging from Tony's left hand. He then saw his roommate on the floor not moving but instead looking directly at him as he moaned. Looking back at Tony, who was now within arm's reach, he noticed the thick working gloves on his hands.

"Aren't you Tony Gable," he asked, eyes now wide open.

"Yep," Tony answered. Tony then swung his glove covered right fist straight into Walton's face, causing a cracking noise and crunching his nose and upper lip. The force of the blow shoved Walton back against the wall, against which he crumpled to the floor. The boy began crying immediately, with both of his hands over his face.

Walking over to where Walton was now on the floor, Tony said, "Where are the copies of what's on your computers?"

Walton looked up and, holding his hand over his nose and lips, said in a muffled voice, "We don't have any copies. There's nothing to have copies of."

Tony walked over to Walton, put the bat on his shoulder and then, holding it with both hands, swung it down hard on Walton's upper right arm.

Walton let out a scream.

"Okay, you two. One more time, where are your records of all of those credit card numbers and bank accounts that you have been hacking?"

167

The first boy quickly answered, "On discs, safety… deposit … box …at a bank."

"Oh, now we are making progress. Where is the key or card to get entry and which bank is it in?"

The boy hesitated for a moment, and Tony edged over to be closer to him again. He then reached over to hold the bat again with both hands.

"No, no. Left drawer, puter desk. Cal Southern bank, Berkley," Walton quickly answered.

"The one on the main drag?"

The kid nodded his head, still holding his right arm.

"And the number of the box is?"

"47010".

Tony then smashed every computer in the apartment. After leaving, he called and arranged for his friend with the local police to get the discs from the bank clearly showing the scam being done by the two boys. He told his local police friend that he would be available to testify against the two boys, if that was needed. He also notified a local newspaper investigator of the scheme. He then leaked the information to a local TV station.

* * *

In Miami, Stanley Rohrbach felt like he was a king. He was 52 years old and had been the head of the third largest drug company, Shetland Rhorbach, in the country for the past six years. With his family owning almost all of the stock in the company, and his now sick, elderly father having turned over the company to him to run, he was in control. Though his father retained the office of President of the company, he was not physically able to even regularly attend meetings concerning management.

Stanley was in control and he was not shy about letting anybody, especially beautiful women, know about his powerful position, not only in the company but also in the industry. Though married and the father of two almost grown children, Stanley had always made sure "pretty ladies", as he called them, knew how important he was and how rich he was. As a result of his pompous attitude and constant bragging, there were usually women around at conventions and in bars after business meetings that he would get to know better as an evening of drinking went on.

After a rather full day of activities at this convention, Stanley went out to dinner with three of his running buddies to a restaurant near the convention center. His room for his stay was located in an adjacent motel, which was usually his arrangement at most conventions. By not having his room at the main hotel associated with or built as part of the convention center, he felt he had more room to hook up with one of the always available women hanging around such conventions. He was usually looking for a standout, well-dressed lady to meet with and talk with in order to let her know how rich and important he was and how smart he was.

After having a good meal, he left his dining buddies and went back to his motel by himself. This meant that he could go into the bar connected to where he had his room and see if any interesting ladies might be available for a few drinks, a conversation during which he might impress them with his intellect, and possibly end up in his room in bed with him. He had done that many times over the years and had even done it at this particular motel the last time this convention had met there in town a little over a year ago.

Walking into the bar, he quickly surveyed the place as he moved towards the main bar area. After locating a spot over to one side, he leaned in towards the bartender and ordered a Scotch on the rocks. Turning to face the crowd in the bar, he continued to survey the group, looking as he usually did for a possible companion.

After receiving and paying for his order, he turned again to face the crowd as he took a sip of his favorite drink. It was then that he saw her! A beautiful blonde woman in a dark blue business suit, which consisted of a well-fitted jacket and pleasantly tight, just above the knee skirt, walked in the doorway and appeared to be looking for a place to sit. As he watched her, she did not seem to be meeting anyone, at least anyone who had yet arrived.

She looked over the nicely packed room and slowly made her way, in her five-inch heels he noted, towards the opposite side of the bar area. Stanley decided he needed to move fast, before any of the other males seeking companionship could get up the courage to move in on such a nice package. He was able to rather quickly get over to that opposite side and fit himself in next to her before she could even order.

He quickly introduced himself to her and was greeted by a pleasant smile, whereupon he offered to buy her a drink. Expressing appreciation, she ordered a bourbon and coke. After some very amiable conversation, during which she said she was from Fort Lauderdale and was in the area for the first time on business, and during which they shared a few quick drinks, he invited her to his room at the motel, where they could have a few more drinks. Appearing now to be somewhat tipsy, she agreed, and they soon left for his room.

Getting to his room, he offered to mix a drink for her while she went into the restroom. She came out, dressed only in a black lace bra and bikini panties, still in those heels. He wanted to play with those large breasts she had ever since he had first seen her walk in the bar. He came over to her and grabbed each of her large breasts as he began giving her a deep tongue probing kiss. She then pulled back and said that she would mix him a drink while he went to the restroom to take off his suit, shirt, tie, tee shirt and underwear, which he promptly did. He came out a few moments later wearing nothing. As she cradled her drink in her left hand, she offered him his drink with her right hand. He took his drink from her and they clicked glasses, with her saying, "To our new friendship. May we both enjoy what happens." Then they each took a full sip from their glasses.

Three hours later, Stanley began to wake up. He at first did not remember anything but gradually began at least to realize he was still nude. Pain started to get his attention. He thought back and vaguely remembered that he had met this beautiful woman with a large pair of perfect breasts in the bar, who had come with him to his room, and who was now nowhere around. He thought for a moment and vaguely remembered her, at some point, giving him a shot in his upper left arm with a hypodermic needle.

Immediately he felt pain, which quickly grew more acute. It caused him to shift his eyes to look at his right hand. He couldn't see! He had heard about criminals having acid put in their eyes, so they would not be able to see again. But those were criminals. He was the head of a massive Wall Street company!

He tried to move his fingers of his right hand up to his eyes to feel. He had NO FINGERS! They were all gone!

He tried to move the fingers of his left hand.

He had NO FINGERS on his LEFT HAND! They were all gone!

He now felt pain coming from his feet. He tried to look down at his feet. He still couldn't see! But he could tell!

He had NO TOES, on EITHER OF HIS FEET! NONE!

That was when, as much as he could, he screamed out.

"AAAAAAAAAAAAAAAGGGGGGGGGGGGGG!"

After screaming out, he tried to look down at his penis, but couldn't see anything. If he could have, he would have seen something white in the tip of his penis. He would later find out that the white stuff was super glue, which had been injected into his penis up most of the length of its urinary canal!

Chapter Eleven

Coming back to the Gulf Coast from LA gave Tony time to think about other things his father had told him as they had sat on the bench in Sicily overlooking the straits. The older Tony had gotten, the more comfortable his father had felt telling him at least some of the things that had happened while his father had been in Mississippi. This time, Tony remembered an individual his dad had talked about who had been sent down by the federal government to investigate the illegal shipping of booze to the area.

His name was Charles Lovelady and he wanted to use his efforts on the Gulf Coast to get himself a good reputation. His father was third in line of officials in command of the Treasury Department in Washington, D. C. and had no trouble getting his son assigned to south Mississippi, of all places. The feeling had been that certainly Charles would be able to build up his resume based upon what all he was able to get accomplished on the gulf coast.

Tony remembered his dad chuckling when he talked about Charles. It was one of the few times he could remember his normally very serious father doing that but do that he did. Twice actually, and both times it was when he was talking about Lovelady. He had told Tony that they had a good information system on the coast and usually knew what all the federals were looking into and where they would be.

When Lovelady had gotten to town, he had gone to the house that the federal agents had leased to serve as their headquarters for their operations. The five agents already there wanted to make Lovelady feel welcomed and had wondered what they might do that would accomplish that. The most senior agent, Lance Bottrell, suggested that they each chip in some money for the purchase of a special gun for their new boss. One of the men had recently seen a sliver automatic .38 pistol and thought that might be something that would create a favorable impression with their new chief. All of the men agreed, and the purchase of the silver gun was made a few days before Lovelady got to town.

When Lovelady first arrived at the house, he was greeted by the men and welcomed to their hangout. After their initial comments, Bottrell walked over to Lovelady and, with the men standing around in the living room area, presented him with the very shiny, bright silver pistol. As he held it out for Lovelady to take, Bottrell said, "We just wanted to welcome you to the area and give you something that will remind you of our welcoming you here. Now, be careful. I don't know if you have ever handled one of these types of guns before, but they are really great to have. This one is very special because we have fixed it for you so that it has a hair trigger, which causes the gun to fire even if the trigger is just barely touched."

Lovelady was feeling very special and with a big smile on his face, said while reaching for the gun, "Why, that is so nice of you boys. It really is. Thank …."

It was while he was saying that word of appreciation that Lovelady had put his hand around the beautiful silver pistol and, as his forefinger had barely touched the trigger of the gun, immediately it happened.

"WHAM!"

The surprise of the loud sound of the pistol shot caused Lovelady to instantly touch the sensitive trigger again.

"WHAM!"

As the second shot was being fired by the now totally shocked Lovelady, four of the five agents were trying every way possible to find cover. One literally dove behind a couch as the one that had been standing next to him ducked behind a large, wooden chair. Another agent quickly dove through an adjacent doorway, immediately disappearing behind a wall. An agent standing not too far from Lovelady just hit the floor facedown almost right in front of him. Lovelady was so shocked that his shaking trigger finger could not help but touch the sensitive to the touch of a feather trigger of that gun again.

"WHAM!"

And again.

"WHAM"

After the fourth shot, Bottrell was able to reach over from the side of Lovelady, grab the gun and pull it out of his hand.

Lovelady stood there, eyes stretched as wide open as they

could get, with the hand that had held the gun visibly shaking. Gradually, agents began to try to recover. The agent behind the couch looked over the back of that couch with only his eyes barely showing. The agent behind the high back chair gradually peered from around the side of that chair. The agent behind the wall slowly moved his head so he could look around the side of the doorway. The agent on the floor rolled over, now with his own gun pulled and pointed at the man that had just held and fired four shots from the silver pistol.

Tony outright laughed as he recalled what his dad had said, with a smile on his face, that he had been told that Bottrell had said, as he now held the silver gun, "It looks like we may need a little practice with this."

Tony also remembered that his dad had told him that Lovelady, in spite of that first experience, not too long afterwards wanted to go out and get on the front lines of the feds' investigation. Tony's dad had arranged for the agents to get information that would cause them to be misdirected. The result was that they were guided towards areas of the swamp that were not actually included in any activities that were going on.

After a couple of trips out into the Mississippi Sound on boats with fellow agents, Lovelady seized on some of the, unbeknownst to him, mis-information they had received which led him to believe the shipments were coming into Biloxi, which was several miles to the east from Bay St. Louis. The feds were also guided more to the east to the town of Ocean Springs and eventually even more so further east over to Pascagoula. There had been what the agents had thought were a few sightings of boats possibly carrying shipments over in that area, but no seizures of any type had happened as of yet.

Lovelady decided, considering himself smarter than the others, that he would explore the coast more in the area around and near Bay St. Louis, but he was not going to let the other agents know anything about his efforts until he had found something. Then he could claim all the credit and such success could be utilized to more quickly get him a promotion. He might even be able, with his father's help, to become head of the southern regional section of the Department. That would certainly make his father proud of him.

One day, while the other agents in his office were over on the eastern side of the coast, he was able to get one of the guides that had recently been employed by their office to take him to an area that had not been explored so far. That area was the vast swamp and bayou somewhat north of Bay St. Louis, a large part of which was known as Devil's Swamp.

Tony's father told him that Devil's Swamp was huge, over a hundred thousand acres, and that it was easy, extremely easy, for someone going out in that area to get lost, and stay lost out there, for quite some time. A person going there, who was not familiar with that area, had to rely completely on their local guides to help them go anywhere in there. Even more so, once they had gotten into that huge swamp, they had an even more difficult time getting out of it.

His dad mentioned that Lovelady just had to try to show off so everyone would know how much smarter he was than everybody else. As part of that effort, he insisted that his guide take him into at least a portion of that swamp. The guide suggested that, if he was shipping booze into the area, he would consider locating in the area to the north and northeast of Bay St. Louis.

There was a massive, elegant hotel up there known as the Pine Hills Hotel. It was the most elegant hotel between Dallas and Atlanta at that time and was visited regularly by literally thousands of visitors from all over. There were massive parties there all the time and certainly there may be booze being shipped to a location near there. There might even be a landing area not too far from the hotel itself that could possibly be used for handling shipments.

Lovelady agreed, so he and the guide, Bobby Boudreau, known as Bootie for short due to his success with the ladies because he was so handsome, set a date to go in that direction while everyone else was spending their time over on the eastern side of the Mississippi coastal shoreline. What Lovelady didn't know, Tony's father had told him, was that Bootie was working with Tony's dad's operation and was paid very well to keep people away from the area that was actually being utilized for shipments. He was also to make sure Tony's dad had access to any information Bootie was able to find out.

Upon hearing about Lovelady's upcoming trip, Tony's dad sent word to Bootie the night before to take Lovelady to one particularly dense swampy area just to the north past the Pine Hills Hotel. Bootie was told to let Lovelady get out of the boat at some point to explore the area, so he could see there was nothing going on up in that area, but to not lose him out there. He was told also to make sure Lovelady knew that there was a lot of voodoo that had been practiced up in that area for well over a hundred years, since back when that area was just part of the Mississippi territory, even before it ever became part of the state.

At six the next morning, the two launched in a small boat from the docks in the harbor at Bay St. Louis. From there they made their way north on the body of water known as the Bay of St. Louis up to and past the location of the Pine Hills Hotel. Lovelady got excited and was continually searching for any indication that might lead him to discover a dock or landing area that could be utilized for the shipment of booze.

After a while, the open water bayou gave way to swamp land and then, even more so, to nothing but tightly packed marsh grass. As they worked their way more deeply into the thick marsh grass, they came up on a strange object stuck in the thick mud. Hanging from it was what appeared to be the remains of some animal, and groups of feathers. The object grabbed more and more of Lovelady's attention the closer they got to it.

"What is that?" Lovelady asked as he stared at it.

Taking a moment before he answered, Bootie said, "Looks like some sort of voodoo thing."

"What does it mean?" Lovelady asked while still staring.

"It means that whoever it belongs to don't want us out here going past that marker," he answered as he also continued to stare at it. "Let's move on by it, if that's alright with you. We don't know what might be out here on the other side of it, so let's get on by it."

"Sure," Lovelady responded as Bootie was already trying to maneuver the boat away from the marker.

As they moved further away from the post and its trimmings, they both moved the scanning done by their eyes in a lot of directions. Movement by the boat was becoming more and more difficult.

Lovelady finally fixed his gaze on what he saw in the far distance might possibly be a group of trees.

"Bootie. Fix the boat so it won't float away. I'm going to get out and go see if I can work my way to that group of trees over there. Maybe there is something located there."

Wearing some almost knee-high boots which he had bought in Bay St. Louis just for this purpose, he swung both legs over the side of their small boat and began to push aside the tall swamp grass reeds, so he could make his way into the thick overgrowth. It wasn't but a few steps and he was already out of sight.

"Can you hear me," he yelled back to Bootie.

"Yea, I can hear you," answered Bootie from the boat.

Lovelady worked his way further and further into the high overgrowth of the swamp. After several steps, he yelled back again, "Can you still hear me?"

There was no response. He turned to the side and yelled over his shoulder, as loud as he could, "Can you hear me?"

Again, there was no response. Then he thought he heard something in the marsh grass area now behind him. He quickly turned completely around and immediately found himself looking at what looked like a black belly button of something. As he gradually scanned up what was beginning to look like a torso, he finally got up to the head of what looked to be about a 7-foot 4-inch black human being. The body was wearing only all sorts of feathers and beads around his head and neck! Immediately, raising his long black arms and holding them out wide as if he was getting ready to grab his target, the figure opened his mouth and let out a loud growling sound, which then went into an even louder, deep base level laugh.

At that point, Lovelady did something he later said he had never done before. He passed out, falling backwards and landing on his back in the swamp grass.

When he gradually came to, it took him a few seconds to figure out he was laying out in the swamp grass. It took him less than two seconds to figure out that a large, at least three-foot long snake was laying partially on top of his stomach and moving slowly up towards his chest! Lovelady immediately let out a scream! As he tried to back away from the head of the snake, it quickly slithered off of the side of the human.

Tony remembered his dad laughing at this point while telling the story. He told Tony that Bootie had gotten to Lovelady just as the snake had disappeared off into the swamp grass. He said that Bootie had told him that, after he had gotten Lovelady to stand up, it had taken no time at all for Lovelady to run back, even without Bootie's help, to the boat, even though he had fallen down three times while trying to hurry back to it.

Chapter Twelve

Jean's Saturday morning tennis matches with her three friends, which she had put together while a member of the New Orleans Lawn Tennis Club, was one of the activities that she really enjoyed. She had continued to participate in and enjoy the group's matches when they had moved them to the tennis courts at City Park. They had moved due to her losing her membership at the Club because of her divorce. She continued to participate in the matches except when she had to go out of state from time to time because of her job.

She had wondered, the first time they had played after her experience in North Carolina, if the girls could sense in any way the fact that she had just experienced having sex with a black man! Oh, she felt that they could tell somehow, but of course nothing seemed out of the ordinary from the way she was greeted by her friends.

She had also felt that way after her experience with Mary Jo and Ronnie. But the girls seemed to have no idea about that either as she had been greeted again and a fun filled match had been played.

Today, she was again wondering what her friends would think once they had gotten together and started playing. It was a beautiful day with few clouds in the sky and a light breeze was in the air. So many varied thoughts were on her mind, much more so than any of the previous times they had played at City Park. She had been thinking about what she was going to wear and decided that she should go ahead and try to enjoy life, even though her mind was constantly going over all of the things that had been happening in her life.

Mary Jo had called her and told her that she wanted to see her, badly. Jean loved that, having thought so much about, not only all the other things that had recently happened, but also about how much she had enjoyed Mary Jo's, and yes also Ronnie's, successful efforts in taking her, mentally and physically, places sexually that she had never been. Thinking about that had gotten her mind off of most things. It also made her think about why shouldn't she try to have some fun and tease Mary Jo just a little. So, she invited her to come out to City Park and watch her play some tennis Saturday with her friends. She just hoped upon hope that none of her three friends had been to that bar that Mary Jo hung out in and seen her there.

Jean had bought a new tennis outfit one of the last weeks of her membership in the Club and had not worn it yet. Maybe wearing that would take her mind off things. It would be interesting to see what reaction Mary Jo would have, if any, once she saw Jean in that skirt and top. The top was a three button, sleeveless, white, almost sheer blouse. Underneath, she wore a white French cut, lace cup bra, which in itself was not something she would normally wear to play a tennis match. The straps would constantly be coming down off of her shoulders with all of the motions of her arms, unless she made them rather tight, which she did.

The skirt was what had caught her attention in the Club's store. It was a black, mini pleated skirt that was of the style that had recently become so popular. Instead of the skirt being one and three-quarter inches longer in back, thereby almost completely covering her panty covered rear when she bent forward at her waist in a ready position, this skirt was the same length down from the waist, all the way around. That meant that almost a half of her rear would be exposed by the motion of the skirt as she walked around the court and when she ran, but especially when she bent over at her waist in the ready position.

Her rear would be made even more obvious by the fact that, instead of wearing the black panties that had come with the skirt, Jean chose to wear white panties. While the panties did cover all of her rear, the cut of the skirt allowed more of her rear to show all of the time, but especially with every motion. Most of the stylish female players on tour made sure these days that those were the type of skirts that they wore.

Jean got several compliments about her outfit from her friends when they had first gathered. She thanked them all and said that she had gotten the outfit because her former husband had seen it and liked it. Of course, he had been so up into drugs that he wouldn't have ever been where he could have even seen something like that in the store. She had seen it and decided that she was going to show off a little bit. She might as well. She still had a good figure, she felt. But to cover herself, she expressed a little concern to the girls about what all the skirt did not cover.

185

Her group assured her that what she was wearing was certainly the style these days.

Two games after they had started playing, Mary Jo pulled up and parked her MG near the bleachers at the rear of their court. She got out, dressed in loose beige shorts, a white blouse and tennis shoes, and walked over to sit on the end of the second row of the bleachers. She quickly put on a pair of sunglasses and began checking things out.

Jean waved at her, feeling that it would be better to recognize her than let her just sit there and ignore her. At the next changeover, she told her group about her visitor being there and that she was somebody that she was doing some business with. She almost had to stifle a smile when she said that because it caused her to think, for a brief second, about how many times she had been made to totally lose it, sexually, by that woman now leaning back on that bleacher. That thought quickly took her mind off her tennis match, at least for a few moments.

After the first few points had been played, Jean decided to make sure she was bending over at her waist as she waited for the next point to begin, whether she was up at net or near the baseline to receive service. She made sure that, though she was being prepared, she was also at the same time putting on a good show for her friend, although pretending to not be aware of that at all.

After a while, Jean felt that there was no suspicion by any of the three girls as to just how far Mary Jo and her relationship had been taken. She made sure that she paid attention to the match and made every effort for her team to win. From time to time as the foursome was changing courts, she would look over at Mary Jo to see how she was doing. She would get a smile in return and one time received some limited applause from her after a particularly good shot Jean had just hit. She took deep breaths after running hard for some of the shots hit to her, making sure with each breath that her breasts were pressed tightly against her blouse.

It was about that time that a ball which had just been hit rolled over next to the players' bench, which was up on one side of the net post. Jean had to walk over to retrieve the tennis ball. She was able to quickly see that her partner was getting one of their other balls from a player on an adjacent court while their opponents were both talking with a player also on that same court. She decided to take her time and put on a little show for Mary Jo.

She walked up to the ball and, instead of using her tennis racket to pick up the ball by pressing it against the side of her shoe, she slowly bent over from her waist, without bending her knees at all, and taking her time, picked the ball up with her hand. By doing that, her skirt rode up so high that almost all of her white panty covered rear was showing. When she stood up, she slowly turned while checking to see if any of the other girls had noticed anything. As she walked back towards the baseline, she gradually shifted her eyes until they met Mary Jo's. She slightly smiled and Mary Jo smiled in return. When Jean turned around, she noticed that one of the girls on the other side was looking at them, but that girl quickly turned her head to answer back to a player on the adjacent court.

As the match went on, Jean performed the same ball pick-up maneuver she had done before but did not look over at Mary Jo to see what her reaction was. When she and her partner were close to winning, a shot was hit short to Jean's side of the court so that she had to run to try to get it. Mary Jo thought that, when Jean started after the ball, she wasn't going to get to it before it bounced the second time, but Jean tried anyway, causing her massive breasts to bounce, a lot, as she made her effort. Watching Jean do that really taxed Mary Jo's efforts to not show any reaction to Jean's movement on the court. She momentarily turned her head and when she looked back, she saw Jean looking at her, along with the same girl who had looked at them before. Mary Jo tried to act as a loyal fan by showing another effort at clapping, as if for her effort. What the two of them knew was that the fake clapping had not been for her effort. It had been for the bouncing show that Jean had just put on during her run for Mary Jo.

Once the match was over, Jean went to net and shook hands with her friends. After putting her things together and saying goodbye, she made her way over to the fence gate. Once through the gate, she walked over to where Mary Jo was sitting on the bleachers. Seeing her watching her friends make their way to their transportation, Jean smiled and said, "Did you enjoy our match?"

Without looking at anything but Jean's face, she answered, "Oh yes. And do you know how hard it is to just look at your face right now, doing that because I know I am probably being watched by your friends?"

Jean chuckled and, after looking as her friends now in their cars began pulling away from the courts, said, "They're not watching you now."

Mary Jo smiled and, moving her eyes so that they looked at Jean's very large breasts, said, "And you see what I am looking at now."

Jean then moved over closer to where Mary Jo was sitting, where she dropped her bag on the ground and leaned the racket she had just been using up against it. She took her right foot and placed it up on the end of the second row of the bleacher. Then she leaned forward, putting her right forearm on her upper right thigh and putting her left hand on her left hip. Those motions caused her already short skirt to ride up.

Grinning, she looked at Mary Jo and softly said, "See anything you like?"

Mary Jo quickly looked around, pitched her head back and laughed. Then she looked back at Jean's pose and with a big smile said, also softly, "You've been killing me." Then she just shook her head a little from side to side. Looking back at Jean, she said, "I wanted to go out there on the court and take care of you a long time ago, you hot little girl."

Jean arched her back as a slight smile began to come over her face. She slowly twisted her shoulders from side to side, pretending she was trying to loosen up her back as she now looked at Mary Jo's eyes, enjoying Mary Jo glancing again at her breasts, which were showing so nicely underneath her almost completely see-thru blouse.

"You're going to get arrested wearing that out here and doing that," Mary Jo said as she looked around again to see who might be watching. "Come walk with me to my car, you tease", she said as she stood up and began to move to get off of the bleachers.

As Mary Jo landed on the ground, Jean said, with her lips drooping down in a fake sad face, "You don't want to look anymore?"

Mary Jo looked back at her, laughed and said, "Oh honey. Yes, I want to look, but I also want to touch, and I can't do that out here." She began walking towards her car.

"Oh, is that all you want to do, touch?" Jean asked, acting like she was pouting. She picked up her bag and tennis racket and began to walk with Mary Jo away from the bleachers.

When they got over to her car, Mary Jo said as she opened her car door, "Get in the front seat, tease."

Jean opened the other front door and put her tennis bag and racket on the floor. After she got in and sat down, she pulled the door shut.

Mary Jo looked around to see who might be watching. Seeing nobody paying special attention to them, she began to lightly run the fingers of her right hand up Jean's left thigh to the edge of her tennis skirt.

"You were trying to turn me on," Mary Jo said. Now turning her head to look at her, as she continued to run her fingers lightly over Jean's left thigh she said, "I'm not somebody you can tease and get away with it."

Jean took a deep breath and said, "You know you're going to make me hot doing that."

Mary Jo looked back at Jean and said, as she continued to gently move her fingers, "And you know I can take care of that. I'm going to take you back to where you were feeling the last time you were like that with me, except this time I want it to be at my house. Think you can follow me to my house, tease?" Mary Jo queried, with a smile on her face.

After taking another deep breath, Jean looked back at her and, now smiling, answered, "I think I can handle that." After a short pause, she added, "The question is, do you think you can handle me after I get there?"

Mary Jo laughed and said, "I know I can handle you, honey." She then removed her hand, grabbed her car keys and put them into the ignition as she said, "The real question is, can you handle what I've got in mind for you." Then she started her car.

"Mmmm, promises, promises" Jean said. She eased herself out of Mary Jo's car, grabbed her tennis bag and racket, and shut the car door. She walked over to her car and got in. She did start to wonder what she might have gotten herself into. After all, Mary Jo had just made her hot.

Mary Jo led the little procession with Jean following close behind in her car. While driving, Mary Jo picked up her phone and pushed a button.

"Hello?" Ronnie said.

"The target is following close behind. We'll be at my place in about thirty minutes or so. She is one hot girl. I'll get things started. Be ready to come make your appearance as soon as you see my number come up on your phone. Just like we did with the last one."

"Okay."

"We may not have to use the dust again to get things started with this one. Depending on what happens, but we may not even need it this time. If we do need it, I'll just bring it into play after we get things started. She is so hot! You had better be ready. Go ahead and call Susan and Katie. Get them to be ready. If things work out, they need to start making their appearances, one at a time, Susan first at about 4:30. Katie at about 4:45. I'll call Lindy. She's on notice and is set to get involved at about 5:15 or so."

"Do you think you can get it started?"

"I think so. We are going to find out in just a little bit. It almost just got it started in the parking lot at the tennis courts. You remember that one about five times back," she said, not wanting to identify any of their prior targets on the mobile phone. "We had doubts about that working out, but it did. That one eventually turned out so well she was calling us. We did alright with that one, remember?"

"Oh, yes. Would be nice to have another one like that," Ronnie said.

"This one might be. If it does work, around 6 or 6:15 or so, an hour or so before it gets dark, our motorcycle friend and her young rider will probably want to show up. I'm going to make that contact if it works out and try to have them lined up so just be aware that is a possibility. She said she wanted in if we had a place for her on this one, but she wanted to bring her friend along to watch and maybe be part of it also."

"Now, that would be something I would like to be around to see, if that happens."

"Well, by that time, if everything works out, it should be a GBP," she said as she laughed. She knew that Ronnie would know that GBP stood for "Gang Bang Party".

"That would be wonderful! I think I am about to get excited. That has happened to me at least the last seven times we did this, you know," Ronnie said, now also laughing.

"It'll have to go some to beat that one three times ago, but you know me. I'll try my best. This one may have possibilities. Let me get gone so I can put Lindy on alert."

"Okay. I'll be looking for your call. If it goes, any particular way you want to get started?"

"No. Just ease on in and start using those talented fingers of yours, me in front and you in the back. She seems to really enjoy talented fingers. And after we get going, don't forget to get her positioned for me to take some more pictures of you with her."

"Okay. I'll be waiting with my phone for your call," Ronnie said.

"Bye for now," Mary Jo said as her mind went on to what needed to happen next.

She quickly called Lindy, who had been put on alert that the evening might be something she would want to participate in for at least part of the time. She was very excited and was looking forward to hopefully getting a call later about coming over at about 5:30 or so.

Ronnie called Susan and Katie, two of the other basic core members of their group and put them on notice as to their possible times of appearance.

Mary Jo pulled up and was able to park almost in front of her small house on a side street just off of St. Charles Ave. Jean parked a few spaces away down the street. Mary Jo waited for her in front of her house and had the pleasure of watching the former beauty queen walk down the street towards her in that lovely tennis outfit. She could not believe her good fortune. Little did the former beauty queen know what Mary Jo had tentatively already planned for her.

They walked up the three stairs from the sidewalk to the little front porch. Mary Jo unlocked the front door and in they both walked to her cozy little place. The living room had a fireplace facing the front door with a couch on the right side and a table next to it. A TV was over the fireplace and a padded chair and foot stool was on the left side.

Mary Jo quickly showed Jean around the other parts of her small house. Entrance to one bedroom was to the right while the doorway to the larger bedroom was down a rather narrow hallway to the left. Both bedrooms had a small closet area, except there was an entrance with a door to a closet area for the larger bedroom. The larger bedroom had a king-size bed while the other bedroom had a double bed. A small chair and a chest of drawers were also in each bedroom.

The entrance to a small kitchen was down the hallway on the left. Inside the kitchen area was a small table with four chairs around it.

"That is a kitchen, they tell me, but I don't cook hardly ever so I don't know that much about it," Mary Jo said, after which she laughed as she grabbed a small cooler.

Behind the kitchen was a bathroom, which could be entered from either side. Mary Jo pointed toward that room, as she began filling the small cooler with ice from the refrigerator, and said, "That is the biggest problem about this little house. It has only one bathroom. Whoever designed this place should have been shot for doing that," she said as she picked up the cooler.

"This is very nice," Jean said as they both began walking back up the narrow hallway towards the front of the house.

"It's all I need. That couch up front folds out into a double bed. That helps sometimes with company. Let me make you a drink," Mary Jo said as she pulled open two small doors to a wooden glass cabinet next to the fireplace. She pulled out two glasses as she said, "I seem to remember it was bourbon and coke you like." She then pulled out a bottle of bourbon from behind the doors on the bottom shelf.

"You're going to get me in trouble serving me a drink this early in the day," Jean said as she smiled.

After handing Jean her drink and then quickly mixing her own scotch and water, they walked over to sit on the couch.

After they clicked their glasses together, each then took a nice sip of their drink.

"I enjoyed watching you play tennis. You're pretty good," Mary Jo said in a complimentary voice.

"Thanks," Jean responded and then took another sip of her drink. "We have a good time with our matches. I'm not quite as good as they are, but I am getting better."

Mary Jo took another sip and then said, "There is something I have to tell you."

Jean looked over at her, glass in her hand and quizzical look on her face.

"You remember that I took pictures of you while you were enjoying things with Ronnie and me," she said as she now looked back at her.

"I do, and I have wondered several times since then about what you were going to do with them, and when you were going to get rid of them."

Mary Jo took another sip, knowing that what she was going to say next was probably going to change a lot of things concerning her relationship with this still beautiful woman. She replied saying, "Well, that is what I want to talk to you about." Taking a moment, she looked at her and then said, "I want to take more of you."

Jean's mouth fell open and then she exclaimed, "Of me? You've already got more than you should have of me."

Jean immediately thought about what might happen if anybody saw those pictures of her with Ronnie and Mary Jo. Especially if they showed up on the internet after what she had just done!

After taking a sip of her drink, Mary Jo said, "I have sold a lot of pictures to lesbian clubs in Bucharest, Hungary; in Montreal, Canada; and in Charlotte, North Carolina. Have made a lot of money, and some of the other girls have too, by us doing that. There is a huge market out there for pictures of regular, every-day girls, just like us, doing what we enjoy doing."

"Mary Jo, you can't do that, not with any pictures of me," Jean said, now leaning forward towards her. "Honey, I just cannot let any pictures of me being part of that get out. I mean, I work for a major company. I can't let my clients find out. I have a daughter who has problems that I don't want to lose custody of, which could possibly happen if something like that were to ever get out. I'm still fighting with my husband about things in our divorce and that certainly would be used against me if it ever came out. My garden club, I mean, I wouldn't even be able to show my face there if word of something like that were to ever get out about me."

Mary Jo looked at her and said, "You might be surprised about some of the things that members of your garden club have been involved in."

That comment caused Jean to think for a few seconds about that club. It was a very exclusive club, made up only of women who lived in the Garden District area of New Orleans. Most of its members were from multi-millionaire families who were in the club because of their money, their heritage, their family names or their connections. The only reason she was in it was because of her having been married to the son of one of the old-line New Orleans families and their owning a house in that very upper-class area. Some of the club members hadn't figured out a way, because of her divorce, to get her out of the club just yet, though she knew her ex-husband's two sisters had been talking with some of the members and they were looking for a way. She didn't want to give them a reason to get her out of the club. She certainly did not want pictures of her with another woman to get out.

What had really hit her hard was when Mary Jo had mentioned pictures of some of the other girls being sold to a club in Charlotte, North Carolina! Oh, not only could her new former football player client friend potentially become aware of them but, more importantly, what about if somehow her face in the pictures was matched up by investigators with pictures in videos taken at other places, one other place in particular. She absolutely in no way could let that ever be a possibility!

"Mary Jo, listen. I cannot, under any circumstances, have my pictures be out there. I just can't. I can't! I mean, you can talk about other things, but you cannot let those pictures get out. At all! I mean, you can't send those out. You just can't."

Investigators, she knew, were getting more and more sophisticated in comparing literally thousands and thousands of computer-generated pictures in unbelievably small amounts of time in order to find suspects in crimes. The matching up of computer-generated pictures was not the problem it used to be for anyone needing those capabilities.

Mary Jo felt it was time to ease back a little bit and try to close the deal. She had been at this point with other girls several times before and, only after messing up a couple of situations, had she learned that there was a point where it was better to work out a deal to, at least, get the girl to start being a part of what Mary Jo had in mind. Several times before, such deals like that had been agreed to and gotten started. Eventually, once the reluctant girls had become involved, it had been possible to move most of them into doing more and more, especially once actual money started coming in from the sale of the pictures she had taken.

"Aren't you worried about your pictures showing up somewhere?" Jean asked after taking a big sip from her drink.

Mary Jo wasn't about to tell her that she had not let her own face be showing in any of the pictures she had sold, and she was definitely not going to tell her that now.

"Let's just say I am not worried about something happening from the clubs I mentioned. They are glad to get the pictures. They love seeing girls from everyday lives enjoying themselves. But if you don't want me to, I won't send any out of you. I won't do anything to cause you a problem. Me just watching you enjoy yourself and having more pictures of you for myself would make me happy. Are you willing to do that, for me?"

Mary Jo looked at Jean knowing that, based on other experiences like this, now was when the decision was going to be made by the target to do it or not.

After watching Jean think for a moment about the situation she was now in, Mary Jo said, "You've enjoyed yourself so far. I will try to get you to enjoy yourself even more. Just spend time with me. You turn me on so much. You always have, even back in college. I was so glad we got together out in Texas, and again when you got back from your trip. And, honey, you really had me hot in the parking lot. It seemed like you were enjoying it too."

Jean had to admit to herself that she had not wanted what was happening in the parking lot earlier to stop. That was why she was here. What Mary Jo had gotten her involved with before had been so exciting. She started wondering what else she might have in mind for her. She decided to see what she had in mind, at least for right now.

"Okay. I did. I really did. You just reminded me that you took something that belonged to me in Texas, remember?" she asked teasingly.

Mary Jo smiled and said, "I think I do remember that. And I also remember telling you that you were going to have to earn them back. Are you ready to do that?" She now began to feel like she had made some progress in getting Jean's involvement moved along.

"Just please be careful with this, okay? Don't ever send any pictures of me being involved with any of this out to anybody. Okay?"

After being quiet for a few seconds, Mary Jo said, "Okay. I won't send them out. Pictures of you will just be for me personally. But I do want more of you, for me."

"Ohhh, honey."

Thinking quickly about what all could go wrong if those pictures of her did get out, Jean said, "Fix me another drink. A strong one. I think I am going to need it. What do you have in mind?"

"Oh, a lot more of the same, honey. We've just gotten started. You're going to love it. You've already had fun. There are going to be a few other things that can happen that you are really going to enjoy. I'll make sure of that," Mary Jo said as she stood up and began fixing Jean another drink, this time discretely adding a pinch of the white powder that had been used before at the bar. She knew the powder would make it easier to get Jean to let things happen. Once she handed the drink to her, Jean began by taking several full swallows of it.

The more Jean thought about it, the more she knew that she was going to need the drinks. She knew that she had enjoyed being with Mary Jo and Ronnie the last time. It was true that her experiences with Mary Jo so far had been very enjoyable, so enjoyable that was why she was there today. She wondered what else there was to look forward to. It sure looked like she was going to find out, and it was going to be soon. She began to wonder if it actually might be even more exciting than it already had been.

Mary Jo walked over and took a camera off of the bookshelf. Opening the top drawer under her liquor cabinet, she pulled out Jean's white thong that Mary Jo had taken in Texas. Holding them up as she turned to face Jean, she said, "Okay, tease. Start earning them back. You know what I want you want to do. I want to see that fabulous body of yours that you were teasing everybody with out at the tennis courts. So, start taking your top off, slowly. I want some better pictures of you, for me."

"Oh, honey. But promise me, promise me again, that you won't ever, ever let any of these pictures get away from you. Okay? Please, keep them locked up here somewhere. Is there a place you can keep them here so that nobody can get to them?"

"I have a place I can keep them. You don't have to worry about that. There's a safe place, right there in the back of my closet, where I can keep them locked up. But I can get to them and look at them when you are not here and are out on one of your week-long or ten-day long business trips. Having them will keep me thinking about you and about things I can come up with for you that you might enjoy the next time we get together. It's the same place I have kept your thong locked up."

Mary Jo began twirling the thong on the fingers of her right-hand and said, "Now, it's time for you to start working to get these back, honey," as she smiled at her. She placed the thong on top of the bookshelf and then positioned herself to begin to take pictures of Jean. As she did that, she pulled her phone out of her pocket and pretended to place it on top of the bookshelf also. While placing it there, she gently pushed the button to let Ronnie know it was time for her to come on over.

Within five minutes, there was a knock on the door. Jean's blouse was off as well as her shoes and socks. Mary Jo let Ronnie in and, upon seeing Jean, Ronnie said, "Well, hello there, beautiful girl. What do we have happening here? Looks like I got here at just the right time."

Mary Jo answered, "Jean has decided she might enjoy more of what she has experienced with us already. She's a little worried about the pictures we took the last time. I have told her that they will be just for me."

Ronnie walked over to Jean and said, "Don't worry about that, pretty lady. I'm not worried about it at all and you shouldn't be either. The pictures she takes will just be for her. You just need to be thinking about how good we are going to make you feel."

Mary Jo took the now dazed Jean's left hand with her right hand while holding her camera in her left.

"The fun was just about to begin," Mary Jo said as she began leading Jean into her bedroom.

As the rest of the afternoon and evening went on, the schedule went almost exactly as Mary Jo originally had set it up. At the appropriate times, Susan and Katie were sent signals by telephone that gave them notice that it was time for them to come on over. By the time they got there, the music was on and Jean had finished off two more drinks. With the additional very small pinches of white powder that Mary Jo had added to Jean's

201

next two drinks, along with the expertise practiced by the two additional girls, Jean was at the point of enjoying the attention being shown to her by Susan and Katie. She was into what was happening to her so much that the pictures now being taken by Mary Jo were not even on Jean's mind.

Not too much later, Mary Jo's twenty-one-year-old former stripper-student, Lindy, who had been called earlier, showed up at Mary Jo's house. When she got there, she immediately asked, "Where is our play toy?" Then she tilted her head towards the bedroom door and asked, "Is she in there?"

Mary Jo smiled and said, "She's in there and she's ready for you. It is your turn. It's time for her to experience being with a younger girl." With that, she eased the door to the bedroom open. Jean hardly even knew Lindy had arrived, at least until Lindy took her turn with her. It was soon apparent that this was not Lindy's first lesbian experience where multiple girls were involved. Mary Jo again used her camera to take additional pictures of Jean now with four girls.

After another hour of activity and occasionally more picture taking, Mary Jo felt good. She decided to not even call the motorcycle rider and her friend this time. She would save them for the next time. She was thinking even more that, at some point in the future, when she thought the time was right and that was going to be soon, she was going to make a lot of money selling pictures of Jean with at least the four different girls she had already been with to the clubs in Budapest and Montreal. But the most money, she knew, would come from Charlotte, when she eventually made the sale of Jean's pictures there. She had recently talked with her contact at that club and they were ready for the next batch of pictures of newly seduced, previously straight girls from Mary Jo. Jean would never know, Ronnie didn't care, and Mary Jo could use the money.

Mary Jo also remembered that she had made almost twice as much money from Charlotte in the past than she had made from the other two clubs combined. There were two very wealthy girls in that club who had enjoyed knowing that the pictures provided by Mary Jo were of actual formally straight girls being taken further and further into "other" activities. If things worked out, the two girls and members of their club would actually get an opportunity to meet and possibly be with some of the girls in Mary Jo's pictures later on in the year at a discrete national lesbian gala in California. Mary Jo knew that the former beauty queen would be a hit at that convention, if she could just get her there.

Ronnie left at about 8:30 to go to her bar tender job, returning to the GBP at about 2:30 a.m. after working her shift. By the time Jean left that next morning, with her thong, Mary Jo had 47 more pictures of her. She wanted many more of Jean, and others, to sell before that convention took place. That meant she had to get Jean back to her house again as soon as possible. She would try to make sure the motorcycle rider and her friend would spend time with Jean at her next party, introducing her to their very special talents, along with two other girls from Lafayette, who had also occasionally been participants at some of her previous GBP gatherings.

Chapter Thirteen

.

Soon after Tony arrived back in Bay St. Louis, he made his way over to Karen's house. He had to find out where various things stood and what, if anything, had happened while he had been away. He had called Karen on his way back and let her know approximately what time he would be arriving. He asked her if it would be alright if he came by and was immediately told that she was glad that he had called because Harry Meadows happened to be over at her house. She told Tony that Harry was a man her daughter had met a few weeks earlier at a meeting of parents of autistic children. She wanted Tony to meet him while he was there. Tony told her that, if Harry was somebody she wanted him to meet, he would be happy to meet him.

When Tony arrived at Karen's house, he walked up onto the front porch and knocked on the door. Karen opened the door with a smile on her face and walked out onto the porch area, followed by a medium built man about six feet tall with full curly brown hair.

"Harry, this is the friend I told you about. This is Tony from LA," she said.

Harry stuck his hand out with a big smile on his face and said, "Hi Tony. You're the movie star I have heard so much about, right? Nice to meet you."

"Nice to meet you, Harry," Tony responded with a smile on his face as he took Harry's hand in a friendly, firm handshake. "I'm afraid I haven't been told anything about you so you kind of have me at a disadvantage."

Karen said, "You know that Jean's daughter is autistic. Well, Harry is also a single parent of an autistic child, like Jean is. They met a few weeks ago at a support group gathering of parents with autistic children. Since then, they have gone for a few drinks after their group meetings."

"Oh, good," Tony said as he looked over his shoulder and moved so he could sit in the porch swing. He loved the light breeze he had previously felt by gently swinging back and forth while seated on that swing. That motion, along with the light air movement generated by the fan slowly turning in the ceiling above the porch, made a perfect blend for pleasant and enjoyable moments.

Karen motioned for Harry to sit in the rocking chair not too far from the swing, as she eased herself onto the swing next to Tony.

"Man, I've never met a famous Hollywood actor before," Harry said. "This is special. Does this mean I can get the chance to meet some of those famous, beautiful actresses and starlets?" Harry now had a wide grin on his face as he leaned forward in his rocking chair so as to not miss a word that Tony would have to say in reply.

Tony had to laugh before he answered. "You might be really disappointed. Well, you've already spent some time with Jean so you know how pretty she is. You would have a hard time finding somebody as beautiful, and as nice, out in Hollywood."

Harry answered, "Yea, but you know all those famous girls out there. You could get me a date with some of them if I was to come out there, couldn't you?"

"Well, I probably could get you a few dates out there, but very few of them would be as nice as those I am sure you can date around here."

With that, Tony leaned back and began making the effort with his legs to cause more of that pleasant breeze to flow past his face with every movement of the swing.

Karen said, "Harry has been a long-time good friend of ours. He and the Sheriff spent some time together every now and then. Harry helped the Sheriff out on some of his campaigns."

"Now, shhhhh Miss Karen. He always kept that quiet because, if he didn't, all sort of other candidates would have been wanting me to help them in their runs for their offices. I didn't want to help anybody else, and never did help anybody but the Sheriff," Harry said as he sat back in his rocking chair.

At that point Tony felt he just had to say, "I bet you were just making sure that, just in case there was ever any time you maybe, well sort of like, needed the Sheriff's help, you knew you had a little pull with him. Anything to that?"

"Now of course I would never, ever, need any help or anything like that," Harry said, at which time they all laughed. "But he did tell me about this guy he once knew when he was a nobody, who later went on to become a really famous Hollywood person, but before that had been involved in some things he really didn't want to provide me with any details about."

With that, both Tony and Harry had a big smile on their faces as Karen's eyes quickly went from one to the other and then back again.

"Our friend was a smart man, wasn't he?" Tony said, to which Harry quickly answered, "He certainly was. And if he was your friend, he was your friend. You could count on him."

At that point, Jean walked out onto the porch, at which point both Tony and Harry stood up.

Karen said, "You remember your father's friend, Tony Gable."

"Yes, I do," Jean said as she stuck out her hand for a handshake.

Tony grasped her hand and said, "It's good to see you again."

"Thank you," she answered. "It's good to see you again also."

Karen then said, "So you have had a little luck getting Emily to take a nap?"

"Yes," Jean answered as the men eased themselves back into their seated positions. "She finally settled down. We'll see how long she stays asleep. Probably won't last more than an hour or so, but she was tired."

"Why don't you two go ahead and leave while she is asleep. Y'all are going out tonight, aren't you?" Karen asked.

Jean responded, "He did ask me to go out for dinner and then maybe go dancing. We thought we might go try out that new dance place over in Slidell."

Karen said, "That sounds really nice. If you are going to do that, go ahead and go so that you are not around when the little one wakes up. You know she is not going to want you to leave if you are here then."

Harry said, "Well, I can't leave until I get his telephone number so I can go out there to California and meet some of those rich and famous pretty ladies out there."

Tony said, "I'll give it to Karen, and you can get it from her. But I'm telling you, you are not going to find a more beautiful woman out there than the one you are going to be with tonight. And on top of that, I bet this one will even be nice to you. Almost none of the ones out there will be as nice as she will be."

Jean said, with a sincere smile on her face, "Aw Mr. Gable. That is so nice of you to say that. Thank you."

Tony replied, "Well, I meant every word of it. You two be careful out tonight."

With that, Jean and Harry made their escape, quickly and quietly.

That evening, after they had eaten at a nice restaurant, they went to the night club nearby. When the music started playing, Jean immediately took Harry's hand and led him out on the dance floor, a move he somewhat resisted because he was no dancer. Once on the floor, he tried to move around a little bit, but only managed to timely hit a beat occasionally.

But there was one thing he did do well. While moving around at a minimal, he kept his eyes solely on Jean, as did almost everybody else in the place. The reason was that she did not miss a beat and, wearing the tight, white, button-up-the-front blouse and the very short, very tight, white mini skirt she had on, almost everybody, except jealous other girls, wanted to watch every move the beautiful, sexy former beauty queen made on the dance floor. Watching her, Harry had to agree with Tony. Jean did look good, really good. Almost every man there was envious of him, and almost every woman in the place was jealous of her.

Later, on the way home, Harry did not take Jean to his house. His mother lived there with him and helped him take care of his autistic son, which she was doing this evening. He instead revisited the parking area near the 16th hole of a nearby golf course, a place he was familiar with from his high school years. There was no objection from the former homecoming beauty queen. What he didn't even think about was that maybe she had been made familiar, a few years before he even was, with that location also, but she wasn't going to let him know that.

* * *

At the meeting of the drug manufacturers, there were a lot of expressions of dissatisfaction with the authorities investigating what had happened to Stanley Rhorback in Miami. While he was not dead, his body and lifestyle had definitely been changed. Not the least of what had changed was the fact that surgery had been performed on Stanley which put a hole in the lower part of his body below his stomach area. That had been necessary in order to let him be able to urinate when he had to. Having to do that, in addition to learning how to use what was left of his hands and feet again, was somewhat difficult for him, especially with the additional limitation of now being totally blind. His lifestyle was certainly now changed.

In order to try to impress Stanley's new company representative at the meetings, the leaders of the other companies felt the need to express their extreme disappointment that no progress was being made on the investigation of what had happened. Sometimes, a couple of them even expressed their dissatisfaction by raising their voices, on occasion reaching the point of yelling at the person reporting the status of the investigation being done by the officers and officials responsible for the actions being undertaken.

It soon became apparent to the group that a special effort was going to have to be made if any progress was going to be the result. The situation finally reached the point where the group agreed that their badass "special" investigator should be contacted. He needed to, ever so quietly, be brought in to do whatever he felt was necessary in order to investigate and find out who was responsible for what had happened. They did not necessarily want to bring him in because most of them didn't really like him anyway. But he did get results when they had assigned him something that needed to get done that might not be appreciated by law enforcement. Even more important was that their "special" investigator needed to find out why what had happened had ever taken place. The group wanted to know, more so as time went on, whether any of them might have someone wanting to do something similar to harm them, or members of their families. That led the group to agree to put into action plans to quietly direct their investigator to do whatever he felt he had to do in order to find out more about that horrible, frightful incident.

It was agreed, after much discussion, but also with some reservation on the part of chairman Bruce Rushton, of the company Ballard, Tinkersly and Lowell, that an agreed-upon contact for the group should be designated to meet face to face with their "special" investigator at an out of the way location, where there was no possible way the discussion could be recorded. In such a situation, the emphasis could be expressed that there were basically no limits on what had to be done to make sure the efforts of him and his associates were successful. The one thing that the person getting in contact was to make sure of was that the investigator understood that, under no circumstances, was he to provide the group, or any member of the group individually, with any information about how he conducted his investigation. They did not want to know anything at all about it. The only things they wanted to know was who had butchered Stanley and why.

After a two-week period following the discussion that had reached that conclusion, the designated contact of the group met with their "special" investigator. The location as picked by the contact was an out-of-the-way country restaurant in the middle of nowhere in the hills of eastern Kentucky. There, the two men were able to discuss the purpose of the investigator's work and how he could basically make his own rules, if he needed to, in order to be successful. That fit the "special" investigator, Robert Stone, just fine. He didn't like telling his clients about his work or methods anyway. He sometimes ended up having to do things that his clients didn't need to know about and wouldn't like to know anyway. The only thing he really needed to discretely let them know was what he found out. Then, as had been the situation a few times before, if there was a problem, deal with it. Just go solve it, whatever it took, but don't let them know what he did.

Chapter Fourteen

Jean was now so mixed up about herself that she thought it would be good for her if she did something to take her mind off things. What she had done originally with Mary Jo and then with Tyler, and now, she just had to have something else to think about. Workouts may be the answer, she decided.

She had noticed a gym in an area she traveled through sometimes going from the office she maintained on the edge of the French Quarter to her parents' home over in Mississippi. She had noticed a lot of cars and trucks in a parking lot next to the entrance to the facility. She decided she needed to go take a look at it and see if she might like working out there.

When she did go inside, she was pleasantly surprised at the number of people in there, especially women. She quickly saw why. Though there were numerous men of various ages in attendance, almost all of the instructors were nice looking younger men, she guessed, in their mid-twenties to early thirties. It was obvious that the girls working out there were enjoying the attention they were receiving from the instructors, who were white, black, and Latin American. Some were more handsome than others and were constantly being asked to show those in attendance how to utilize the equipment and do various exercises. What appeared to be mostly women about her age, with a few that appeared to be in their late twenties, were making every approach possible to somewhat discretely gain, and keep, the attention of various members of the mostly younger staff. She also noticed that there were a few men in tight workout clothes that seemed to be around her age or younger. She soon realized she was spending a lot of time not thinking about any of her immediate past activities.

Thinking membership at the facility might really help her physical and, more importantly, her mental state, she signed up for membership. On her first trip to the facility one afternoon at about 3:30 to actually work out, she came already dressed in some of the clothes that she wore playing tennis. She noted that most of the women at the facility had come already dressed for their activities. Many had worn outfits that really showed off their figures. She had worn old brown, baggy tennis shorts with a white nylon bra under a white cotton tee shirt.

She immediately appreciated the attention she received from some of the male exercise leaders there. In particular, one extremely sexy and muscular young man, about 5 ft 7 inches tall and looking to be about 26, walked over to her. Appearing to be from a Mexican background, he introduced himself as Rodriguez. With a big smile, he offered to help her get more familiar with a one of the pieces of workout equipment she was trying to use. He made sure he took the time to patiently and physically show her, closely and slowly, how to utilize the various possibilities of that machine.

As she began to use the machine by riding it, she could not help but notice how his eyes were checking out every square inch of her body, especially her large breasts. She was so happy to see that. The more she watched him watching her, and his lightly touching of various parts of her body, the more she realized she was getting excited by his efforts, but especially the way he looked at her. She soon noticed that he was almost continually moving his eyes over her body, but he began to almost stare mostly at her breasts, particularly her nipples. His look became more and more obvious as she continued her workout. She had not even thought about that possibly happening prior to coming there. Now, she realized she was putting on a show for this handsome young man.

She somehow managed to escape after not being there too long, making the excuse that she had not worked out much lately and did not need to do too much too soon. The real reason was she didn't know what to do with this young man's obvious interest in her whole body.

Leaving the facility after about an hour of workout, she felt the urge to get new workout clothes, clothes that could help her show off what she thought was her still fabulous figure. Once she had gotten back to her office downtown, she caught herself checking in her mirror for wrinkles, and not really finding any. Yes, she may be a little heavier than she had been in college, six or seven pounds maybe, but in her eyes, she was still attractive, she thought. Rodriguez had apparently thought so too by the way he looked at her. Yes, she could compete with those girls at the gym, especially those close to her age but also with those younger than her. But she had to get newer, and maybe even sexy, workout clothes. Not too long thereafter, she went shopping and bought clothes that she thought would help her stand out in that crowd. She put a complete set in her tennis bag with her tennis clothes and began to always carry them in the trunk of her car.

Three days later, she went back to the gym, again at about 3:30 in the afternoon. This time she wore tight, black spandex mid-thigh pants with a white spandex workout bra. Her tennis shoes and ankle socks completed her outfit. She didn't think her nipples were going to give her away as much this time as they had before.

The place was full again. Looking around the room as she entered, she saw that her Latino friend was with another woman. She walked over to and started on the same machine she had worked on with him the last session. From time to time, she would cast an eye around to see where he was. She had to admit that she missed the attention from him. Maybe he was just being nice to her. Maybe he was just teasing her. He was so much younger than her. She realized that even more so as she glanced over at him. Thinking about his being so much younger than her, she wanted him, even more so, to pay attention to her. She had not been aware how much it had meant to her to have that attention paid to her, especially in the way he had done it. She had to admit to herself, again as she had done so many times since that first work-out, that he had gotten her excited with just his eyes and smile. Of course, he was so hot to look at. He really was, and today he wasn't paying her any attention, at all.

After working out on her machine for several minutes, she decided to take a break. She stopped and began just sitting there on the seat of her machine, with her hands on her hips as she breathed somewhat heavily. Then she felt warm air on the right side of the back of her neck. It was him! She quickly turned her head to the right but didn't immediately see anybody. She turned her head to her left and there was that wide smile on that handsome male.

"Hi there," he said through his smile.

"Oh, hi there," Jean answered, trying to act normal, even trying to not smile.

Then he said, "I missed you. You have not been back since our meeting."

He had missed her. At least he said he had. But he was a man. Men had said things to her before that they hadn't meant. This one was no different. He was just saying that. But then she noticed. Oh, did she ever notice. He was looking at the nipple of her left breast. Then, with that smile on his face, he shifted his eyes to the nipple of her right breast. She so much wanted to look down and see if they were showing. Her nipples had always, always been so large. She just knew they were probably now giving her away again!

So, she did the one thing that she knew she should not have done. She arched her back, slowly, with her hands on her hips, making sure she was sitting up straight while watching his handsome face. She could have sworn he almost lost his breath! She loved it! "Eat your heart out," she thought to herself.

For the next forty minutes, he worked with her, making suggestions as to different uses of the machine she was on and then watching her as she used it. She could not resist putting on a show for him, making sure every now and then that she did what she knew every man loved watching. That was, making sure her breasts bounced as she rode her machine. And she made sure she watched his eyes as she did her little exercise continually in a way that made that happen.

He finally walked up to her and, while now standing by her, asked, "Why don't you come with me to my place when you finish here? We can have drinks there."

She looked back at him and so badly wanted to say "yes", but she couldn't. She knew what that might lead to and she could not do that. At least not this soon after meeting him. Not yet, at least. But he was so handsome and so sexy and such a hunk. She could not believe she was thinking in such terms about him, a male! But oh, what a male. Well, he wasn't anywhere near her age, or at least she didn't think so.

"I can't do that," she answered. She noticed he did seem a little disappointed. "Not today, at least." She did notice that seemed to perk him up a little.

"Are you married? Is that keeping you from doing it?" he asked.

Taking a moment, she then said, "No. I am not married."

"Oh, good," he answered. "Then maybe another time". He looked at her and added, "Sometime soon, I hope."

She thought that was sweet. He did not have to say that, but he had. That was nice. Maybe it would be sometime soon, she caught herself thinking. Soon afterwards, she left.

She kept thinking about Rodriguez. Doing that certainly kept her mind off other things. She felt she had to go back to the gym again soon and she did that the following Tuesday. She also made sure she looked good. She wore her tight black spandex shorts and tight white latex top. Underneath she wore only a white thong. Her white tennis shoes and socks completed her look. She wanted Rodriguez to want to spend time with her, if that was possible.

Arriving there about 3:30, she looked for Rodriguez and saw him helping a woman about her age, but not as attractive, she thought. She would get him away from her quickly. She went to her exercise machine and mounted the seat. Ten minutes later, over walked Rodriguez, a big smile on his face as he immediately began checking out her breasts. She could already feel herself get excited, knowing this gorgeous hunk of a younger man was now getting so close to her from behind that she wondered how long today it would be before he touched her, somewhere.

Not only did he come up close to her from behind, he began to lightly run his right hand over her back as he said, "I was wondering when you were going to be back in here. I wondered if it was possible for you to look as good again as you have each time I have seen you, but you look even more beautiful."

Jean was about to melt already, wondering how long it would take him to get to the part about coming with him to his place for a drink. He took his time, and after working with her for a few minutes, brought it up.

"Are you going to come and have a drink with me today? I get off in about thirty minutes and you can ride with me to my place."

"I don't know about going with you. Where do you live?"

"It's safe. I've lived there for several months now and nothing bad has happened. Besides, I'll be there to protect you," he said, again with that wide smile on his face.

She made her decision. For one thing, she loved the fact that this younger, hot Latino stud was flirting with her. For another thing, he definitely was keeping her mind off of other things.

And for another thing, she was beginning to wonder what it would be like to be with him in bed. She had been with a black man. She had been with the girls. How would this experience with a Latino be? If for no other reason, she wanted to find out if she could keep up with this hot, younger, sexy Latin man. What was she waiting on? She wasn't getting any younger herself. It may be fun trying to keep up with him. Maybe.

"Ok. I am not going to ride with you, but I will follow you when you leave. Just for one drink, ok?"

"Great!" His big smile showed happiness while his eyes again looked all over at what he hoped to become more familiar with soon. "I'll meet you out front in about five minutes, after I am finished with work. I'll be driving a grey Torino."

"I'll be in a black Lexus."

And meet out front they did. She followed him to his area of town, which was an area where she had heard a lot of foreign people lived. It was a little run down, but a neighborhood about where she would have expected him to be living. The roads around the place where he was living were somewhat narrow with mostly older cars jammed packed into parking spaces in front of the continuous rows of small two-story houses.

He was able to park his car just down the street from the front doorway entrance to his building. She pulled up as he was getting out of his car that he had just parked.

He walked over to her car and said, "Find a place to park. You may have to go to the next block, but I'll be standing here waiting for you," he said with his wide smile showing.

She drove down the street and around the block but was only able to find a parking spot around the corner. She had not seen but two people, both rather heavy Latino females, talking with each other on the sidewalks as she had circled around. She parked and got out, leaving nothing visible in her car and taking her cell phone with her. As she walked around the corner of the street she had parked on, she could see him waiting for her at the top of three stairs leading up to the building.

Once she got to him, he turned and walked inside the opened front door. She walked up the few stairs and, after she entered the hallway area, she noticed doors on both sides of a small hallway leading to the back of the house. He opened the door on the left side of the hallway and, while saying, "It's not much but it's home," stood aside to let her enter first, which she did.

There was one couch, which was unfolded into an un-made bed, and two sitting chairs in front of a coffee table and a TV screen, which was hanging on the wall. A chest of drawers was over near the bed.

She took a few steps forward and noticed what appeared to be an open doorway to a bathroom on the backside of the room.

It was at that point that he very slowly moved next to her and, putting his arms around her, gave her a very long and deep kiss. He then took his tight tee shirt off and immediately began to ease the shoulder straps of her top down, allowing her large, now sensitive breasts to become available. He bent over and began using his active tongue on her nipples. Within a few seconds he had eased her onto the couch bed. He stood up and slowly pulled his pants off, making sure she had a show to watch as he did it. Then he kneeled on the bed and slid her workout shorts off, and next her thong.

For the next forty-five minutes, he took her to a level of excitement she had not experienced recently with a man, other than the black man in North Carolina. Now, here she was with a Latino. She was again glad she was on the pill. After finishing his effort, he rolled over and laid next to her as she attempted to catch her breath. Yes, it had been almost as good as she thought it might be and she wanted more. Then, after a few moments, it happened.

Through the door to the room came a burley 5-foot, 6 inch, slightly overweight Latin man with tattoos on his wrists, up his arms and around his neck. Seeing the two of them laying on the bed, he said, "Ah, so this is the puta."

Jean was shocked and immediately began looking for a sheet or something to cover herself with but could only start tugging at her pulled down shoulder straps.

"Alberto, meet Jean. Jean, this is my roommate, Alberto," Rodriguez said as he sat up on his elbows in the bed.

As she tried to pull her straps up and began to put her breasts back inside her top, Alberto moved towards the bed as he said, "Now it's my turn."

Jean, now horrified, looked at Rodriguez and said, "I am not going to be with him." As she said that, she began to try to get off of the bed.

Alberto grabbed her left wrist and Rodriguez grabbed her right wrist. She turned to look at Rodriguez in shock. He looked at her as they both forced her to lay back on the bed.

"Now, sure you are, honey," Rodriguez said. "He just wants to use you for a little while like I did."

Lying on the bed with her wrists held tightly by the two Latinos, Jean yelled out, "Use me?"

It was at that point that Alberto used his left hand to deliver a back-handed slap across Jean's face.

Stunned, she looked back up at Rodriguez as he said, "Now

Jean, if you start fighting and screaming out like that, he's going to beat you. And Jean, he loves beating women."

Alberto let go of Jean's wrist and stood up, beginning to take his clothes off. "It's my turn to be with you, puta."

Jean didn't know much Spanish, but she did know that the word "puta" meant whore. She tried to use her now free left hand to grab at Rodriguez's grip on her right hand. He then quickly grabbed her free hand and held it tightly.

"Don't do this, Rodriguez. Please don't let him do this," she begged with a tremoring voice as she looked at him. "I didn't come here to be with him. I came here to be with you."

With all of his clothes now off, Alberto got back on the bed and began to spread her knees apart, positioning himself between her legs. She could now see tattoos all over his body as she tried to keep her legs together, but she was no match for the strength of the stronger, younger man. With Rodriguez still holding both wrists, Alberto entered her and began pumping. The shock and effect of it all now caused her efforts to stop what was happening to her to weaken.

"That's right, puta. Just lay back and enjoy yourself. You can't stop me," Alberto said as he continued his efforts.

After a few minutes of that, Rodriguez gradually lessened his grip on her wrists, eventually letting Alberto hold her wrists with his hands as Rodriguez pulled her top up over her head. She was now nude, except for her shoes and socks.

After laying next to them for a few minutes and watching the look on Jean's face as she was being worked on, Rodriguez got off the bed, stood up, grabbed his pants and began putting them on.

223

Seeing that, Jean managed to utter, "Where …. are …. you … going?"

Now pulling his shirt on over his head, Rodriguez answered, "I'm going to see my girlfriend."

"Your …. girlfriend!?" she barely managed to get out as she looked over at him while getting continuously pumped.

"Yes. My girlfriend," he answered looking at her on the bed.

"Whyyyyy … now?" she asked as Alberto really began to get into his efforts.

Now with his pants and shirt on, Rodriguez walked back over next to the bed. He bent over and, with both hands on the bed, said, "Because she is a very beautiful, much younger Latino girl, who just loves sex. She is not old like you are. She is 17. And the good thing about her is she really enjoys sex. Wants to do more of it. Really gets into it, doesn't just lay there like you do."

He then stood up, turned and began walking across the room. After putting his shoes on, when he got to the door of the room, he turned and said, "You know what to do, Alberto. Do the same thing with her that we did with the others. Carlos may like this one because she is older. She's not married so we don't have to worry about that. But don't beat her unless she gets out of hand. If she does that, do what you have to so that she stays quiet."

Alberto looked back over his left shoulder at Rodriguez and said, "I'll take care of the puta."

"I'll tell the others that you've got her, and she is available here for them later tonight. Let's plan on shipping her out at about four this morning. I want my money for her, don't you? You know, like the others, the faster we get her down there, the quicker we get our money. Besides, there may be one more I will have to send with her. That one will be much younger than this one, if I can get that set up." He then turned and left the room, shutting the door behind him.

Others? What others? Money? She was going to be sold? She had heard a little bit about sexual slavery along the border, but this was New Orleans. Jean did not know what to think.

About fifteen minutes later, two other younger, heavily tattooed Latino men walked into the room. She heard Alberto call the bigger one Gonzo and the shorter one Pedro. They each began talking about taking their turns with the puta. Gonzo immediately took Alberto's place when he had finished, while Pedro stood next to the bed watching. As Gonzo was mounting her, she yelled at them, "Nooo! Don't do this to me! Let me go! You're raping me!"

Alberto quickly moved over close to the bed and shoved his right fist in her face, stopping only inches away. "Shut up, puta! Next time you yell, I hit you with this!" Jean started to tremble and sob.

Backing away a couple of feet, he said as she was now beginning to be continually pumped by Gonzo, "You came over here to get some sex, puta! You're getting it. Rodriguez didn't force you to come over here. He's good at getting girls like you to come here with him. Once he gets them here, they get what you're getting. Gonzo and Pedro are our gang brothers. They live across the hallway, and we have good news for you, puta. Six more of our gang brothers live a couple of buildings down the street. Rodriguez is going down there now to tell them that, in a little while, they can come here and take their turns with you, puta. We've got to make sure you are ready for Carlos for when we get you down south of the border. He's the head of our gang. He's gonna like you, puta."

Finally, after each one had finished working on her while the others watched and commented, Pedro got up, left the room and went across the hallway to get his phone, which was ringing. Alberto was in the bathroom and Gonzo had walked over through the doorway to the bathroom. Jean knew that, if she was ever going to escape, she had to take the chance of getting away now, if she could physically make it. She knew she would probably get beaten if she got caught, but she might not have another chance.

They obviously were not expecting her to try to escape because they had kept her nude, except they had not paid any attention to the fact that her unobvious shoes were still on her feet. But she knew that she could not try to put her clothes on before she made the effort. She quietly and quickly eased off the bed, grabbed her phone which had ended up laying on top of the chest of drawers, and moved as fast as she could to the doorway and out of the building, barely touching the stairs. She stumbled down the street, not hearing any noise coming from where the men were until she had gone to the other side of the street and around the corner of that block. Then she began to hear them yelling as they ran out of the building and down the stairs onto the street. But they did not know where to look for her because none of them had seen where she had parked.

She barely made it to her car in the middle of the block. She quickly used the keyless entry, got in and locked the doors. She grabbed the keys out of her center car pocket and then pulled her loaded pistol out from under the front seat, laying it on her lap. Looking around her and not seeing anybody in the street or on the sidewalks, she started her car and quickly pulled it out of its parked position. She then drove off down the street at a high rate of speed, escaping into the night. As she got further away, she realized that her workout clothes were still there, but there were no personal markings on them because they had not been taken to the cleaners yet.

Once she was back on her side of town and had driven around several blocks, she pulled into a vacant parking lot adjacent to a church and stopped her car. She got out and opened up her trunk. She pulled shorts and a top from her tennis bag and quickly put them on. After closing her trunk, she got back into her car and drove around for about another twenty-five minutes to make sure she was not being followed. She finally pulled into the garage next to her house on St. Charles Street. She turned the motor off and sat there in her car trembling. Soon she began crying, uncontrollably.

Chapter Fifteen

Tony was sitting in the swing on Karen's front porch gently swinging back and forth, which movement causes a nice enjoyable breeze of the somewhat heavy air. Karen was inside the house dealing with Emily who was at the moment being peaceful and attempting her very limited amount of schoolwork. Tony began thinking about, now that he had solved Karen's credit card problem and her problem with the cost of the funeral with the funeral home, what else might he be able to do to ease the transition of life for Karen to being a widow with a divorced daughter whose autistic child was an absolute challenge to deal with day by day and minute by minute.

Looking across the street, he noticed the extremely tall and large live oak tree across the street from Karen's house. The huge trunk of the tree was about the size of eight men standing together with the first huge limbs beginning about seven to eight feet from the ground. The breeze was also causing a slight movement of the smaller limbs of the huge tree.

It was at that moment that he began thinking about another of the stories his dad had told him so many years ago. They were again sitting on a bench in Sicily overlooking the body of water between his home country and Italy. There was mention by his dad of something that had happened way back when he was on the Mississippi gulf coast. That particular story involved an oak tree that Tony imagined could have looked like the one he was looking at now.

His dad had told him that the government agent he had mentioned before, Lovelady, had still been wanting to be the hero of the government's efforts on the coast. He just knew that, by finding at least one of the shipping locations that he was convinced were also being utilized in the Hancock County area of the Mississippi coast, his father would be proud of him and be able to help him get promoted. That way, he would be more likely to be moved up the organization's management ladder and get out of the mosquito infested swamp area known as the Mississippi gulf coast.

Oh, for sure there were some attractive locations down there, the elegant Pine Hills Hotel location at the head of the Bay of St. Louis being one of them. But any shipment operation was not going to be located in an area that would make it easy to find. Lovelady concluded that meant that he should look not only in areas like Biloxi and Gulfport, which did have nicely built hotels, but that he should also look in areas not too far from the Pine Hills Hotel.

Tony's dad had told him that he had instructed their plant inside of Lovelady's operation, the guide know by the name of Bootie, to try to direct the efforts of the government agents towards areas away from where the actual operations were taking place. Since the shipments were mostly taking place, very successfully, in the swamp areas, Bootie was finally able to get Lovelady to look in some of the upland areas of the more northern parts of Hancock County. In those areas was land that was sometimes used as pastureland for cattle. The best thing about such land was that those areas were nowhere near where the actual shipments were taking place.

On one occasion, Bootie had gotten Lovelady out in the woods of rural northern Hancock County and was able to direct him towards an open pastureland near a wooded area only accessible by a dirt road. Bootie convinced the energetic agent that having such a road would be a great place for any shipment operation to conduct its efforts. From there, product could be sent all over and thus would be an ideal place to be located either in the area or nearby.

After taking him up into that area, Lovelady saw a nice pasture next to the road and told Bootie to stop and let him get out of the car and check things out. Bootie pulled the car over and turned off the motor. He felt safe doing that because he knew the actual distance to any portion of the operation, which he was secretly part of, was miles away with none of it actually close-by.

"You stay here with the car while I go see what I can find out around here," Lovelady said as he made sure his silver gun was in its holster on the belt around his waist.

"You be careful out there now, you hear?" Bootie said to him as he walked over to get in the shade of some nearby tall pine trees. As Lovelady checked the surrounding property out, he looked over the nice open pasture and noticed what appeared to be about six or seven head of cattle way back away from the road.

After walking over to the two railed wooden fence, Lovelady found a way to crawl though the fence between the two rails. Standing up once he had gotten on the other side of the fence from the road, he began to walk over toward the more open area of the field.

"Don't get too far away from this road", Bootie yelled out to him as he motioned to the narrow dirt path road they had just driven up on. "You don't know what might be out there."

"I'll be okay. I've been down here a while now, so I am not as concerned about things as I was when I first got down here. Besides, I've got my gun with me," he said as he smiled while looking over his shoulder at Bootie as he patted his gun in its holster. He then again began surveying the land as he walked further out into the pasture.

Bootie leaned against the car and with his arms folded in front, scanned the countryside for whatever he might be able to see. To himself, he was thinking about how absolutely stupid this agent was, but he wasn't going to complain. This guy was exactly what they needed to have looking for the operation on the coast. If anything, they needed to look out for him and make sure something didn't happen to him. If something did, they might send somebody in who had some sense, and that could be dangerous.

Lovelady wandered across the field but was not seeing anything of interest. He looked back to check on Bootie and saw he was doing exactly what Lovelady had told him to do, staying with the car. Bootie was now even leaning on the hood of the car, which was in its shady place under some tall pine trees. Lovelady continued his walk away from the road and eventually moved over the gentle rise of the pasture, but he was still able to barely see his driver. As he was beginning to have a good sweat coming out over his body due to what was now intense heat, he stopped to pause for a moment to catch his breath.

It was at that point that he noticed something coming slowly up over the rise in the property. He could see the cows in the distance and noticed that they all seemed to be looking at him. He immediately wondered why that was, but more so he was wondering what this was coming up the side of the little rise in property. It immediately came into view. It was another cow, except this one had horns. Big horns. Horns?

The cow moved into full view and stopped, not too close to him but not too far away either. It was at that point that the cow started to dig at the ground in front of him with his right front hoof. He also began making a noise that did not sound too friendly. It rather quickly began sounding somewhat like a snort coming out of his nose.

Lovelady decided that it was time for him to move away from what he suddenly realized was a bull. He shuffled a few steps in a direction away from the bull, but the bull also moved a few steps towards him. Looking quickly around him, then back at the bull, he realized that he had better start moving quickly because this large creature was beginning to edge towards him, taking small steps but still moving and in his direction. He looked over and saw Bootie moving away from the car and trying to wave him in the direction of the fence Lovelady had just crawled through.

Lovelady immediately took his guidance and began to walk rather quickly towards the fence, which he now saw made a turn across the field on the side of the road Lovelady was on. Beyond the fence was a forest of what seemed to be the type of trees that had been identified to him as live oaks. As Lovelady now began to run, he looked over his shoulder and saw that the bull was starting to run also! Breathing harder and harder, Lovelady was finally able to make it to the fence and immediately worked himself through that fence, climbing over the lower piece of wood and under the upper piece. Distancing himself a few steps over from the fence he just crawled through so that he was next to the nearest tree trunk, he looked back as he tried to pull his gun out of its holster.

What he saw at that point in time was a very large, now clearly mad bull crash through the fence Lovelady had just climbed through, easily cracking those two beams and knocking them aside! He fumbled with and then dropped his silver gun. He started to bend down to pick it up, but he looked up and saw the huge, mad animal now charging towards him. He then quickly turned, grabbed a low hanging limb and tried to pull himself up onto that limb of the live oak tree he just had been standing next to. He was able to get himself up on the first large lower limb next to the trunk just as the clearly irritated bull arrived at the base of the tree. Now the bull just stood there, looking up at the treed federal agent.

Lovelady held on to the limb next to the trunk and started screaming out, "Help! Help"! He would look down at the bull, then back up to see if he could find Bootie.

"Help!" he yelled out, again and again, as he quickly looked down at the animal and then up to see if he could yet find Bootie.

Bootie had seen it all happen as he was running to where Lovelady and the bull were. As he got closer and could see Lovelady was up that big tree, but was all right, he could not stop from breaking out in laughter. And a hearty laugh it was. He was still on the other side of the fence from that bull but close enough so that the bull turned his head to look at him when he had started laughing. It was then that Bootie determined that he had better do something really quick or that bull might decide that Bootie needed to be up a tree also, if he could find one in quick enough time to get up.

Bootie pulled his gun out of his holster and fired it at the base of the tree that was now holding Lovelady. The noise of the gunfire, plus the closeness of the bullet's impact, got the bull's attention. Bootie then fired two more shots, somewhat spaced apart to make sure the bull was affected by each of the loud sounds. If the bull did not turn now and get away from that tree, and them, Bootie was going to use the next bullet, at least the next one, to solve their problem. He was not going to let his male friends be able to kid him about being run up a tree by a bull.

Thank goodness, after the third loud shot, the bull decided that it was time to leave. He had defended his territory, and his cows. It was time to at least leave the immediate area, and he did. Bootie fired a fourth shot as the bull was moving away from the tree. Once he felt the bull was far enough away and giving them some immediate room, he yelled to Lovelady, "Get on down out of that tree, before he comes back."

Lovelady did not climb down immediately and only did so after Bootie yelled to him again, "Either come down out of that tree right now or else I'm going to leave you up there. Then you'll be out here all by yourself, because I'm leaving."

Only then did Lovelady, with a lot of effort, work his way down out of the tree. The two of them went down the road to their car as quickly as they could. As they were driving away, they both noticed the bull standing near the base of the tree that Lovelady had been up in, watching them as they left.

Tony's dad had laughed so hard when he had told that story. Tony had to admit that he had laughed that day also, when he had heard his dad tell that unique, special story about what had happened one day in south Mississippi.

What made the story even funnier was that, only when they had gotten back to their headquarters did Bootie let Lovelady know his special silver pistol was missing. Bootie had noticed it missing when they had gotten back to the car, but he didn't bring it up to Lovelady until after they had gotten all the way back to their headquarters.

Lovelady had wanted to get some of his workers and go back out there to look for it right then. Bootie convinced him that was not a good utilization of manpower and that having so many people out there would signal to everybody that they had been out there looking. He was able to convince Lovelady to let him handle it quietly, to which he agreed.

It had turned out that the landowner was a good friend of Bootie's and that Bootie had made sure all was clear out there before they went to the property. Bootie was therefore quietly able to let the homeowner know about what had happened during the trip. Bootie was able to then go out and find the pistol the next day, returning it to its owner a couple of days later. His story to Lovelady was that he had been able to quietly go out there and search around for it, becoming a hero to Lovelady.

Now that Lovelady had been up there and not seen anything, he was sure the property was clean. It wasn't too long after that, due to his providing a helping hand to Bootie, the landowner wanted to make a little extra money. Bootie cleared the request with Nick and the operation started making some shipments to certain areas in the northern part of the county through and near the owner's extensive two-thousand-acre cattle farm.

Not close to, but also not too far north of the large farm, was a honkey-tonk with good booze and, on some nights, good music.

Tony was able to find out that on one particular evening, while Aunt Madeline was actually trying to leave the locally rather well-known establishment, she had been forced to pull a gun, put it under the chin of an admirer, and have him get on his knees when he had tried to force sex on her in her car. When he tried to get up from his knees after she had backed away from him, she had fired her gun, placing a bullet right between his knees as he was kneeling on the ground near her car.

Tony remembered being told that there was one thing the guy had been telling people afterward that he remembered while he was on his knees in front of her. That had been that when he had started to get up too soon, before she had told him to, she had fired that shot. The one thing he said that he became aware of afterward was that, when she fired that bullet, her hand holding her gun had not been shaking, at all. That meant that she knew exactly what she was doing with that gun. The man had decided to stay put and not move from his knees, until as she was driving off.

It was at that moment that Tony's cell phone rang. His memories were brought to a halt. He checked the number on his caller ID and saw it was from the New York number for his cousins. He immediately answered.

"Hello?" he asked, wondering which one of them was calling.

"Hey there. Am glad you answered." He recognized Conrad's voice on the line. "You need to get up here as soon as you can. There are some things we need to talk about, face to face, tomorrow if possible."

Tony could tell from the tone and seriousness of the voice that he needed to get to New York as quickly as it could be arranged. Since it was mid-afternoon, he said, "I will get there as soon as I can. I can leave here right now, but I'll have to make arrangements to get up there. I don't have any idea how big of a problem that might be, but I will let you know as soon as reservations are made."

The voice answered, "That would be good. Do what you have to so that it happens as soon as possible. What I have to tell you needs to be said soon and in person."

"Okay. I will let you know," Tony answered.

"Good. I will look forward to hearing from you on this line." Then there was a click.

Tony got off the swing and went in to let Karen know he was going to have to leave for a couple of days to take care of some things and that he would be back as soon as possible.

Karen was surprised but, knowing that if Tony was telling her this, there was good reason for him to go. She gave him a quick hug and wished him a safe trip. Tony gave Emily an easy, quick hug as he told her, "I'll see you in a couple of days." She looked at him but did not have any response. Instead she looked back at the specialized book she was working on.

Tony was able to get a late-night flight out to New York going through Atlanta. He called to let them know when he would be arriving. He was told it would be best for him to use the same method of getting to them that he had used before.

After settling in his window seat on the plane, he looked out over New Orleans and the lighted land, roadways and adjacent water areas as the plane made its turns from takeoff and proceeded towards Atlanta. As he looked at the dark areas below, he wondered just exactly where his dad had been referring to when he had told what few stories he had related to his son. He remembered the story he had thought about on his way back to the coast from LA. He again thought about how that particular story was one of the few his father had actually laughed about as he told it.

That thought brought his mind another one his father had told him that had also brought a smile to his dad's face. His dad had again mentioned how much the IRS guy, Charles Lovelady, was always wanting to try to make himself look good so maybe he would get really quick promotions. After his encounter with the seven-foot four-inch black man wearing nothing much but feathers, his dad had said that it took Lovelady several weeks before he was ready to go back to the area where that encounter had taken place. He was much more comfortable going over to the eastern part of the coast of Mississippi. However, eventually Lovelady did let Bootie know that he again wanted to go out by himself, of course with Bootie going with him as his guide but with none of the other agents, to the swampy area just west and north of the elegant Pine Hills Hotel.

Bootie tried to persuade the federal investigator to continue going back to the eastern part of the Mississippi coast but, during several discussions, Lovelady was insistent that Bootie take him back to the area that they had visited before. Lovelady told Bootie that he just felt there was something going on over there not too far from the Pine Hills Hotel. It was finally decided that they would go explore some of that area they had been in before and, again, it would be done without any of the others with them and without their knowledge. Lovelady told Bootie that he was bringing along his silver automatic pistol that had been given to him by the agents when he had first arrived. Lovelady assured Bootie that his gun would be loaded, and he would be ready for action. He recommended that Bootie be fully armed also, which suggestion Bootie easily agreed to.

On the appointed day, they met again down at the docks of the

City of Bay St. Louis and boarded the little boat that "Bootie" had again procured for them. This time, they left not too long after lunch since it took Lovelady some time to make sure all of his guys were away on their assignments to the east side of the coast. It was a somewhat cloudy day and "Bootie" again tried to discourage Lovelady, but he was insistent. They were going out that afternoon so go out they did. There were a few people down at the docks who watched them as they left the area on their excursion.

After they had passed to the west of the Pine Hills Hotel at the head of the bay and had been on the bayous for some time, they again got into more shallow water and eventually into thick swamp grass that required them to stop. Nick's dad had told Tony, with a smile growing on his face, how things had gone once they came up on another pole stuck in the swamp grass which had the remains of some animal hanging from it with all sorts of feathers attached and flowing in the light breeze. Lovelady again had Bootie go past the marker and, after about a hundred yards, dismounted the boat and began, with his silver gun in a holster on his hip, to work his way into the reeds of the tall marsh grass.

"Now stay sort of close to me, you understand?" Lovelady said looking back at Bootie.

"Well, last time you told me to stay with the boat. Do you want me to do that this time or come be near you," came the appropriate question from Bootie?

Lovelady thought about it for a moment and then said, "Stay kind of close, at least in hearing range."

"Ok, I will. Just don't get so far away you can't hear me. Okay?"

"Yea, sure. Now come on and let's go find us a shipping dock, or something like that which could serve as a shipping point," Lovelady said as he turned and started pulling the reeds aside, so he could try to walk through the thick growth.

It wasn't too long and the two were out of sight of one another. Lovelady could hear Bootie yelling out suggestions as to which direction he should go as he worked his way further into the swamp.

As Lovelady made his way further, he kept pressing forward, even though now he was not hearing any directions from Bootie.

Tony's father told him that at that point, Bootie could not then be seen by Lovelady. When Lovelady turned around to look over his shoulder to see if he could find Bootie, he saw something immediately that got his attention. It was the seven-foot four-inch black man, now standing about thirty yards away from him in the marsh grass! Lovelady also saw a man dressed in what looked like a pirate's outfit holding up a sword above his head not five feet to the left of the tall black man! He next noticed another man dressed in a long red coat holding an old musket standing about ten feet to the right of the tall black man! Standing with them with a bandana around his head was another man holding up a pistol!

Lovelady began shaking and tried to pull his silver gun out of its holster. As he did that while looking at the four men as they began slowly walking towards him, he fumbled with his gun and it fell off into the marsh grass. The four men began to walk faster as they made their way towards him.

Lovelady quickly looked down for his gun but did not see it. When he looked back up, the four men were much closer to him and began screaming out words in some sort of language that Lovelady had never heard before. He immediately made the decision that it was time to run. To hell with that gun, he had to get away from these strange looking and now strange sounding people. So, he ran, or at least he tried to. Briefly held up by tripping and then falling over in the marsh grass, he screamed out, "Bootie! Help!"

Getting himself back up, he could see that the men were getting closer and screaming out more words in their strange language. He tried to run faster and, thankfully, began to find a little more solid ground on which to run. He dug in and tried harder to run as fast as he could, in a direction away from the four men, but it was also away from where he thought Bootie was.

Tony remembered that it was at that point that his dad really started laughing. His dad then said that Lovelady was running so fast that he must have sensed some success in getting away and turned around to make sure the screaming men were not gaining on him. It was at that point that his feet no longer continued to make contact with the ground. That was because he had run off of the remains of a small bluff and began to fall through the air with his legs still moving as if he was running. Then he hit the water of a bayou with a loud splash!

Coming to the surface of the water, he looked over and saw three alligators begin to slide off of the opposite side of and into the approximately forty-yard-wide body of water. He quickly turned around and began to now try to quickly make his way back to the side of the bayou from whence he had just come. Finally, able to drag himself out of the water and up onto a small three-foot wide sand beach area, he heard it.

WHAM! WHAM!

It was gun fire and he turned to look up to the top of the small bluff he had just run off of. There stood Bootie, who had fired his gun at the alligators.

Lovelady turned to look in the direction of where the alligators had slid into the water as Bootie began working his way down the side of the small bluff. When he got down to the little sandy beach, he saw that Lovelady's clothes were completely wet.

"You alright?" his guide asked him.

"Yeah. Did you see'em?" Lovelady asked while breathing very heavily.

"See what?" Bootie responded. "The four guys up there? Is that who you are talking about?"

"Yeah, the bootleggers!" he exclaimed.

"Bootleggers?" answered Bootie.

"Yeaaah, the bootleggers!"

"Charles, those weren't bootleggers," Bootie said. "Those were swamp people. They live out here and have for a long, long time."

"Live out here?" Lovelady said with his eyes about as wide as they could get. "In this swamp?"

"Yes, Charles. They live out here."

After quickly looking around the area to see if there were any to be seen, Lovelady then put his eyes back on Bootie and asked, "What do they do out here?"

Looking around quickly also to see if any were visible, Bootie then shifted his eyes back to Lovelady and said, "They practice their voodoo worship out here. And sometimes Charles, sometimes, they cut people up and eat them out here."

"WHHHHHHAAAAAAAATTTTTTTTTT ?" Lovelady yelled back.

"And that's exactly why we need to get the hell out of here,

243

Charles. Now!" Grabbing Lovelady's arm to help him walk, Bootie said, "Come on! Let's go!"

With that, Bootie began to basically pull Lovelady over to the side of the bluff, so he could help him climb back up to its top.

Tony couldn't help but chuckle to himself as he sat there in his airplane seat. His dad had told him it was quite some time before Lovelady wanted to go back out anywhere unless it was with several of his federal agents accompanying him. His dad had also told him that Bootie had not been able to retrieve the silver pistol from that trip into the bayou. He had tried but could not find it. As Tony thought about that story, a smile stayed on his face as the plane began its approach into New York City.

Chapter Sixteen

Out at the compound on Long Island, Tony was again well received by everyone. This time though, he was more immediately taken into the back building. He saw six men working at various computers around the room. They all stood up to greet him and seemed happy to meet this famous movie star that Tony had become. After kind words were said all around, he was taken into the solitary room by Conrad and the door firmly shut.

"This must be really something for a person like you, who has seen so much, to give me a message like you did. You seemed a little concerned," Tony said as he took his seat next to his host, who had eased himself into his chair.

"Well, let's just say I have run into a few things that we needed to talk about sooner rather than later," Conrad said as he eased into his chair. Looking over at Tony, he began.

"I mentioned a little bit to you before about how so much more is available to people these days, especially people who are dedicated to spending the time and effort and the money to find things out. A person or entity, be it a country or a corporation, can basically find out what they want to find out. If they are dedicated enough to the effort, then it is usually just a matter of time before whatever is being looked for becomes available."

Turning a little more towards Tony, Conrad looked at him as he said, "There is really not anything that cannot be found out these days. Everything, regardless of how well-hidden, can be found out. In most instances, it is just a matter of how long it takes."

After glancing away for a moment, Conrad looked back at Tony and continued, "The girl your friend asked you to look out for, his daughter named Jean, is involved in some things that may shock you, or at least surprise you, but these days I would just tell you that things are different. Please understand that I am going to tell you what I am going to tell you because you asked me to find out about her. Well, I have been able to do that, but a few things have happened with her that I think her father would have wanted to know about. At least then, he could have dealt with them, if he had decided to. Those are decisions you will now have to make. But she is on the verge of having, not just one thing, but at least more than one thing happen to her that you need to know about."

Tony kept his eyes on the speaker. He had great comfort in knowing who was going to be telling him whatever it was he was going to say. But otherwise, he was at a complete loss of having any idea what Conrad was leading up to.

"First of all, as some background for all of this, you know she is divorced and the mother of two children. One, her eight-year-old son, her sorry ex-husband and his wife have custody of and her other child, her six-year-old autistic daughter, she has custody of. She, of course, was a beauty queen, is now thirty-six but does appear to have maintained her beauty to this day."

"You have done your research," Tony said, impressed that Conrad was as far along as he was.

Shifting a little in his chair, Conrad continued, "The family she married into is very wealthy, involved in the international shipping business out of New Orleans and does a lot of business in China. They are members of upper crust society and are thought of as one of the "old" families of New Orleans. Her ex is now married to his former secretary and they both are deeply involved in drugs."

Tony was surprised, but not shocked by the news. He had seen so much of that during his time in the movie industry out in LA.

"Jean has tried to keep things together, mostly for the sake of that poor autistic child. She did not get enough money in the divorce due to the influence and control her husband's family exercises in that area, and specifically over that particular judge. Jean has really struggled and has received and is receiving as much help as she possibly can from her parents. But after all, he was just a Sheriff and they don't make much money, at least legally. Your friend, though, was very honest and would not succumb to payoffs and all. It is said that he was probably one of the most, if not the most, honest Sheriffs in that state."

"That's nice to hear," Tony said. "At least I won't have to worry about that side of things."

"I'll say one thing about your friend, and his father. When they died, and the funeral was held, a very large number of people showed at each of their funerals. Huge numbers, at each one."

"I had heard that," Tony said.

"They were both well-thought of down there, that is for sure. I'm not going to get into all of the details, but I do need to let you know what has happened and is happening."

"Okay. What happened? What's going on there?"

Conrad answered, "While checking around on things down there, I took a look at the boy she married. In particular, I wanted to know more about him, and his family. Well, come to find out that group is into a lot of things. They are highly successful in their shipping business and make a lot of money, each year, doing mostly things with the Chinese these days, as I mentioned. Her husband got into drinking a lot in college, then even more so when he went to work at the family company after graduation. Then he got into taking drugs, usually with the secretary that worked for him at the business. He ended up getting divorced after their autistic child was born and eventually marrying the secretary. But there is a little more to the story."

Tony leaned over a little closer to concentrate more on what was being said.

"The boy's two sisters, Gertrude and Josephine, are both older, single, and not good looking at all. But the worst thing about them, especially Gertrude, is that they are horrible people. They are not nice to anybody, have nothing complimentary to say about anybody, are not helpful to anybody, and are basically just arrogant, horrible people."

"That bad, huh?" Tony responded.

"That's not even the worst part. The worst part is that both sisters continually tried to break Jean and her husband up and eventually were successful in helping get that done. After the marriage, the two of them constantly, even to this day, bad mouth Jean every chance they get. But here is the worst part. Once the divorce proceedings were filed, Gertrude got one of the company dock workers, Sammy Jeffery, to appear at a preliminary hearing to testify that he was having an affair with Jean. Jean denied it, said it wasn't true, and fortunately one of her sorority sisters from college testified on her behalf that Jean's husband was having an affair with his secretary, which was true."

"Glad her friend helped her out", Tony said.

"I am too, because we were able to find out that Gertrude was responsible for setting all of that false testimony up, for getting that Sammy guy to testify, and for promising him that he would get paid $28,000 spread over about four months for lying about it all. She brags about that from time to time to her sister, but she still has not paid him all that she promised him. I think she is one of those people that likes to jerk people around because they can. She seems to just enjoy seeing if she can get away with that sort of thing. Of all things, they sometimes even laugh on the phone about all of the different problems they have been able to cause Jean."

"Does their mother and father know about all of that?" Tony asked as he wondered what the answer was going to be to that question.

"They have to know about most of it. That Sammy guy spent an hour or so on the witness stand talking about being involved sexually with Jean at the hearing. The mother and the two sisters were sitting right there while he testified."

"Sounds like Jean got involved with a group of bad people," Tony said as he looked to see what Conrad's response would be.

Conrad looked directly at Tony and answered, "I'm just getting started. There's more. A lot more."

Shifting in his chair, he then continued. "Jean, is now intimately involved with a former college sorority sister, a girl named Mary Jo. And that is not the only girl she's involved with."

"Really?" a surprised Tony responded.

"Yes. That sorority sister, Mary Jo, has coerced Jean into being with other girls. She was going to send pictures of her being with other girls out to three different lesbian clubs, one in Budapest, one in Montreal, and one in Charlotte, North Carolina. They were going to be sent out for money, which the Mary Jo girl could use because she is a Sociology teacher at a local college and not making that much. She was going to split the money she made from providing the pictures, about $12,000, with Jean. Most of the other girls introduced into having their pictures taken and sent out end up wanting or needing the money that Mary Jo usually splits with them. So, they end up letting the circulation of their pictures happen. Some have even ended up posing for additional pictures, thus making more money."

Taking a brief pause to see if there was going to be a reaction so far, Conrad saw that there wasn't, so he continued.

"Well, Jean, for a very good reason that I will tell you about, did not want her pictures sent out at all. But Mary Jo needs the money, or shall we say she likes having the additional money. So, she put pressure on Jean, telling Jean how she could probably also use the extra money that she would make. Jean knew there was no way she wanted her pictures out circulating around, especially in one particular location Mary Jo had mentioned. It meant so much to Jean that her pictures not be circulated that she basically agreed to more or less do sexually whatever Mary Jo might want for her to do and with whoever Mary Jo wanted her to be involved with, in order to make up for the loss of the money for Mary Jo."

Tony then asked, "How is that being dealt with?"

"Well, you might say that Mary Jo is a lesbian hunter. She enjoys converting straight girls into being lesbians. She has a small group of about four or five girls that go out each week looking for new conquests."

"Are you kidding me?" Tony almost exclaimed. "I mean, are you serious?"

"As serious as I can be. Mary Jo's little group plans the seduction of straight women that they run into, mainly at one particular bar near the New Orleans Airport. After a while, they actually do what could be called "assign" newly seduced girls to be the girlfriends of certain experienced members of the group, though the new girls don't know that is what is happening. It is amazing how planned out some of the situations are. As of right now, Jean has been with Mary Jo and four other, different girls. It is Mary Jo's intention to get the total number of girls Jean has been with up much higher, though Jean has no idea that is what's happening. Then she will be paired off by Mary Jo, unbeknownst to Jean, with one of the other girls she has already been with in a more permanent relationship, at this point probably with a weight-lifting bartender named Ronnie."

"How did you find out all of this?" Tony asked with some astonishment.

Conrad looked right at Tony and said, "Anybody in our business can basically find out anything they want to these days. It really is only limited by how long it will take us to find something out."

"So, it is possible to find out things that no one would ever really imagine could be found out?" Tony asked with genuine interest.

"Yes. It really is. Anything can be found out. Anything. For example, you have probably heard that the over thirty thousand emails, that were supposedly destroyed on Hillary Clinton's computer and system, were not retrievable and that they are gone forever. Let's just say that piece of information is far from the truth. Any capable professional can get that type of information, if they want it bad enough. It only takes time and the amount of time depends basically only on how badly somebody wants it. There are now several mammoth new buildings out west that were recently built as a place to keep all that sort of stuff stored. That way, should we ever need anything from the past, regardless of how recent or how old, we can always go to what they now call the "cloud" and, if enough time, effort and expertise is dedicated, eventually find it."

Taking a moment to let that sink in with Tony, Conrad then continued.

"The problem is that you never know these days who is watching who. Who is listening in on who? Who is getting access to whose line and locations? I will just tell you, like I think I mentioned to you before, that those who know what they are doing can eventually get into anywhere they want. Some are not as good as others but some, like the Russians or the Chinese, are in places you would not imagine. The Russians are good, but the Chinese are really good, and aggressive. At one time, they even had a pre-installed software in a lot of phones that secretly sent messages back to China every 72 hours. The clandestine features of that software kept up with where users went, who they talked to and what they wrote in text messages, as well as transmitting full contact lists and other data. Recently we were looking into something and found, after taking a little time, that they had gotten into somewhere they should not have been. While they were in there, they left forty-three back door entries for themselves into the system. Forty-three! When I retired, our people were still checking on that one to try to make sure we got them all closed so the system could be secure again."

Shifting in his seat, Conrad then said, "But Tony, concerning Jean, I am just getting started. It seems that Jean is now doing well as a drug sales rep. She struggled for a while and did not seem to be able to make her business commissions grow enough to support her and her autistic daughter. Then she had a very important meeting, in Charlotte, North Carolina, of all places, with a man who is responsible for doing all of the buying on behalf of a major corporation, which business includes six major hospitals. He is a very well-thought-of former All-American football player from one of the major colleges in that state. Well, she is now intimately involved with him, which I think happened in order for her to get the contract she recently got for her company, that she really needed to have. There is no question that they were getting ready to move her on out if something did not happen for her company to get that order."

After taking a brief pause, Conrad then said, "Tony, there is one more thing you need to know about that situation." Looking again straight at him, Conrad said, "That guy she got involved with there, the former All-American football player. Well, he's black."

Seeing that this last bit of news had caused Tony to raise his eyebrows, Conrad quickly said, "I guess she just felt that she didn't have a choice. She seems to feel so badly about how her child ended up. Evidently, she was taking some prescription pills during her pregnancy due to all the aggravation she was having with her sorry husband. Research seems to indicate the possibility that taking some of those pills may lead to having autistic children. Now here she is, a former beauty queen, being put in a situation where she probably feels that she has to make herself personally available to him in order to close a deal she felt she had to close so that she could afford to take care of her child."

For a moment, the room was quiet. Tony was at a loss for words. Seeing this, Conrad said, "At least he's a nice guy. I mean, he is well-liked by almost everybody. And he is not married. He has a white girlfriend, who has lived with him for about three years. I think they get involved in some things sexually with other white girls, but at least they do not seem to be involved in any drugs. He just seems to have this thing for white girls."

After looking away for a moment, Conrad then said in somewhat of an attempt to change the subject, "Taking a look at everything around this girl, your friend's daughter, I was surprised about a lot of the information available about the drug companies. I mean, their profits are just huge, each one of them, and it seems that they have known for a while now about the possibility of harmful effects of some of their products on members of the public."

Tony quickly said, "That is exactly what her mother told me when I first got down there right after my friend's death from Agent Orange illness. They had done whatever little research they could, and they thought certain pills taken at certain times during pregnancy led to types of things like autism and that the companies knew about it. She said that the companies know that they are responsible in large part for the increase in autism, but potential liability for the problems caused by their products would result in such a hit to the drug companies' bottom-line profits that they decided to do whatever it took to make sure that such a hit did not happen."

Conrad replied, "Tony, not only does it look like they knew about it, it appears that they purposefully did not change them, advise doctors to stop prescribing them or stop issuing them because they were making too much money."

"Those bastards!" Tony exclaimed while looking at Conrad. Conrad nodded his head in agreement.

"But Tony, that's not all." Conrad shifted his eyes away from Tony for a moment.

Tony said, "That's not all? What else do you have?"

After taking a moment, Conrad said, "There are hundreds of thousands of parents who are devastated about their children being autistic. Some were that way when they were born, possibly due to drugs taken during pregnancy. Some got to be that way possibly after they were given shots when they got to be about two years old. There are other possibilities, but taking drugs just before pregnancy, during pregnancy or after birth seem to be what many, many parents think is what happened. Then they found out that the drug companies went to the United States Congress a few years ago and, almost in the middle of the night around Christmas time, they were able to get a provision included in legislation on other subject matters that gave them what amounts to a significant amount of immunity from litigation".

"Really?"

"Yes. A limited amount of money was allocated to a fund set aside to make payments by a board that was set up for the damages to victims. That had to be done so that the law could not be determined to be not valid. There were so many children in such bad shape that the companies did not want to have to spend so much money taking care of all the damages. Making huge payments would hurt their bottom lines and their profits. By putting a little something in the fund, I think it was like a million and a half dollars, and not leaving it totally unfunded, they were able to get around having to come up with a huge amount, which could easily be up in the billions of dollars, which is what it would probably take to deal with all of them."

Seeing he had Tony's complete attention, he continued, "After a few years of thousands of families filing and trying to get something to help take care of their children, the first case came up, was tried, and ended up with an award being made in court of around a million two hundred thousand dollars or so. With there being such a small amount left in the fund, you can see where that left the other families. Yet the companies continued to make billions of dollars from their products, claiming first of all that the harm was not caused by their products but that, even if it was, they were covered by that fund and limited to that amount of money. You might guess that a lot of people are very upset about all of that."

"That is exactly what my friend's wife told me after he had died, when I first got down there. She said the very same thing." Tony then shifted his eyes to stare off at the wall in front of them.

After a few moments, Conrad said, "Tony, like I said though, still, that's not all."

"That's still not all? What do you mean?" Tony asked.

Conrad shifted in his chair and began, "Not too long ago, one of the heads of one of the largest drug companies making those kinds of drugs was at a convention down in Florida. He picked up this beautiful girl in a bar down there and took her to his room. After having a drink she made for him, he passed out. When he woke up, Tony, the man had no fingers. He had no toes. They had been cut off. And he had super glue up in his penis. Also, Tony, acid had been poured into his eyes."

"Yikes! Damn! Are you serious? Wow!" Looking over at Conrad, Tony could tell he was serious. "Damn!"

Then Tony knew he had to ask, "Why are you telling me this?"

Conrad just looked at him, not saying a word.

After a moment, Tony knew he had to ask again," Conrad, why are you telling me this?"

After waiting a moment to let it all sink in a little more, Conrad answered, "Checking things out on Jean, Tony, we ran up on a private investigation agency that has been hired to look into the hotel attack on that guy down there in Florida. The lead guy of the agency is a totally unethical, ruthless guy, a complete jackass, who will stop at nothing to find out who caused the event that took place with the company president. He seems to think that he has been able to uncover who did all of that to that corporation's president in that hotel room and is now trying to trace the person they think it is. It looks like they are trying to find a girl that looks a lot like Jean."

Tony was quiet, thinking, and letting what he had just been told be absorbed and evaluated by the analytical side of his brain.

Looking at Tony, Conrad continued, "We ran into him and his little group while we were taking a look at a few things on Jean and her computer setup and arrangements. We started seeing what all they were up to. So far, that investigative unit has kept what little information they have to themselves. We've been able to keep up with them, seeing what they are doing and plan to do. The head of that group likes to try to take advantage of people, especially if they are female, and they don't even have to necessarily be nice looking. He likes to make himself look good, so he does not usually share any information about anything with anybody in his investigations until he has to. That includes his clients. Not until he has a chance to squeeze what he can out of those who become involved as the targets of his investigation."

After a quiet moment, Tony said, "Do you, Conrad, do you think that Jean is the one who did all of that stuff to that guy?"

Conrad looked at Tony and a scowl came across his face that Tony had rarely if ever seen on him. It was a look of experience and of total conviction.

"Yes, Tony, I do. There is not much doubt in my mind. I can't say that I blame her. She had to have access to information about him, where he was going to be, and when he was going to be where. On a computer, someone trying to cover their tracks would likely pay for and use a very expensive, specialized data tool, but commercial tools leave a money trail. With one of her computers, there was one. They would try to overwrite free disc space to hide previously deleted files. She did that. There are things a person can do to make it difficult for anyone trying to find and recover deleted files and emails. She did that. Some cell phones send out a GPS signal. Because of that, a person has to remove the battery from their cell phone so as to be free from being traced. At a key point in time, for a few hours, we have been able to figure out that she did that. Free software can be downloaded and used with complete anonymity, unless it is somebody checking who is very knowledgeable and experienced, like we are. As you may have heard in the Hillary Clinton situation, bleach bit can be used if there is something a person really does not want the world to know. It looks like we may have run up on a situation where that item was obtained. I am going to guess that, if we go check one particular location, we are probably going to find that it has been used. The only thing is, so far, they have not been able to find her. But it looks like that may be coming soon."

Taking a moment to watch Tony as he thought about what he had just been told, Conrad decided he now had to tell him about something that was going to be very hard to tell him.

"Tony, there is one final thing else I have to tell you. It is really why I called you to come up here so quickly. You will understand when I tell you."

Turning to look at Conrad's face upon hearing the tone in Conrad's voice as he said that, Tony said, "It will really have to be something to beat what you have already told me."

"I'm afraid it is, Tony."

After taking another moment, Conrad said it.

"Tony, I'm sorry to tell you this, but Jean was raped three days ago."

"Raped?!" Shocked, Tony leaned forward toward Conrad to make sure he could hear all of his answer.

"Yes. She eventually got away from them, but before she could get away, she was gang raped. There seems to have been four guys involved. The best I can tell, there was one Mexican and three others that seem to be from El Salvador. All of them are illegal aliens and part of one of those big gangs down there."

"How did you find out about the rape?" Tony asked, barely able to finish his question.

"Her telephone. That has been one of the ways we have been using to check on her. I've told you a little bit about what all we have done with our technology, how we have capabilities that nobody fully appreciates or really knows about outside of those of us who have dealt with it all."

Shifting in his chair, Conrad continued, saying, "We've been able to keep up with her with some of those capabilities. The guys I used to work with have let me have access to some of the unique capabilities that we had. I had to ask them for that special access to some of it because I am now retired, but I still do help them with some things from time to time. So, my contact said that I could monitor her, and some others I have been keeping up with concerning her, by utilizing some of those, shall we say, very special capabilities."

After a moment's pause as he thought about how far to go with telling Tony about what happened, he continued.

"I did not like doing that, asking for that special access. I was doing alright keeping up with everything with what I already had access to but, as you now know, other things started happening. To make sure I could keep up with where she was, now at all times since I started to get concerned about her situation, I made a call and got a favor from a long-time friend and former business associate to make sure I could get access to that one capability I felt I needed, and he agreed. I did that because I was getting worried about that private investigator. It was a good thing I had already done it because, right after I did it, she hooked up with this Mexican guy, Rodriguez Lopez. He was an instructor at the workout facility she had started going to."

Taking a deep breath, he continued.

"Well, he started coming on to her. He was telling her how beautiful she was, how much he wanted to be with her, how she just had to come have a drink with him, at his place. There were two episodes of that, and each time she turned him down, but she started responding to his approach. I was listening each time through her phone. I had turned it on when I first started checking on things so that I could hear what was going on all the time, regardless of who she was with or where she was, and regardless of whether her phone was on or off. We can do that these days without that much of an effort. That's why I am able to tell you so much. But up to now, there was no reason to get back to you about things. As I just told you, there were other things going on that she was involved with."

Taking a brief pause, he then said, "But Tony, this rape thing was different. Her Mexican paramour, Rodriguez, got her to his apartment that he shares with his roommate, Alberto, a Salvadoran. After his session with her, in walked Alberto. Well, he wanted his turn with her, and Rodriguez agreed. She tried to get away, but Alberto grabbed her and threw her back on the bed. Rodriguez even helped hold her down while Alberto got started. Then Rodriguez left to go see, as he told her - he told her this - to go see his girlfriend, who is much younger than she is, 17, and better in bed than she was, he said! He told her that, on the way out the door."

"What an asshole!" Tony exclaimed. "How is Jean? Is she ok?"

"Well, let's just say she eventually got away. I don't know how okay she is, but at least she did get away. She was able to get up and run out, even though she was nude, after the third Salvadorian guy had finished with her. By that time, it was dark, and she somehow managed to run down the street and around the corner away from them. She was able to grab her phone as she left and took it with her. I don't know how she did that, but she did. Got to her Lexus, which was parked on the street a block over, which was a blessing because they couldn't find her before she used her keyless lock. She got in her car and started it up with an extra set of keys she had in her middle car pocket. She was able to pull away in her car just in time."

"I am glad she got away. How is she now? Is there any way you can tell?" Tony asked as he showed his genuine concern.

"No, not really. She has not talked about it at all, to anybody. She didn't report anything to anybody. I am going to guess that she is a mental wreck, after what all happened to her. She probably feels bad enough about it in that she did voluntarily go meet the guy at his place. She did go to have sex with him, but I am sure she had no idea that there were going to be three other guys involved because she did try to get away. She screamed out one time, when the first guy, Rodriguez, grabbed her, but Ricardo hit her and told her he would beat her if she didn't shut up. Rodriguez told her that Ricardo enjoyed beating up women and that she needed to just lay back and enjoy what was happening to her."

"He hit her in her face, with his fist?" Tony asked.

"Well, he backhand slapped her," Conrad said as he turned more to face Tony. "After he finished with her, two of their fellow gang members, who live across the hall in the same building, took their turns with her."

"He had two other guys have sex with her?" Tony asked.

"Yes, and not only that. Rodriguez said before he left that there were six other gang members that lived down the street and he was going to let them know that she was available for them."

"What a total shithead!" Tony exclaimed. "What happened?"

"It seems that they have been doing an operation where Rodriguez, being a good-looking guy, gets various girls to come to his place, thinking they were going to be with just him. Yet, when they go there, after Rodriguez does his bit with them, his roommate gets involved and also eventually some of the other members of their gang that live nearby. They then arrange to either take the girls themselves or have them taken over to Texas and across the border into Mexico. There they are delivered into sexual slavery to the various crime boss heads down there. Some of the more attractive white girls, like Jean, are targeted to be sent to the lead people of the Mexican gang they are members of. All the girls are paid for and most are kept at out of the way ranches in deserted areas of the country to be made available and passed around."

Taking a deep breath, Conrad continued.

"It had already been mentioned that Jean was going to be sent to the head of the gang Rodriguez was a member of, at least initially. They get paid rather well for each girl they send, depending on the age of the girls and of course their looks. Some of the bosses want really younger girls, down to about 12 to 14 years old. There was going to be a lot of money given to him and his guys for Jean at the border, along with money for another much younger Latino girl that was going to be sent down with her. That girl, who is fifteen, ended up being with Rodriguez. She was grabbed and worked on by several of the guys in their group in New Orleans. We found out she was sent down to Mexico night before last. They liked Jean because of her looks and being white, but they were also worried about her being older. Some of their discussions indicated that they worry about older girls because they try harder than younger girls to resist or get away from what they are being taken into."

Conrad shifted in his chair and said, "If any of the girls cause problems, they go ahead and get rid of them. With respect to the older girls, they eventually just go ahead and get rid of them anyway. They do that, usually not by killing them, but by selling them to other similar groups that are in what is sometimes called the "Tri-plex" area of South America. That is a jungle area with limited access where the borders of three countries come together. There are a lot of things going on there. I was doing some work there from time to time a few years ago because of everything and everybody going through there. Lots of drugs, lots of really bad people, from places like Syria, Pakistan, Iran, Iraq, Afghanistan, Saudi Arabia, and a surprising number of Chinese. Even had a few Russians and Cubans in there. We kept up with that stuff until Obama's people had us stop doing that, and they also had us stop keeping up with who all was coming into this country and going in and out of the Moslem enclaves in local places like Michigan, Maryland, Wisconsin and Minnesota."

"Did you say Chinese?" Tony asked.

"Yes. Jean would have probably ended up down there in the "Tri-plex" area eventually. They usually send the white girls down there when they are finished with them in Mexico. They don't want to take a chance on leaving them somewhere in Mexico. Sometimes, a few of the girls end up in El Salvador or Guatemala. They also pay out big money for white girls in those countries. So, it is a real blessing that she was able to escape. It really was. If she had ended up down there, in all likelihood she would have never made it back out."

Continuing, he said, "Once I got to checking on those guys, it looks like Rodriguez got a 15-year-old girl the very next night. It seems to have been a Honduran girl that he had met at a convenience store. He was able to find out that she didn't have any family with her and had only recently come up through Mexico and across the border with a girlfriend. She appears to have thought New Orleans would be safer than Texas. She probably also thought Rodriguez was going to take care of her, but he's a predator. His whole group is nothing but predators. After Rodriguez and his group had their way with her, she was taken back across the border and delivered to their cartel contacts. They have teams of guys, and girls, out looking for girls that may be targets for kidnapping so they can get them, and then deliver them to their contacts. They get paid a lot of money, thousands of dollars, for delivering girls into that sex trade. Jean was very fortunate to have gotten away from those animals."

Tony looked at him and said in a firm, level tone, "There is a special place in hell for people like that."

It was all quiet as Tony stared at the wall in front of him for a moment and thought about everything he had just been told.

Then he softly said, "I'm not doing a very good job of taking care of my friend's daughter."

Conrad looked over at him and said, "Don't be too hard on yourself. After all, she did go to his place voluntarily. She had no way of knowing that all of that was going on in that neighborhood. And fortunately, she did get away."

After thinking for a moment, Tony said, "I need to get back down there."

Then turning his head to look at Conrad, he said, "Do you think you can get me any information on those Latino guys?"

A smile came across Conrad's face. He leaned forward with a slip of paper already in his hand, and said, "I thought you might want that, so I went ahead and put this together for you. It's their names, the address of the place where they are staying, and I took the liberty of finding out where they are working and what their hours are."

Reaching out and taking the offered piece of paper in his right hand, Tony said, "Thanks, Conrad." Then he said, "Look, I'm going to need some help."

Conrad, now standing in front of him, replied, "We got out of that business a few years ago, Tony."

Tony thought for a second and then, after he had stood up, he said, "Conrad, this is special. Looks like a few things are going to have to be dealt with. Taken care of."

"What are you thinking about doing?" Conrad asked as he intently looked at Tony's face.

Tony looked back at him and slowly answered, "Whatever it takes." After looking away for a moment, he looked back deep into Conrad's eyes and continued, firmly saying, "I am interested in doing whatever it takes, to get even. But I'm going to need some help."

Conrad looked back at him and said, "I understand. I'll run it by the guys, see what they say."

Flying back to New Orleans that evening, Tony began thinking about what all he had just been told. He had no idea how he was going to try to deal with everything involved in the situations he had just been told about, especially the rape. He felt so sorry for that poor girl. Going over what all he had been told caused him to get even more upset.

Thinking about various things eventually brought to mind another story his dad had told him when he was a teenager sitting on the bench with him in Sicily. His dad had told him about the so-called "war" that had gone on between their group, Capone's, and the infamous "Purple Gang", a gang made up of mostly Jewish men in Detroit.

Because of Capone's efforts to take over booze and other illegal substance shipments in the Detroit area, shooting had broken out between the two outfits. In fact, the shooting had gotten so intense that most descriptions labeled it as a "war". The hatred became so intense that there were numerous killings of gang members on both sides. Each side got to be so intent on winning that they kept increasing the incidents and events. Both sides were determined to raise the level of violence so high that each was sure the other side would give up.

His dad told him that one day they were unloading the most recent shipments of illegal booze from Cuba at the dock up the bayou. From that location, they could unload the barges that had been filled up with the most recent shipments and put those shipments on different means of transportation to be moved to various locations in Louisiana, in parts of Arkansas and Mississippi, and in Texas.

On this particular day, they were about to finish unloading the barge that was tied to the dock when, all of a sudden, around the bend just to the east came two fast, small fishing boats. In each of those boats were two men, with one man holding a submachine gun in the front and the other man in the rear driving the boat, but also having a submachine gun close by. The minute they both made eye contact with the dock, the lead man in each boat opened fire on the dock.

Due to a prior attack by a competing Chicago mob, his dad had made sure that the group working at the dock had at least two submachine guns on site. Because of that, the two workers nearest to those weapons grabbed them and dove for cover. The other three workers had pistols with them, which they each quickly pulled as they dove behind cover. A gunfight ensued which consisted of a steady brand of heavy fire. One of his dad's men had been wounded in the initial gunfire on the dock.

The attacking men quickly settled into positions on the opposite side of the bayou from the dock. From those positions, they maintained a steady stream of automatic fire on the positions of his dad and his men. The gunfire was continuous, and his dad told him that he was surprised that more men were not killed or wounded.

After a few minutes, it seemed that there was a standoff. The gunfire lessened as both sides realized that they did not have an unlimited supply of ammunition. They began to level brief spurts of gunfire at what each side thought were sites worth taking a shot at, but no serious damage was being done by either side. After about ten minutes of that, things changed.

A very loud bang was heard from behind the raiding guys positioned on the opposite shore. His dad said he saw one of that group literally get blown up out of his position. The other men quickly turned around to see what had caused that to happen and two more of them were also shot, causing them to be thrown out of their positions. As the fourth and final one was now turning around and trying to aim his gun in the direction behind him, another extremely loud sound set forth and the final one was also literally blown out of his position.

After quietness crept in over the battle site, first one and then other figures dressed in all-white outfits and on horseback road out of the swamp grass and up onto the berms that had been protecting the shooters. His dad said he yelled out to his men to not fire anymore, that these men were their friends. The lead rider directed his horse up to the top of the berm, reached up and pulled off the hood of his Klu Klux Klan outfit.

He then yelled out, "Heard some gunfire. Thought you might could use a little help."

His dad yelled back at him, "We sure did. Thanks so much for showing up." He noticed that each of the riders was carrying a Winchester rifle. He knew that each of those fired a bullet big enough to bring down a bear or a wild hog. A man didn't stand a chance.

His dad said he then yelled out at them, "Since you helped us, come on over and let us show our appreciation by giving you and your guys a little something to take with you."

The lead rider yelled back, "Well now, that would be awfully nice of ya. I think we'll do just that. It'll help make our ride home a little easier."

As he began riding up the edge of the bayou to where he knew the shallow water crossing was, he yelled back, "Follow me, boys." With that, all ten of them crossed over and, one by one, road by as his dad's men gave each of them a bottle of booze to take with them.

As the leader rode up to his dad, his dad said, "Thanks again for your help."

"Glad we could help you out, partna. You're gonna need to be careful around these parts. There's some bad folks hangin out around here. Right boys?" With that, they all chuckled and added words of agreement.

Then his dad asked, "What were you guys doing down here? You still looking for that Leroy, the black guy that you said raped the white girl?"

The leader said, "Yea. That's why we were back down here. We found him just a little bit ago not too far from here. But we also found out, barely in time, that the boy didn't rape nobody. She had been leading that boy on and, when some people found out about it, she made up a story, lied about it. Said he was trying to make her be with him. Girl's daddy found out the truth about it. Let us know, just in time, what had happened. We were just up the road letting him go, getting ready to leave and heard the gunfire. Thought we might come down here and find out what was going on. When we saw it was you and your guys, well, we thought we might see if we could help you out."

"Sure am glad you did. Thanks again so much. You have a safe ride home," his dad yelled out.

With that, the leader turned his horse around and rode into the water and back over to the other side, followed by his men, each one now carrying his own bottle.

As they began to ride off into the swamp, the leader caused his horse to rear up. Once it had all of its feet back on the ground, he waved to everybody, which wave was returned by his dad's men. He then turned his horse into the swamp and road off, disappearing into it, as did his men.

Tony said his dad had one last comment about that shootout. He had said that, after the Klansmen had left, he had been asked by Bootie, who had been out there when the shootout had taken place, what were they going to do with the bodies? After checking the pockets of the men, they were not able to determine for sure where they were from, but they thought possibly they may have been men under contract with their competition in Detroit.

His dad told them that, when the Chicago group had attacked the dock at the house, they had taken those bodies out into the Gulf of Mexico, cut them up and fed them to the sharks. This time he didn't want to fool with that. Instead, he said for Bootie to get in touch with the swamp people and turn the bodies over to them. He was sure they would see to it that the bodies were never found. That is exactly what happened to the raiders.

Tony's mind explored what his possibilities and alternatives were in dealing with his present situation, all the way back to New Orleans. One of the things he wondered about was, if there were any still around, would it be possible to get in contact with some of the swamp people.

Chapter Seventeen

The drug company's "special" investigator, Robert Stone, began to quietly knock around to find out what had happened to Stanley Rhorback in Miami. Stone directed that his two computer experts spend all of their time on Rhorback's case. Stone first began spending his time by looking into the facts concerning what had happened. He rather easily found out that the damages Rhorback had suffered happened during a convention that some of the officers of Rhorback's corporation and of some of the other major drug companies were attending.

He then checked the list of attendees at the hotel where the convention was held and looked over the identities of people who were attending it and those who were not. He immediately assigned his two computer whizzes to run identity checks on each name revealed. Checking the video of entrances and hallways of the hotel where the attack took place, the gurus were able to identify the people that had not been staying there. In particular, he was able to find Rhorback and the unknown woman in tapes covering the bar, the entranceway and the hallway to his room.

Investigating further, Stone was unable to identify the woman who had been with him as being a person who was staying at the hotel. She simply didn't exist at the hotel during any day of the conference. He then began the time-consuming effort to see if she could be identified, by using a poor picture from one of the videos of her in the hallway near Rhorback's room, as having been at a nearby hotel or motel. He eventually found a video of her parking the car she was using in a parking lot of one of those hotels. Gradually he began to make progress after finally identifying the car as having been rented from a company in another state. Now he began the process of trying to find out which state that might have been.

* * *

Upon Tony's return to Bay St. Louis, Harry came by Karen's house to see him and to talk to him about a friend of his, Jack Lancaster. Lancaster was a Special Assistant Attorney General from the Mississippi Attorney General's Office who was on the coast preparing for a major trial concerning a portion of Devil's Swamp. Lancaster had helped Harry with a legal matter and, during that effort, had expressed an interest in finding out more about the history of the area while preparing for the upcoming massive trial.

Tony had initially said no, but Harry was persistent, saying that Jack was a friendly guy and just wanted historical background information with no particulars as to the names of individuals who were involved. He was interested in general information as to what all had gone on in the area back in the 1920's. Jack had mentioned to Harry that he had previously heard about a few things that may have happened back in that era.

Harry encouraged Tony to meet with Jack and make his own decision as to what all to tell him. Tony finally agreed to meet with the Special Assistant Attorney General at the café of a small gas station in an area known as "the Kiln". Jack encouraged Harry to go with him to the meeting, if that would make Tony feel more comfortable. Harry mentioned that possible arrangement to Tony, but assured Tony that he would be quite at ease meeting and talking with Jack. Tony finally agreed to meet Jack without anyone else present.

Walking into the small café at the appointed time of 10 a.m. on a Thursday morning, Tony stopped just inside the doorway to search out the person he was to talk with. One booth had two men carrying on a conversation while having what appeared to be their morning coffee. Moving his eyes around the room, Tony could only see a young, nicely dressed man sitting by himself in one of the booths on the opposite side of the room. Tony began slowly making his way towards that man as he continued his search of the room with his eyes.

Arriving at the booth, Tony stopped and said, "Are you Jack Lancaster?"

The young man easily smiled and said, "Yes, I am. And you are Tony Gable?"

"I am," Tony responded.

"Please have a seat, Mr. Gable."

Tony eased himself onto the bench seat of the booth where Lancaster was seated. "Please call me Tony."

"Okay, Tony. Thank you so much for agreeing to meet with me. I work for the Mississippi Attorney General's Office and am down here on a massive case involving part of this over one hundred-thousand-acre swamp down here known as Devil's Swamp. Harry is somewhat familiar with my efforts to find out some of the background of this area. I have always been interested in history and have found some of the history about the area the subject of this lawsuit I am involved with to be potentially very important for our case. Harry tells me that you might know some background information about Devil's Swamp that I might be interested in."

For the next almost two hours, the two men engaged in a very amiable and informative conversation. Tony mentioned many different pieces of information about the history of the area that he had learned years ago. Jack was impressed with Tony's knowledge and listened intently to his in-depth answers to Jack's numerous questions.

Near the end of their meeting, Jack asked Tony if it would be possible for Tony to think of other people who might also have knowledge about the area and of eras gone by. Jack had been particularly impressed with the remnants of the old massive Pine Hills Hotel from the roaring 20's. Tony responded that he would think about others who Jack might be interested in talking with that might know more about the area in that era.

With the agreement for Jack to get back in touch with Harry in about a week in order to find out when he might meet with Tony again, the two men parted company.

Upon meeting with Harry on his way back to his hometown of Jackson, Jack was told that he needed to go by a black man's house. Harry told him that the rumor around that area of the county was that the black man had possibly been involved as a teenager in the shipment of illegal booze on the bayous during the roaring 20's.

After receiving directions to the black man's house, but not his name, on his way out of the area Jack pulled up a short, narrow, dirt road to the dilapidated house as sunset began to darken the area. Jack noticed that no lights were on in the house or in the area surrounding the house, and that the front door was shut.

Thinking the least he could do was get out of his car and call out, Jack did that as he now stood next to his opened car door.

"Hello in there. Anybody home?"

After a moment of silence, there was a response.

"State your business," was the reply in a deep, baritone voice.

"I am a lawyer with the Mississippi Attorney General's Office. I am down here working on a case and was told that you might have some background information that may be useful in the preparation of our case. Would it be possible for me to schedule a meeting with you so we might discuss that?"

After a short, quiet moment, a response came back.

"No, I don't think so. I don't have anything I want to talk about."

Jack thought for a moment and then said, "Look, it would be really helpful to me in getting ready for our case. If need be, we can get a judge to encourage you to give us information."

The voice immediately replied, "Mister. I don't know who you are, but I do know this. Back in the 1930's I was taken to court in Louisiana where they tried to force me to talk. I didn't talk so they put me in jail for four months. I didn't talk then and I ain't talking now."

Mississippi Special Assistant Attorney General Jack Lancaster made the only decision that was left to him. He immediately got in his car and drove back to Jackson.

277

* * *

Karen's granddaughter, Emily, seemed to be responding to country music more now, particularly the music of the group, Little Big Town. Karen thought it would be great to take the child to Nashville to the Country Music Awards and see the group live. She thought that such an experience might be good for her granddaughter. Tony agreed to go with Karen as she took the child to Nashville. Karen and Emily would stay in one room and Tony would stay in an adjacent room. The child's mom, Jean, could not go because she was working out of state.

While they were at the awards show, Little Big Town performed its hit song, "Tornado", which is about a woman "coming after you". As he listened to the song, it dawned on Tony that may be exactly what had happened to the drug company official that had been attacked. Somebody had gone after him. It was then that he realized it could have been somebody who has a child affected by their drugs. For the first time, he considered that he couldn't blame Karen's daughter, or any mother, if they had done something like that.

While in Nashville Tony agreed, after being asked, to meet Jack again at the little gas station in "the Kiln". During the course of their conversation there, Tony told Jack more about what he knew concerning the "Bluffs" and let him know that there had been a magnificent mansion built out there in the mid 20's. Jack said that he would certainly like to see that site at some point. He said that he had always found that seeing something, whether it was a location or building or an event, had always added to his appreciation and understanding of what he had been told about it.

The day after the return from the concert, during which Emily had reacted somewhat to the playing of the music, Tony received

278

information from Conrad about the activities of an investigator, Robert Stone. Conrad had been monitoring the investigator's internet and telephone communications and had found out that Stone was now focusing on a woman from the New Orleans area. Tony had Conrad check and he was able to figure out that Karen's daughter was out of town for several days around the time that the attack on the company president had taken place. He asked Conrad to make sure he was now constantly monitoring Karen's daughter's locations and communications.

The next day, about mid-morning, Karen grabbed Tony by his arm in the hallway and said, "There are two black men out in front of the house, on the sidewalk. I think one of them may be your friend."

Tony walked towards the front of the house, wondering what it possibly was that would cause two black men to be where she said they were. Opening the screened front door and walking out onto the wooden floor of the open porch, he saw the two black men. One was on the sidewalk and the other was back by a car on the street that they must have been riding in. Looking at the man on the sidewalk, Tony recognized him. It was Martavias.

Tony walked down the three steps of the stairs looking at Martavias as he said, "Hey guys. How are you doing?"

Martavias didn't say a word but motioned with his right hand for Tony to take a few steps to bring him closer. As Tony did that, Martavias looked over his right shoulder and searched up and down the street with his eyes. Turning back around to face Tony, he said, "This here es Elton. He needs to tells ya sumthin."

Elton took a few short steps to get closer to where Tony and Martavias were now both standing on the sidewalk.

Martavias said, in a lower voice, "Elton saw sumthin yesterday while he was cutin grass down the street. Told me bout it. Knows you ben visitin around here. He told me what he saw. Since you be here, I wanted to make sure you know about it."

Tony looked at Elton.

Elton first looked at Tony, then at Martavias, back to Tony, and then said, "Ther was two ov'em. Tall one was driver, short one in front seat. Drivin a black Mercedes, four door, black windows." He took a breath, looked around him, then back at Tony.

"I was puttin my clippins in the trash can in the alley, the one behind yor house here. Was just three down from here. And they called the cat. The cat walked over to them. The little short fat one picked it up. The tall one standin next to him, lookin around, saw me. So I walked back over to the fence behind the house." He motioned down to his right. He shifted on his feet again, looked around, as did Martavias, and then said, "The short fat one started tryin to choke dat cat." Elton then looked at the ground, shaking his head back and forth. "That cat don't bother nobody. Dats a friendly cat. Walked right over to that fat one. He ran his hands over that little cat's head and then grabbed him and just started tryin to choke him."

So that was what had happened. Tony could tell it was hard for the man to tell him about it. He could hardly continue but Martavias said, "Go head. Tell him what happened next."

Tony did not want to hear it but had to. It was now very important to him to know what had happened next.

Elton continued, saying, "The tall one opened the trunk of the car, took out a paper sack, pulled out a hacksaw." He started shaking his head back and forth. "He was gonna use that hacksaw on dat cat. Right there. On da trunk of dat car. But when da fat one started tryin to choke him and dat cat saw that hacksaw, he must hav' sensed somethin' cause, when I yelled at um and da fat one jerked around, dat cat jumped right straight up, got on da ground and ran away. I watched em from behind da fence down there. Dey tried to grab him but couldn't get him."

The man's voice by now was almost stuttering. After a pause, he said as best he could, "Dey were gonna saw dat cat in half. Dey was smilin and laffin the whole time. I yelled out at um. Dats little Miss Emily's cat. They saw me looking at um. Dat cat jumped up out of his hands and ran right away. Dey put dat saw back in da trunk, got in da car and left. Drove right by me on the way out. Black windows up and all."

Tony could tell by the sincerity in the man's quivering voice that, what he was being told, had happened exactly like it was being told. He looked at both men, first at Martavias then at Elton again, and then at the ground.

Martavias looked down the street and then said, "Elton said dat he thought dat was Miss Emily's cat."

Tony nodded his head and said, "It is. It's Jean's daughter's cat, little Emily. She has autism and that cat is one of the few things she reacts to. Loss of that cat would have been devastating to her."

The three men stood there with nothing being said for a few moments. Then Martavias said, "Elton did something else."

Tony looked up, first at Martavias and then at Elton, and said, "What did you do?"

Elton slowly reached into his right pants pocket and pulled out a crumpled up small piece of paper. As he pushed his hand holding the paper towards Tony, Martavias said, "He wrote down da tag number of dat car."

"You did?" Tony almost exclaimed. He took the piece of paper from Elton, opened it up and there it was, a Louisiana tag number. From what Tony had previously seen on a tag for his own rental car, he guessed the tag numbers were also for a rental car.

Looking back at Elton, Tony said, "You wrote this down?"

Elton said, "Yas sir. Always carry a pencil with me when I'm workn da yards. Helps me keep up wid thangs. Don't remember like I used to. Haf to write things down, when I mow, when I get paid, all dat. So, I wrote it down. Hope dat heps."

Tony said, "You better believe this helps. Thanks so much. And Martavias, man, I can't thank you both enough."

"Thought you might want ta have dat. When he told me about it and where it happened and all, well I knew we had ta let you know if we could," Martavias said as he looked at him.

"Thanks, my friend. You were so right. I needed to know this. We shall see what we can do with it."

Tony called the compound in New York after Martavias and had Elton left. Before nightfall, the two men in the rental car had been identified and their offices in Kentucky located. Tony began to have a few ideas about what should happen next. So did New York.

Tony felt that he needed to go back to the church one more time, especially now that things seemed to be spinning out of control. He noted that it was about 9:45 on this particular night as he parked his motorcycle in the same location he had during his last visit. He then made his way across the street to the front door of the church. The same faint light in the church was viewable from the street so he hoped that the door was open once again. It was.

282

After making his way down to his pew on the left side of the center aisle, he took his seat, again looking around to see if anyone else was in the area. Not seeing anyone, he began to focus on the altar as thoughts about Jean's situation began to demand his attention. He wondered how much, if anything, Mark had known about all of that before he passed away. The more he thought about it, the more he felt that somehow, in some way, Mark was aware that things were not right and that was why he had wanted someone he could trust to look out for his daughter, and his family. He had tried his best to be around to take care of them, but his illness had not allowed that to happen.

It was at the point where Tony had been thinking about everything for what had to be at least thirty minutes when he heard something. He had been in such deep thought that he wasn't sure that he had in fact heard anything, but he turned to look around anyway. As he looked back over his right shoulder on his way to view the doorway entrance, he was totally surprised to see someone kneeling in one of the rows on the opposite side of the church a few rows back from him. Focusing his eyes as best he could, he saw a somewhat hazy figure. It looked like the same figure that he had seen all those many years ago! Checking himself to make sure he wasn't dreaming, he realized, and was comforted to know, it was indeed a figure very similar, if not exactly the same, as what he had seen so many years ago.

He couldn't help but literally exclaim, "It's you!" He continued to stare at the figure, not wanting to even blink his eyes so as to not lose his view of what, he now more clearly saw, appeared to be the same black man he had seen there years before. He leaned back in his pew with his body turned so he could maintain his gaze on the figure. He noted there was no response.

"I was hoping upon hope that you would be here," he said as

the figure now turned its head to look at him. "The last time I saw you, you mentioned something that really helped me at that time. It really did. It was such good guidance. I have wanted to thank you for that, ever since then. So, I will say, 'Thanks', for what you did."

The figure then, ever so slightly and ever so slowly, nodded his head affirmatively, while continuing to look at him.

Taking a deep breath, Tony continued, "Now, there is another situation. A real mess." He paused for a moment and, not seeing or hearing any response, he continued. "I have to do something to try to take care of it. The hard part is, I really do not know what to do." Tony finally took his gaze off the figure to quickly glance around the altar area to see if anyone else was there. There wasn't. He was hoping, when his eyes returned to that pew, that the figure would still be there. He was happy to see that it was and that it was still looking at him.

A moment of silence came over the sanctuary. Tony looked away again, thinking that maybe this was not the same guy or that maybe he was asking for too much. After the moment of quietness, a deep, smooth baritone voice began to speak.

"He has moved mountains, and He will do it all again."

Tony could not believe it. What the figure had just said was in the same tone he had heard so many years ago. And it was exactly what he needed to hear now. It gave him confidence to move forward. He looked back at the figure, which was now looking toward the altar area. Tony now felt the Lord would be standing by him, regardless of whatever happened. He turned to face the altar, his mind jumping ahead, trying to figure out how things might play out given this guidance. He knew one thing. He had to move and move quickly.

He got up from his seat, edged out of his pew, and turned to walk up the middle aisle. The figure was gone. His eyes quickly searched around the whole room, but they did not see him. When he got to the row where the figure had been kneeling, he stopped, turning to search the other pews. Nothing was there.

After he had scanned the altar area, Tony turned and walked towards the rear entrance of the church. He knew, once he got to the doors and reached for the right door handle, that he had to turn and take one last look, even though he knew what he was probably going to see. And that was exactly what he did see, which was absolutely nothing. The figure was gone.

Tony glanced one last time around the church and then again brought his eyes back to the now vacant pew. He closed his eyes and said a quick prayer of thanks. Then he exited the church.

After he had walked across the street, he put his leg over his motorcycle and straddled the bike's seat. Sitting there, the one thought that came to his mind was that sometimes, at some point, it is to every interested party's benefit, that something happens.

After thinking for a few moments while sitting on his bike, he took his cell phone out and called Harry. He had to talk with Harry. He didn't have any choice.

"Harry? It's me. Meet me at Karen's front porch in about thirty minutes or so. There is something I need to talk with you about."

"You wanna talk with me? A famous movie star wants to talk with me? This must be serious, calling me at this time of night. Have you got somebody you can fix me up with? Is one of your starlet friends coming to town?"

"This is serious."

"She must really be something, with you calling me like this, at this time of night. Okay, I'll be right over," Harry said.

"I told you that you already have somebody who is better than anything you could meet out there. See you there in a little bit." With that, he chuckled and hung up.

Arriving at the house, Tony eased his cycle onto the driveway as quietly as he could. Right after he got it settled in place, up drove Harry.

Tony walked over to Harry's car and, as Harry was getting out of his vehicle, Tony put his fore finger up to his lips in a hush position and motioned for Harry to follow him away from Karen's house. After walking about twenty steps down the sidewalk, Tony stopped and turned around so he was facing back down the sidewalk towards Karen's house.

Looking at Harry while now standing about two feet away from him, Tony said, "I need your help."

Chapter Eighteen

Jean did not recognize the number that was now calling on her phone. It had been on there several times in the past two days but had no identifying information. She had just felt that she should not answer it, but the number kept calling. The repetitive attempts to call her finally got her convinced that, whether it was good or bad, she needed to answer the call. She was in a rural area on the edge of a major city and felt that, even if they did have a location device trying to trace the call, if she kept it short, she would probably still be alright.

"Hello?"

"Jean Favreaux?" a male voice asked.

"Yes. Who is this?"

"So, you finally answered. This is Robert Stone. I am a private investigator working for a certain major drug corporation."

"Yes?" she said as she quickly began looking around her location to see if someone may be watching her.

"You and I need to meet as soon as possible so that you can answer a few questions."

"A few questions about what?" she answered now more quickly looking around her.

"Well now, that is what the meeting is going to be about."

"Well Mr. Whoever you are, you can forget about that, and quit calling this number or I will have you arrested," she said with a firm voice.

"Ms. Favreaux, it will be in your best interests to meet with me or I will be the one going to the police. I will do what I have to do, unless you cooperate with me. And if you don't meet with me, things will get a whole lot worse for you real quickly. Do you want to have something happen in front of your family? Do you want something to happen in front of your home? Do you?"

"You are threatening me, mister whoever you are. I am getting ready to hang up."

"I am trying to give you a chance to deal with what I have found out concerning you that I have not yet told the company that hired me. Just meet me at Garneau's bar in the Quarter tomorrow night. You have been a very bad girl, but I am willing to meet with you and talk with you about how my information concerning the company I represent may be dealt with. But I have to meet with you, privately, to do that."

Robert pated himself on the back. He was really getting good using this approach with the women he had to deal with. They all were such weaklings. Though he had not seen a clear picture of this woman's face yet, he had an idea that she was of a better class than he had previously dealt with. That was all the reason more why he wanted to get to her, before he had to turn her over to the authorities. This one intrigued him, not only for what she had done, but also because she seemed to be smarter than the others. But he felt, talking with her now, that he would be able to handle her just like he had handled the others. He was just too smart for women. None of them could outsmart him.

"Tell me really quickly what you want, or I am getting ready to hang up," she said after a brief pause.

"Does the name Stanley Rhorbach mean anything to you?" he said in a very determined voice.

"No."

"Well now my information indicates you know him very well. I guess the term 'intimately" may be the appropriate word," he said in a low, cool tone of voice. After a moment's pause, he continued, "I am giving you the opportunity to talk with me unless you want me to go on and let other people know what all I have found out. So, meet me at Garneau's at midnight tomorrow night and let's talk."

Jean knew she had to meet with him, but she wondered about that.

"Do I need to bring my attorney with me?" she asked.

"I don't think that would be a very smart idea. I am trying to work with you here, Jean. I am trying to tell you that the fewer people that know what I have found out that I want to discuss with you, the better off you are going to be. If you bring your attorney, then I know there is no possibility of working out a deal with you. Do you understand what I mean, Jean?"

If the case wasn't so big, and if all the higher ups at the company were not on him to do something about finding out who she was, he would have just gone ahead and had her arrested at her house in Bay St. Louis. But something about her was intriguing. Maybe it was how she had done the things she had done. Maybe it was how nice she appeared to look, even though the pictures he had were not complete.

"If I meet with you, will Mr. Rhorbach know about it?" she asked.

"Honey, that is what I am trying to tell you. No, he won't know about it, and may never know about it depending on how our little chat goes. So, tomorrow night at midnight at Garneau's"?

After a few moments pause, Jean said, "Okay. I'll meet with you. But not tomorrow night and not at Garneau's. If we meet, it will be after Tuesday mid-night at 2 a.m. and it will be at Francois' Coffee House."

Robert smelled success, but he felt he had to grasp it immediately. "Okay. But where is this Francois place?"

Taking a moment, she said, "It's near the waterfront, just off of the French Quarter."

"Alright, but don't bring your attorney. If you are going to do that, then we will just go ahead and meet at the District Attorney's Office. I am trying to give you a chance here. Look, I don't like Rhorbach either, but we have to talk."

After a moment's pause, she said, "I don't like it, but I will probably be there." With that, she cut off the connection.

After hanging up, she pulled off the highway she was on, put her car in park, and just sat there. Eventually she started crying. How in the world had her life become so turned upside down in such a short period of time? The more she thought about it, the more she cried. The more she cried, the more helpless she felt.

Conrad heard the conversation. He had no choice but to call

Tony as soon as he could. He didn't know how he was going to be able to tell him about what had just happened, but he knew that Tony needed to know everything as soon as possible. Thank goodness, he was able to get in touch with him within an hour.

At the end of their conversation, which took place on one of Conrad's safe phones, Tony said, "I need some help, Conrad. I really do. I need your guys to, at least temporarily, come out of retirement."

"I don't know, Tony," Conrad answered. "We talked about it. As I mentioned before, that would be taking us back away from where we are now and have been for quite a while. Besides, 'vengeance is mine', sayeth the Lord."

After a quiet moment, Tony said, "Maybe I am supposed to be the instrument of that vengeance."

Chapter Nineteen

The cool of the November night was all over the city of New Orleans. A breeze was gently blowing, which caused the flags on display to stand out and from time to time make popping sounds. The streets on this Tuesday night were almost deserted with only an occasional pedestrian making their way down the sidewalk.

Francois's Coffee House and Bar was located on one of the side streets just off the French Quarter. It had been there for many years and was mostly known only by locals who had gone there because of how it was constructed. The slender facility fronted on the narrow street with a three-step staircase leading up to the single wooden door at its entrance. To the immediate left of the entrance were five tables with a wooden bench on each side that were located next to the glass windows that ran the length of the facility. Pull-down shades were installed so that each table could either have their shade down or up, depending on the preference of those particular patrons. Restrooms were located behind the cashier station, as well as a back door which led to an alley where service vehicles delivered their products and the cleaning crew parked their vehicles.

Robert arrived at 1 a.m. so that he could get a feel for who was going to be there and where the other patrons might be sitting. He was guided to the last table adjacent to the windows. He liked that because he could sit with his back to the far wall of the small facility and keep everything in front of him. That way he could see each individual in the place and also see who was coming in and who was leaving. Once a person entered the bar, the worker at the cash register immediately in front of the door would guide the patron to a table or allow them to proceed to the bar, which ran parallel to the line of small tables. The only bartender served as his waiter and took his order for bourbon on the rocks, which he promptly delivered.

As 2 a.m. approached, there were only two couples at one of the tables and a drunk at the bar still hanging around. The couples got up and left about ten minutes before the designated meeting time. The drunk eased his way off his bar stool and stumbled to the front door, which opened as he got there. He stood back to let a person make her way into the entry area.

Robert watched as a woman wearing black sunglasses walked in and then stood there, looking first around and then in his direction. She was wearing a long wool coat, which was completely buttoned up, along with a scarf around her neck, leather gloves and leather boots. Everything she wore was in black, matching her jet-black hair, which was up. The leather purse she was carrying was also black. The only server there, a male, approached her. Seeing that Robert was the only other person in the place, she slowly began walking in his direction. She looked similar to what he had seen in the few pictures he had reviewed of the lady at the two hotels. As she got closer, he slid out of his bench and stood up. She walked up as if she was gliding on air.

"I am Robert. You must be Jean," he said as he motioned for her to sit opposite him, with her back to the front door. She did not offer her hand to shake nor did she say anything. Robert assumed she was nervous and maybe shy. After all, he had threatened to turn her in to the authorities.

She nodded her head, looked at him as she stood there and slowly unbuttoned the three buttons of her coat. Once she had that accomplished, she gracefully moved to slide herself into position so that she was sitting opposite of him. Robert moved onto his bench also, sliding in but not taking his eyes off of her as he did so. Her appearance was so elegant that Robert was almost stunned. He quickly glanced down to where her black blouse was first buttoned, which blouse now showed because her coat had opened a little as she settled into her seat. She still had her sunglasses on. His first thought was that he was going to keep her for himself for at least a year, maybe two, because she was so classy. No wonder the drug company head had hooked up with her. Who wouldn't? She was so sexy, and he reminded himself he hadn't even seen anything yet. He was looking forward to that, seeing more of her attributes. But first things first. He was ready to begin with the same speech he had used on the other girls. He was going to enjoy this.

The waiter came up and Robert asked, "What would you like to drink?"

She looked up at the waiter and said, "Scotch on the rocks." He nodded his head and departed. She then looked back at Robert as she began to remove the gloves from her hands, beginning with the right one first.

"I am glad you came. I'm trying to help you. I hope you understand that." He closely watched her to see if there was any indication of how she was receiving what he had said. There wasn't. Usually, he could tell quickly what they were thinking. He wasn't so sure about this beautiful animal, so he continued.

"I know it was you who was with Rhorbach." He paused for a moment to take a sip of his drink as he continued to take in his view. He was looking forward to really enjoying this one, at least for a while.

Now having both gloves off, she slid them into her purse and positioned her purse on her lap under the table. She continued to just stare at him with her cold black eyes behind the sunglasses as her mind reviewed her situation. She had already spent so much time before the meeting going over her options. There weren't many, and the more she thought about them, the more she became convinced that she may just have to shoot him with the gun that she had brought with her in her purse.

It was her favorite .38 Smith and Wesson revolver which had been given to her by her father when she was in high school. She had practiced with it over the years and was comfortable with it. There was one thing for sure. She wasn't going to let this arrogant male jerk her around, regardless of what he might want. The condition of her daughter had caused her such despair and continued to do so, yet there was no way out of that. She felt that her mom would take care of Emily, as long as she could. She knew she could count on that. She moved her right hand to where it was now inside of her purse and put her finger on the trigger.

"Look, I am willing to work with you so that you won't be

affected by what I have found out about what you did." He looked at her but continued to see nothing but her steady stare. He didn't know if he was making any progress or not, so he decided to go ahead and push it to the edge.

"Jean, what I am saying here is that I want to help you, but you have to help me. If you don't, I may as well go ahead and turn my information over to the Sheriff and District Attorney's Office and start the process. That process will end up sending you to jail, Jean, to jail! And it will be for a long time."

He got quiet after that statement to let it sink in on her. He noticed, though, that she continued to just stare at him. He had to admit he had never seen anything like that. He was beginning to wonder if she was sane.

The waiter brought over her drink, placing it in front of her, and then retreated to the cashier station at the front.

Feeling somewhat uncomfortable, he decided he had to continue, but he was really wondering how much more he was going to have to push. Almost all the other girls had folded, some of them rather quickly, but this one seemed to be different.

Getting a little indignant, he said, "Look. You need to do something for me, Jean. You really do."

She finally looked away for a moment, but then brought that stare back to him.

"What am I supposed to do?" she asked in an even, cold voice.

Ah, he thought. He was making progress. She had it under consideration, he thought. Now was the time to close the deal. It had worked every time before. It was going to work again, and with this beautiful woman.

"You will have to be available for me whenever I am in town.

Available for me personally. It probably won't be more than three or four times a year, but it will be whenever I want you." He looked for a reaction and saw nothing but a cold, angry look.

After a quiet moment, he continued, "Look, I can't blame you for feeling like you do because of your daughter. I really can't. I might even feel the same way if it were my daughter. But the fact is, you did what you did, I know about it, and for me to be quiet about it going forward, you are going to have to do that for me, starting tonight."

For Jean, it was decision time. She was absolutely angry. She was mad about what was happening, and she was mad at herself for getting into this mess. She hated what this man was trying to do with her. And for her, feeling as she did and being so up against the wall, she might as well go ahead and remove this problem. She wanted to cry, about this situation, about her beloved Emily, about her son, about her life. But now, she had this arrogant asshole of a man trying to basically force her into being his whore. She had already been taken down that road with her medical sales. How had it ever gotten this bad?

She made her decision. She was at the end. She probably should just go ahead and take care of this piece of shit and then take her own life. Yes, that is what she would do. She firmly grasped the gun in her lap.

It was then that it happened. There was a loud noise at the front door. She saw Robert look over her right shoulder at the entrance to the coffee house. She next heard a familiar voice. It was her mother!

"There you are," her mom said as she began walking towards her table. Jean quickly took her hand off her gun. "We were so worried about you,"

Jean thought to herself, we, the word her mom had used. What did that mean? She turned to look over her right shoulder and there was her mother, now standing next to their table, and Tony! What in the world were they doing there?

Her mom gently grabbed her right arm and began to pull on it while saying, "Come on. You have got to see what I have to show you."

Robert quickly said, "You will have to excuse us. We have something very important we are discussing."

Tony, now standing next to Karen, said as he looked at her, "You need to go with your mother. She has something very important to show you."

With her mother's insistent pulling on her arm, Jean decided to do what they were asking and began to slide out of her side of the booth.

Tony then said to Robert, "This is her mother and she really does need to go with her."

Robert looked at Tony, then at Karen, and decided that making his deal with Jean was going to have to wait. After all, they both were saying that this was her mother. The facts he had were not going to go away. And Jean was definitely worth waiting for another time to make the effort to get her available for him.

As Karen was escorting Jean down the aisle and out of the front door, Tony slid in to sit down where Jean had been sitting.

"So, who are you?" Robert asked in a huff.

"I am someone who was asked to look out after Jean," he replied. "And I take that responsibility real seriously."

"Oh, you do, do you?" Robert answered as he leaned back on his bench.

"I do."

Robert looked at Tony a little more closely. After a brief examination, he said, "You look like that actor guy. You know, the one that does all that karate stuff, in the movies and all. What's his name?"

Tony didn't say anything. He just sat there looking at the man as he was pondering his thoughts, trying to remember who that was he was thinking about.

After an additional moment, he blurted out, "Tony Gable! That's who! You look just like him! Is that you?" He was now all excited to find out if he was right. "Really. Are you Tony Gable? I think you are him. I am pretty good about that stuff and I think that's who you are."

Tony answered, "I think you have more serious things to worry about."

"Oh, really? Now what would that be?"

"How you are going to quit bothering the girl who was here with you. Think you could do that?"

Robert looked at him and after a moment said, "You really think you can just walk in here and insert yourself into the situation she is involved in just like that?"

Tony paused for a moment and then slowly took his leather gloves out of the pocket of his overcoat and began to pull the first one onto his right hand. As he began to pull the second one up onto his left hand, Tony leaned forward and said, "I am asking you one more time. Do you think you can go on and not bother this girl anymore?"

Having watched Tony pull his gloves on, Robert decided it was time for a show of force. He reached inside his coat to his hip and pulled out his automatic pistol. He held it in front of him, pointed at Tony, and said, "I don't think this is any of your damn business, actor man."

While holding the gun pointed at Tony, Robert began to slide out of the booth. Tony slid out of his side at the same time.

Pointing the gun waist high at Tony, Robert said, "I'm getting ready to leave this place. I've got two men outside monitoring this situation, so don't get stupid. Now get out of my way."

Tony moved over next to the table as Robert stepped by him.

After getting past him, Robert turned to look at Tony, his gun still pointed towards him. With a sneer on his face, Robert said, "You must not be him. He wasn't a wimp like you. But I didn't like any of his movies anyway."

Now standing and facing Robert, Tony answered, "I was afraid you were going to be a problem." Then shifting to balance his weight on both feet, he added, "By the way, you shouldn't have had your men try to kill that cat."

Looking back at Tony while still pointing the gun at him, Robert said, now smiling, "I don't think that is any of your damn business either."

At that time, there was a noise at the doorway entrance behind Robert. Tony looked over Robert's left shoulder. At the same time, Robert turned to glance over his left shoulder to see what Tony was looking at that had caused the noise. He saw two men, much bigger than him and dressed in all black, entering through the front door.

Then, in a split second, it all happened. Using a karate move Tony had done literally hundreds of times, his left fist quickly came up and forward and then swung out to his left, knocking Robert's right hand holding the gun to Robert's right. Then in an almost simultaneous move, Tony's right hand moved with lightning speed so that his glove covered fist struck Robert with full force exactly in his solar plexus. In a split second, a gust of air came from Robert's mouth. He began gasping, trying to inhale air, as Tony took the gun out of his hand.

Robert began to fall backwards until he was caught by the two large men. They grabbed him, literally picked him up and carried him past the restrooms to the back door of the building. The waiter locked the front door and began to turn the lights out. The two large men handcuffed Robert, as he still was gasping for air, and drug him into the back seat of a white van parked in the back alley. Then, while one drove and Robert was still trying to get his breath, the other one put cuffs on his ankles and gagged him. The drive to deliver Robert over to the Diamondhead Airport in Hancock County, Mississippi took only about an hour.

The two men, who in the back-alley of Karen's house had tried to grab the black cat that belonged to Karen's family, did not know that their identities were now known. They knew that they had been seen behind Karen's house as one of them tried to choke the cat while the other one was taking a hacksaw out of the trunk of their car. They both had laughed several times since then about what they had almost been able to do. They had enjoyed on a few past occasions choking dogs or cats and then carving them up with their hacksaw as a way to intimidate people. They had intended to cut this cat up and hang its rear half by its tail with a large clothespin from a low hanging branch of the tree in the back yard, but the cat had gotten loose. Surely dealing with a bunch of rednecks and blacks in coastal Mississippi was nothing for them to be worried about.

Robert had been very upset with them that the cat had gotten away. He had wanted the girl to be scared when he met with her. That way, she would be more inclined to do what he wanted her to do, or at least that is what had happened in other similar situations.

As they waited to monitor what was being said by radio in their car parked in the block next to where Robert's meeting was taking place, two large figures dressed in all black wearing hoods walked up on each side of their car with guns pointed at their faces. They were ordered out of the car and into a black van that pulled up. Once in the back of the van, they were clubbed on the back of their heads with gun handles, handcuffed, gagged and blindfolded and their feet tied. Their rented car was quickly searched, and any identifying information was removed. They were then driven over to Hancock County and taken out to the landing dock on the edge of Devil's Swamp that had been utilized years before for the shipping of various items to and from the mansion location in the swamp.

From the landing dock, the two computer men were taken by a boat, driven in the middle of the moonlit night by Harry, out into Devil's Swamp and eventually unloaded on the cement docks that had been used for the rum-running operation at the former mansion site. The two men were then forced by the two large figures in black carrying guns to walk from the docks to the back side of the racetrack area behind the remnants of the old house. The two were made to go over next to two already dug graves, where they were forced onto their knees. Then they were told by their lead escort, "This is for Emily's black cat that you two assholes tried to kill," right before the two were quickly shot in their heads from behind by a pistol with a silencer. The shots were delivered at such an angle so as to cause them both to fall into their graves. After the graves were then filled, the men left the area and, under Harry's guidance, returned to the landing dock on the edge of Devil's Swamp.

* * *

At her house three blocks off of St. Charles Street out past the colleges in New Orleans, Mary Jo was coming in from a night out on the prowl. Her continuing effort to locate and seduce straight women had been a little unsuccessful this evening. She had gotten a couple of telephone numbers which she planned to follow up on in the next few days, but her efforts had not resulted in having anyone available for her conversion efforts this evening.

As she came through her side door, it seemed darker than usual, so she immediately reached for the light switch next to the door after she had shut it. All of a sudden, a garment covered fist struck her in the side of her mouth! The force of the blow caused her to slam against the wall of her side hallway.

As she stumbled from the force of the blow against the hallway wall, she moved her hands up to her face. Gloved hands grabbed both of her hands as two other gloved hands grabbed her by her throat and by her hair. She was immediately dragged a few steps down her hallway to her living room. Still in shock from the blow to her face, she didn't realize what was happening as her leather vest that she usually wore out was left on her but pulled off of her shoulders and wrapped around her upper arms behind her. She was then harshly shoved down to sit in one of her wooden chairs which had been brought into the living room from her kitchen table area. A piece of cloth, which she later found out was one of her wash rags, was forced into her mouth.

In her dazed state of mind, she was able to see two huge figures and one smaller figure, dressed in totally black outfits that only had a small opening for the eyes to peer out. One of the dark figures brought up another of her kitchen chairs, put it a little to her left side and then sat in it. As that happened, the gloved hand that had held her by her throat gradually lessoned its pressure but did not release its grip. It was then that she heard something far from a normal voice, resembling instead a very deep, gravelly voice, coming from the figure sitting next to her.

"Listen very carefully," the now obviously male voice said, though she was still in such shock she could hardly understand it. She did recognize that it was sounding like a very disguised voice she had heard on TV one evening during an interview that was shown with an undercover policeman.

"If you try to escape or make any noise, we will kill you," the voice slowly said. "If you understand me, nod your head yes, very slowly."

She immediately, but slowly, nodded her head, which still hurt from the blow. She could also hear a slight noise come from the back of her closet as its back wall was being slid across. That wall area was the entry, hidden by her clothes in the back of her closet, to where she kept her discs of pictures of her conquests and experiences. Pictures of thirty-four different women she had been with were in that back room, and one of these guys was now in that room! How did they know about that room?

The gravelly voice continued while still holding her throat, slowly saying, "You have things that you should not have. We know about Budapest, Montreal, Charlotte. We have a choice. We can either take those things from you that you should not have, or we can take your life, and those things you should not have."

After pausing for a moment, he slowly continued, saying, "We have decided to just take those things you should not have, for right now." The voice's eyes were now approximately a foot away from her face as he paused from saying what was being said.

The figure that had been in the back room of her closet, whom she could only see the outline of, almost floated in and said two words, again in a deep, masked voice, "Got it."

The man still holding her throat said, "And the copies?"

They knew she had copies? First, they had to have known she had things, but they also knew she had the copies?

"Yes," the figure answered.

They knew she had them, but they also knew about her copies! How did they know about her having copies? What else did they know about her?

The man in front of her then slowly said, as if he could read her mind as to what she was thinking, "We also know about your trading off your conquests."

Taking a moment, he then leaned in and now, within only about six inches of her face, said, "If we have to come back here and visit with you again because of what you are doing, first we will take a few hours and slowly cut off all of the skin on your face. Then, we will cut off your head."

As she thought about what he had just said, the next blow from behind her to the back of her head was a complete surprise and temporarily knocked her out. When she woke up, she slowly was able to figure out that she was lying face down on the floor. After slowly turning her head to her left, she was able to see that her vest was also on the floor, unwrapped and lying next to her. The rag was out of her mouth. Realizing she was still alive, she was very thankful. She was even more thankful when she was finally able to figure out that nobody else was still in the house with her.

It was a little past midnight when Alberto parked his car down the street a little way from his apartment. The four beers he had inhaled, after he had left work at the oil change business he worked for, had him looking forward to crawling into his bed.

As he reached the doorway to his apartment, he heard a noise and turned around to see what it was. What he saw were three figures in solid black outfits with nothing but their eyes showing. The first one struck Alberto in his face with his powerful glove covered fist. The second figure dashed up the stairs and got to Alberto before he could react. He immediately got behind Alberto and put him in a head lock. He then performed a quick twist of his head that resulted in a somewhat loud snapping sound. That noise let the holder know that Alberto's neck had just been broken.

Alberto slumped to the floor, as the third black clothed man opened the door to his apartment. Rodriguez was in bed in the back room and heard a noise coming from the hallway, and then another noise that was of his door being opened. As the black clothed figure entered the bedroom doorway, Rodriguez quickly jumped out of his bed and ran through the back door a couple of feet away. He was clothed only in his boxer shorts.

The third figure ran over to the back doorway and saw Rodriguez as he jumped over a chain link fence which surrounded the small back yard. He then saw Rodriguez run down the back alley next to the fence, quickly disappearing as he ran as fast as he could.

At that moment, the shirt on Alberto's body was being pulled up in back. Once that was done, the two men lifted his body up so that it hung by the shirt from the top edge of the door. Its head was bent forward as if it was looking at the floor its feet could not reach. There were a few spasms from the arms of the body, but those did not last long.

At that point, the door opposite Rodriguez's apartment opened and both Gonzo and Pedro looked out, each holding a silver stiletto knife in their right hands. They looked up and saw the body of Alberto hanging from the opened door. As they walked into the hallway, through the doorway of Rodriguez's apartment came two figures totally clothed in black. One of the figures stepped in the hallway so his back was to its entrance to the street. The other figure stood in the doorway to the apartment.

Gonzo and Pedro had both spent a lot of time practicing being a badass with their stilettos. Gonzo had actually used his to torture and kill a fellow refugee who would not do what Gonzo had ordered him to do. Pedro had witnessed that incident and was constantly trying to be like Gonzo.

The figure standing in the doorway said, "Parlez-vous francais?"

As Pedro's mind tried to figure out what had just been said to him, the purpose of the statement was accomplished. Enough doubt was created as to what he should do that he hesitated. In that instant, the doorway figure took one quick step and executed a movement he had practiced hundreds of times. He jumped up and planted a size 11 boot exactly in Pedro's face with a front forward snapping kick, driving Pedro's nose back up into his head. Pedro fell backwards, dropping his stiletto as his back hit the floor. Within a split second, the figure picked the knife up and plunged in down directly into Pedro's chest, almost all the way to its handle.

Simultaneously, Gonzo was going to show whoever this was how much of a badass he was. He lunged directly towards the other black clad figure, trying to use his stiletto like a tomahawk, trying to bring it down from above his head. That figure executed a move he also had performed hundreds of times over the years in his many practices. He blocked the plunging knife, pivoted in the same motion, and used Gonzo's own power, as he had been taught to do, to bring the stiletto all the way down as he pivoted and then driving the knife into the center of his body in his diaphragm area. The force of the blow drove Gonzo back into the side wall of the hallway, which he then slid down until he was sitting on the floor with his back against it. The figure went over and, using his right glove covered hand, pulled the knife out of its position in Gonzo's diaphragm. He quickly raised it above Gonzo's shoulder blade and forced the long, slender knife down into his body next to the left side of his neck behind his shoulder blade, all the way to that knife's handle.

The figure, which had seen Rodriquez run out through the back door, jump the back fence and run down the alley, now appeared in the apartment's doorway. Looking at the three bodies, it motioned the other two figures towards the front doorway.

At that point, a short Latino woman looked out of the doorway of the opposite apartment. The figure immediately said, in English but with a heavy French accent, "Tell Rodriguez that we will be back for him."

He then turned and immediately left, following the other two out of the doorway, down the street and into the night. Reaching their car a few blocks over, they got in and were driven, by Harry, on an indirect route over into Mississippi to the Diamondhead Airport.

* * *

There were only three blocks near Gertrude's office at her family's shipping company that did not have cameras on the street corners. The reason for that was the lack of nearby roads due to the closeness of the Mississippi River, except for one road running next to the warehouses and close to the waterfront.

As the short, thin, unattractive Gertrude, who had just finished having a few drinks and dinner with an old girlfriend of hers who was short, overweight, and also unattractive, was walking back to her car which was parked a few blocks away near the family's office building, up pulled a small black van with no tag. Out immediately jumped two large figures clothed in black outfits which showed nothing but the area around each figure's eyes. After being clubbed on the back of her head with a rubber mallet, Gertrude immediately had a thick piece of black cloth shoved in her mouth as she was being physically picked up and put in the van. The van's sliding door was quietly shut, and the vehicle eased into the night.

Later, around 3:25 a.m. when there was almost no traffic on the Mississippi River Bridge, the van slowed down when reaching the bridge's highest point and the side door was quickly opened. Gertrude's barely unconscious body was unloaded, the black cloth taken from her mouth, and her body carried over to the edge of the bridge. From there, it was launched over the side railing and down into the darkness below. As her body floated through the air toward the water, the van's door was closed, and the vehicle slowly eased off to continue its journey towards the end of the elevated portion of the bridge. Gertrude regained her consciousness about halfway down as she floated through the air. She failed to survive her impact with the water of the dark, massive river.

* * *

Upon returning from their missions to the area of the Diamondhead Airport that they were using, Gordon met up with Tony just before they were to leave to fly back to Long Island on the same plane that would be delivering Robert Stone to that area.

"Just wanted to let you know about something we ran up on," Gordon said.

Tony looked at him and quickly responded, "Did everything go alright at the bridge?"

Gordon paused for a second and then said, "Yes, but there is something that you should know about at the other place."

"What would that be?" Tony cautiously asked.

"Well, out at the swamp site, on the far side of the racetrack in back of what was left of the house, where you wanted us to put those guys, we ran into a problem."

"Really?" Tony said with a quizzical look on his face.

"Yes. You see, the area you told us to go to, straight back behind where the old mansion had been, on the far side of the racetrack. Well, when we had first started digging, we found that there was something already there."

"There was? What was it?" Tony asked.

Gordon paused and then said, "Another body."

"Another body? At that site? On the far side of the race tract?"

Gordon nodded his head affirmatively and said, "Yes, and Tony, it was completely dressed, in faded jeans, a red shirt and shoes. It looked like the body of a shorter person, maybe even a teenager."

Tony was stunned. He then thought about the kid that Karen had told him about who worked for Madeline out there for a few years but had disappeared. People had thought that he had gone to California, even though Madeline had not wanted him to leave. He may not have left after all.

"What did you do about it?" Tony asked.

"We filled in what we had dug up there as fast as we could and moved further down that side of the racetrack and began digging again. Thank goodness, we didn't hit another body there. But Tony, that place is spooky. With the full moon out like it was, that was one eerie place.

"What did you do after you finished the burials?" Tony asked while intently staring at the bearer of this new information.

Gordon looked back at him and said, in as firm a voice that he could muster, "We got the hell out of there, just about as fast as we could. With that moonlight out like it was and all that moss swinging from those huge trees in that breeze, man, we got the hell out of there. Compared to that, the bridge situation was no problem at all."

In the darkness of a hangar at the Diamondhead Airport, Robert Stone was transferred to their private jet. After Tony shook each man's hand and then gave each one, still dressed in their solid black outfits, a man hug, Tony said, "Thanks for your help, guys."

Paul looked at him and said, "We had to help you, Tony. We may be out of the business, so to speak, but we were going to stand by you. You're family."

"I appreciate that so much, guys. It was good to see all of you. Take care of yourselves, and again, thanks," Tony said as he now waived one last time to the men as they got on the plane.

Paul was the last one to climb up the stairs. After he got to the top, he turned and said, "Tony, you take care of yourself too. It may be more dangerous down here than it is on Long Island."

With that, he chuckled, waved goodbye, and then pulled up the stairway.

The group took off and flew to Long Island, New York to their private hanger, arriving there not too long after sunrise. There, in their hanger, Stone was packed into the back seat of the family limousine, which had tinted windows, and taken to the family compound.

During the course of that day and into the night, Stone was subjected to three family members practicing some of their old skills, and a few new ones, on him. They were interested in finding out what other efforts Stone had made on behalf of those discretely fronting for the drug companies. They wanted to know how Stone and his group had attempted to hinder or even stop those who publicly had questioned the safety of certain highly successful money-making drugs manufactured by some of the companies.

Utilizing techniques that Conrad had become familiar with during his days associated with intelligence contractors following the September 11th attacks, their efforts eventually began to result in the disclosure of information that Stone had not wanted to ever reveal. The group was surprised to find out that Stone had performed numerous successful intimidation attempts on clinical researchers, who had been finding out information damaging to various companies during the researchers' investigations of drugs manufactured by those companies.

The group was even more surprised when Stone confessed, under lengthy extreme duress, to causing physical harm to seven researchers located in five different states. They were shocked when Stone finally admitted, in order to stop his by then extreme pain, to causing, at the discrete direction of his contact, the eventual termination of the lives of three of those researchers! Each of those deaths had appeared to have been accidents but were revealed by Stone to have been well-planned and well-executed events. The interrogators felt that there were possibly even more than the three deaths specifically mentioned, but they did not have the time to explore obtaining more detailed information concerning others.

"Damn! That guy was worse than our people, in the recent past at least, ever thought about being," Tony was told by Conrad two days later over a secure phone. "Will tell you about it in person the next time you are here. There are some other things he mentioned that we are going to look into further before then that you will probably also want to know about and, maybe now, need to know about."

After finding out, in the time they had, what they could concerning the deaths caused by Stone's activities, they made extensive efforts to make sure that he remembered, while he could, what happened to him during the time he was with them.

At 2:45 a.m., a barely breathing Robert Stone was delivered to the construction site of a new high-rise building being built not too far from Ground Zero in New York City. There he was placed, while still conscious, beneath part of the concrete base being poured in a back corner of the entrance for that building. A large slab of marble was then placed over the concrete and other slabs were soon added over adjacent areas.

Chapter Twenty

The golden hew of the marsh grass was beautiful next to the blue water of the bayou in the early morning sunlight. It was exactly what Tony and Harry had told Jack he would see on a trip out into the swampland. Jack had told them he would like to see the area about which he had heard so much while he had worked on the coast for the Mississippi Attorney General's Office on a case of potential national importance.

Harry had gotten the boat and was driving it at a high rate of speed on the Bay of St. Louis and then up the bayous. Harry's expert management of the boat impressed his two passengers, but both also wondered about the very visible gun that Harry had tucked into his belt.

"Do you even know which end of that thing the bullet comes out of," Tony asked Harry with a hint of a smile.

Harry glanced at him as he maneuvered their boat and said, "I have a whole lot better idea than I bet you do, city boy. And don't even ask the government lawyer." With that, they all chuckled.

After being in the swamp for quite some time, their boat came around a turn in the bayou and, in front of them, was revealed an approximately twenty-foot-high mound with two large cement docks located in the water at its base. Up against what appeared to be this large outcropping of land was a wall of concrete against its face. On top of the mound could be seen six large white, ante-bellum columns. Harry slowed the boat's forward motion and guided it towards the left side of the dilapidated old cement dock. They soon landed next to that portion of the rather large dock.

As they took turns getting out of the boat while Harry held an attached rope, Jack said, "This is really interesting. Something this big all the way out here in the swamp. There should be a good story behind all of this."

After Harry tied the boat's rope to the dock, he said, "You ain't seen nothing yet. Let's go up these stairs to the top."

With Harry in the lead, the three men started climbing the set of stairs on the left side of the dock area. Reaching the top of the stair climb, Jack got his footing and then took a hard look at what was now right in front of them. He immediately asked, "Was this a swimming pool?"

"What does it look like?" Tony answered.

After taking a few moments to look at the mass of dirty water in the lower area in front of him, Jack said, "Well, I'm not sure."

Tony looked at the water, then back at Jack and said, "Why aren't you sure?"

Jack responded, "Because there are no steps into the pool."

Looking at it more, he continued, "There is no stairway leading down into the pool, if that is what it was. And looking at it, there doesn't appear to be any shallow end. It all looks to be at least ten feet deep."

Harry said, "What do you think about the diving board?"

Jack looked at the pool area, then back at Harry and said, "There isn't one and I don't see where there may have even been one back when."

Harry laughed and said, "The lawyer's pretty observant, Tony."

Tony smiled and said, "There may not have been one."

The lawyer immediately responded without thinking, "Why would you have a pool, especially one this deep, and not have a diving board?"

Tony looked at Jack and then slowly answered in a low voice, "Because this is where they used to also do other things, such as drown people."

Jack looked at the water area, then over at Tony, and then quickly back to the water, and then responded, "Here? Right here? In this pool?" After a short pause in the conversation, during which it was totally quiet, he said, "Ya'll are gonna have to tell me more about this place."

Tony said, "There were men's and women's bath houses back a little bit away from both sides of the pool then but, like almost all of the house, those have been blown away."

Jack then looked out over the bayou as he stood next to the edge of the pool, letting his eyes follow the rather narrow body of water as it worked its way around the area. He then looked at the five huge live oak trees located around the approximately ten-acre area, each with many groups of dark green Spanish moss located on its branches and gently flowing in the light breeze. As his gaze over the area came around to the six still standing, large white columns, Jack could not help but say, "That house must have been huge."

Tony walked over closer to Jack, stopped to look at the columns and said, "It was. And it was first class. With the finest of furniture, curtains, rugs, everything. A lot of things for the house were actually bought in Italy and Sicily and shipped back over here."

As the three slowly began walking past the pool and a little closer to the columns, Harry said, "Back there, behind the house, was the racetrack."

Jack said, "A racetrack?"

"Yep, a racetrack," Harry said. "They used to have big parties out here with lots of people coming over from New Orleans and from all over the coast. They used to bring the guests over in the same big barges that they used to bring the horses in to the site."

Then there was a loud sound.

"Elp!" "Elp!"

All three men jerked around with Tony and Jack immediately bending down, lowering themselves to the ground. Harry attempted to pull his gun out of his belt, fumbling with it as he tried, eventually getting it available for use.

Out of the backside of the property walked two animals, then a third.

"Peacocks," said Tony as he began to stand up.

"Peacocks?" said the lawyer as he also began to stand up. "What are peacocks doing out here?"

Tony answered, "Guard dogs. They used them as guard dogs out here. They won't let anything happen without sounding an alarm."

Harry then said, "I'm going back to the boat. Just wanna make sure it will be there when you're ready to leave." He turned and began walking towards the steps, gun still in his hand.

"Be careful carrying that gun," Tony shouted out with a smile on his face. "Wouldn't want that thing going off while you're trying to go down those stairs."

"Yea, yea. I hear you," Harry yelled back as he began to maneuver down the side of the bluffs.

After walking around the area and enjoying the view a little more, as they got ready to leave, Jack said, "I may just have to write a book about this place."

After a pause for a moment, Tony said, "It may take more than one." After taking a few more steps, he continued saying, "It might take two or even three."

They both smiled at one another as they began to make their way back towards the stairs.

"I would have to change some of the names, don't you think," Jack said while looking over at Tony to see his reaction.

Tony chuckled, looked back at him with the hint of a grin on his face and answered, "You might want to change a few things more than just some names."

With that, both men looked at each other as big smiles came over their faces.

Epilogue

The offices of Robert Stone and his two unmarried associates, located on the outskirts of Louisville, Kentucky, were broken into the night after the associates had been delivered to the edge of the former racetrack in Devil's Swamp. Their extensive computer records were taken, and all memory on their computers was removed. Subsequent investigations seemed to indicate that their supposed undercover efforts on behalf of the drug companies may have led to the break-in, their disappearances and the theft of their office records.

Along with the discovery of Alberto's body hanging with a broken neck from the door leading to his apartment, the bodies of the two other Latino's were also discovered on the hallway floor. One body was laying on his back with a stiletto in his chest and the other one was on the floor leaning up against the wall with a stiletto down through his shoulder blade next to his neck. Within six hours, all seventeen male illegal aliens living within eight blocks of the apartment had disappeared. Most of them had found ways to quickly travel back to Texas.

Rodriguez disappeared from the United States. Rumor has it that he crossed the border back into Mexico. He supposedly took up a position with his gang targeting for seduction female refugees coming into Mexico from El Salvador, Honduras, and Guatemala. He was known for identifying young girls, particularly Salvadorian girls sometimes as young as 12 years old, for seduction and eventual captivity. Five months after his return, as he was getting into his car after shopping in early afternoon at a grocery store, his car was blown up by a massive bomb. With both legs and half of his right arm missing, he passed away after three days in the hospital.

About eight months after the disappearance of Robert Stone and his associates, the company of Ballard, Tinkersly, and Lowell announced that their financially very successful drug, which had been suspected of being one of the products made by the industry that had caused such large numbers of cases of autism and other medical problems in children, was being pulled off of the market for further testing. Only after over a year and a half of research did the company make the decision to put their money maker back on the market. The difference was that their drug had been extensively re-formulated.

Gertrude's body was discovered on the banks of the Mississippi

River some distance downstream from the Mississippi River Bridge. Her death remains a mystery though there is an investigation of a dock worker who testified in a case involving her family's shipping company. Apparently, he still has not received all of the payments he was promised by Gertrude for his testimony in that case.

Jean agreed to go to counseling. As her counseling progressed, Harry asked her to marry him. She eventually accepted Harry's proposal and they were married. At a very small service held in the church that Tony had visited on two occasions, he served as Harry's best man. Harry's very successful real estate and oil and gas businesses meant that Jean was able to quit her job and spend time instead with her kids, both of whom she and Harry were granted custody.

Tony agreed to move back to the Mississippi Gulf Coast. Arrangements were made so he could continue pursuing his highly successful movie career from there. After living there for six months, Tony and Karen got married. Jean and her daughter and son took part in the wedding, which was held at the same church as Harry and Jean's wedding.

Tony and Karen made sure that the black cat belonging to Jean's daughter, Emily, has continued to live with them at their new house. Emily's face lights up with a big smile almost every time that she sees and holds that cat. Those smiles continue to be among the few that have been seen on her face since the shot was given to her. Emily's condition has gradually improved somewhat, though, as time goes on.

Tony, Karen, Jean and Harry attended a service at the black Baptist church on the edge of town to hear Martavious Lewis preach. The service had over one hundred mostly black people in attendance. The sermon was surprisingly good, and the gospel music was outstanding. Tony arranged for a sizeable donation to quietly make its way to Martavious for his church.

Rumor has it that information, even that which might have been stored at some point on a disc or a computer that may have been destroyed, might eventually be found and recompiled, if an expert spent enough time and effort looking for it, somewhere in the "cloud".

Author's Notes

This book is fiction. Any resemblance to actual events that may have taken place is coincidental. My interest in writing this book was simply to tell an interesting, hopefully captivating story. I hope I have accomplished that, and that the reader enjoys the time they spend in the world created by my efforts.

This is the third book in a trilogy. The first book is "The Bluffs of Devil's Swamp", which takes place in the roaring 20's, and the second book is "You Just Never Know", which takes place in the 1970's. This book, "Whatever It Takes", is set in today's general time period and purposefully ties back, to some extent, to the other two books.

Coming along through life, I never had any idea that I would ever write a book, much less three. I have always, though, found the Mississippi Gulf Coast interesting. My family spent some time during the summers on the coast as I was growing up. It was always a fun place to visit. My professional career as an attorney and a real estate broker led me to spend a lot of time in the coastal area. My research efforts on various cases and projects on the coast caused me to spend many hours at various historical facilities in the greater Washington, D. C. area as well as in Jackson, Mississippi and at locations along the coast.

The most interesting aspect of my experiences has been the people that I have met and gotten to know from that area. With my familiarity with the history of the area, I have constantly been amazed by the love for life that is almost always exhibited by the people who have long lived there.

One thing that I have always noted my entire life is the courage shown by the people who are from there. I have witnessed, whether it was while working for Senator John Stennis when Hurricane Camille hit or while working on projects when Hurricane Katrina hit, unbelievable amounts of courage exhibited by the people who live in that area. I have always been amazed at their ability to bounce back from such horrible disasters. Their love for life, or "joie de vie" as the French call it, regardless of how bad things get, has never ceased to amaze me.

We have been so fortunate to live in a country that has allowed each of us to be free to pursue our dreams. This most recent state election cycle in my home state reminded me once again that we are so blessed to be allowed to go vote for the people we want to run our government. We do not have to take somebody as an officer in our government just because somebody tells us we have to take them. We really are so blessed to still be able to have that freedom.

One thing that seems to be missing, though, more and more is that there is no retribution. Incidents, such as the killing of an innocent person just walking on a pier with her father, take place and there is no justice. So many innocent people have family members maimed or even killed, as well as themselves, and nothing, absolutely nothing is ever done about it.

A very good man, a close friend of mine and one of the nicest people I have ever known, was merely leaning up against his car in the early evening waiting for his son when he was robbed by four kids sixteen years old and younger. Because he did not have much money on him (only about ten dollars it was rumored), he was shot by one of the robbers. When he ran to try to get away, he was chased down by the kids and repeatedly shot over and over by the two who had guns as he laid on the ground. Repeatedly. It was horrific.

No word was ever put out about if all of them were ever caught and, if they were, when were they going to be put through the justice system. It turned out that one of my friend's main assailants was within ONE DAY of being completely turned loose, without even being indicted, before it was fortunately discovered that NOTHING had been done about processing that guy through the justice system! And, oh by the way, nobody seemed to know exactly what happened with the three others that were in the group while my friend was being robbed and shot, so many times, in cold blood.

This episode, and so many others, cause good citizens to lose faith not only in our system of government, but also in those who run it. Frustration over seeing justice not done and retribution taking place has grown to all-time highs. It is getting to the point that so many people are fed up with some completely worthless excuses for human beings time and time and time again getting away with committing crimes, doing dastardly deeds to innocent people and paying little, if any, price for what they did.

One of these days, if our leaders don't show themselves as having the guts and the backbone to do what is right and necessary to protect the innocent public and their families, then good people will become fed up with seeing nothing happening to this scum as a result of what they did. The good people at some point will begin, more and more, to take matters into their own hands and do "whatever it takes", to get even. They will begin to do what is necessary to protect their innocent loved ones so that hopefully they will not have to endure seeing the continuance of the abject chaos that we are beginning to witness now on an almost daily basis.

May the Lord watch over us and protect us and see to it that justice is brought down on all of those that do dastardly deeds.

About the Author

Mack Cameron was born and raised in Laurel, Mississippi. He was on crutches as a child from the beginning of the first grade to the middle of the fourth grade. Through the grace of God, he got off crutches and took up tennis.

He began playing on the Laurel High School tennis team in the sixth grade. He played as high as number four on the high school team in his seventh grade and started playing in the team's number one singles position in the eighth grade. He went to the state high school singles finals four consecutive years, while in the ninth, tenth, eleventh and twelfth grades, and won the Mississippi High School Singles Championship his junior and senior years. He was a member of Laurel High School tennis teams that won the Mississippi High School State Team Championship his junior and senior years.

He represented the State of Mississippi in five consecutive National Jaycee Tennis Championships. During his senior year, he was also selected, along with other top players from around the country, to play in the nationally respected Sugar Bowl Tennis Tournament in New Orleans. He served as class president his Sophomore and Junior years at Laurel High School and as Student Body President his Senior year.

He attended Mississippi State University (MSU), receiving a Bachelor's Degree and a Master's Degree in Political Science. At Mississippi State, he won four Southeastern Conference (SEC) individual tennis championships while a member of MSU teams that won two SEC team championships and finished as high as number three in the nation. At Mississippi State, he served as Chairman of the Student Judicial Council, as a member of the Student Senate, and as a member of Scabbard and Blade, the honorary military fraternity.

Upon graduation, he worked in Washington, D.C. as Staff Assistant to U.S. Senator John C. Stennis. He then served as an officer in U.S. Army Military Intelligence. Among other assignments while on active duty, being fluent in French, he served as translator for eight French speaking, high ranking military officers from the African countries of Dahomey, Niger, Ivory Coast, and Upper Volta during their visit to the Washington, D.C. area and several military facilities around the nation.

Upon completion of his active duty military service, he attended law school at the University of Mississippi (Ole Miss) where he won the American Jurisprudence Award in International Law, served on the Law School Honor Council, and coached the tennis team. His 1974 tennis team held the record for most wins

(21) at Ole Miss until 1995. He also raised the money for the first two full tennis scholarships ever given by Ole Miss.

After graduation from law school, Mr. Cameron served as Assistant Legal Counsel for the United States Secret Service under Presidents Nixon, Ford, and Carter. During Mr. Cameron's tenure, only the Chief Counsel, Mr. Cameron and one other Assistant Legal Counsel constituted the Secret Service Legal Counsel's Office. While at the Legal Counsel's office, he was responsible for the review of Secret Service documents for consideration of public disclosure under the then newly passed federal Freedom of Information Act. He taught classes to Executive Protective Service personnel of the Secret Service concerning their authority and powers.

Upon his return to Mississippi, he has worked as a Special Assistant Attorney General in the Mississippi Attorney General's Office under five Attorneys General. While at the Attorney General's Office, he coordinated the State of Mississippi's successful efforts to block the Tatum Salt Dome in south Mississippi from being used as a storage site for national and, eventually, even international nuclear waste.

Mr. Cameron is also responsible for the renegotiation of hundreds of unconstitutional 16th Section leases that had been issued at numerous locations across portions of the state for give-away prices. The result of the renegotiations was an increase in millions of dollars in income being received by school districts that were the beneficiaries of the proper leasing of the property.

He represented the State of Mississippi in the case of Cinque Bambini Partnership verses the State of Mississippi which successfully protected state ownership of and public access to submerged tidelands below the mean high tideline. The decision in that case, which was issued in favor of the State of

Mississippi by the lower court and confirmed by the Mississippi Supreme Court and the United States Supreme Court, resulted in significant, positive, economic impacts for the State of Mississippi, as well as other states.

Mr. Cameron is in the State of Mississippi Sports Hall of Fame, the Mississippi State University Sports Hall of Fame and the Mississippi Tennis Hall of Fame. He and his father, C.B. "Buck" Cameron, were the first father-son duo in the State of Mississippi Sports Hall of Fame. He has been ranked the number one singles tennis player in Mississippi in every age group of participation and as high as number one in the South and number eight in the nation in the group of participation.

He is a member of the Mississippi State Bar Association and is a real estate broker. He has served on the Mississippi State Bar Ethics Committee, as President of the Jackson Touchdown Club, and as a member for several years of the Touchdown Club's Board of Directors.

He is the author of "The Bluffs of Devil's Swamp," the first book in this series, and of "You Just Never Know", the second book. This book, "Whatever It Takes," constitutes the third book of the trilogy.

www.ingramcontent.com/pod-product-compliance
Lightning Source LLC
Chambersburg PA
CBHW051330020726
47501CB00007B/2002